Anne
of
Avenue A

Praise for Audrey Bellezza and Emily Harding's
Previous Novels

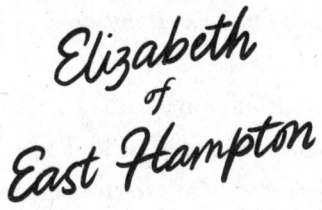
Elizabeth of East Hampton

"Bellezza and Harding put a beachy spin on *Pride and Prejudice*... Austenites will be over the moon."

—*Publishers Weekly*

"Escape to summer in the Hamptons—a Hamptons bakery, to be exact—via the pages of Audrey Bellezza and Emily Harding's latest page-turner. A charming, modern-day retelling of *Pride and Prejudice*, this sun- and sugar-soaked novel will delight even the most discerning Jane Austen fan. Readers will be enchanted—and are sure to add this talented duo to their list of auto-buy authors."

—Kristy Woodson Harvey, *New York Times* bestselling author of *A Happier Life*

"*Elizabeth of East Hampton* proves that the only thing better than an East Coast beach read is an East Coast beach read that doubles as an irresistibly fresh take on the ultimate enemies-to-lovers romance. Endlessly charming and more delicious than the famous sour cherry muffins from Bennet Bakery—which I'm still drooling over—this Hamptons-set romp is guaranteed to delight both die-hard Janeites and *P&P* virgins alike!"

—Nicolas DiDomizio, author of *The Gay Best Friend*

"Equal parts poignant and hilariously witty, *Elizabeth of East Hampton* captures all the charm of Jane Austen's beloved *Pride and Prejudice* and makes it fresh and new!"

—Liana De la Rosa, author of *Isabel and the Rogue*

"Lovers of Jane Austen and romance, rejoice! Bellezza and Harding have taken the bright, tender spirit of Elizabeth and Darcy's romance and transmuted it to the contemporary world, along with fresh, infinitely amusing interpretations of one of the most ridiculous and lovable families in literature, the Bennets."

—Kate Khavari, author of *A Botanist's Guide to Parties and Poisons*

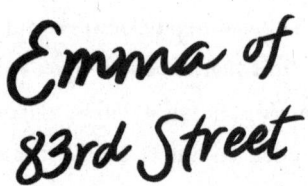

"A glamorous romp that is heartfelt, steamy, and romantic . . . For fans of the movie *Clueless* and retellings of classics."

—*Library Journal*

"The best romantic comedy I've ever read."

—Lauren Layne, *New York Times* bestselling author of *Made in Manhattan*

"A compulsive page-turner with excellent slow-burn tension. An instant favorite!"
—Sarah Hogle, author of *You Deserve Each Other*

"The authors bring plenty of wit to this classic friends-to-lovers tale."
—*Publishers Weekly*

"Delightfully modern and compulsively readable, this made my *Clueless*-loving heart sing—a knockout debut!"
—Angie Hockman, author of *Shipped*

"A delightful debut . . . sweeter than candy."
—Marilyn Simon Rothstein, author of *Husbands and Other Sharp Objects*

"A great summer beach read . . . From its Lilly Pulitzer–colored cover to its Blair Waldorf–type protagonist, this book should be purchased immediately because it's going to ride off shelves like a vintage Jaguar with the top down."
—*Bookreporter*

"Austenites and rom-com fans rejoice: *Emma of 83rd Street* is witty, wonderful, and the best retelling of *Emma* since *Clueless*. I loved every minute of it."
—Sarvenaz Tash, coauthor of *Ghosting: A Love Story*

"A fresh, utterly charming, feel-good retelling of an enduring classic. Whip-smart, pitch-perfect, and newly minted."
—Julie Valerie, author of *Holly Banks Full of Angst*

"Bellezza and Harding balance introspection with a healthy dose of New York glitz... as with all Austen adaptations, the joy—and there's plenty of it—is definitely in the journey."

—*Shelf Awareness*

"Warm, sweet, and funny, *Emma of 83rd Street* is a fun take on a comforting classic and a fresh reminder of all the reasons we love romance."

—Genevieve Novak, author of *No Hard Feelings* and *Crushing*

"A witty and romantic debut novel."

—*The Nerd Daily*

"New York and Jane Austen are two of my great loves, so how could I not fall for *Emma of 83rd Street*? It's a frothy city romp based on one of Austen's most delightfully fun stories. And that's what we all need this summer—a burst of fun. I couldn't have enjoyed this slice of NYC fantasy more."

—Ali Rosen, author of *Alternate Endings*

"A delicious wonder of a book... Bellezza and Harding effortlessly make this contemporary retelling of the classic Austen novel into a delightful romance filled with characters and a love story you'll definitely want to revisit."

—*Sheaf & Ink*

ALSO BY
AUDREY BELLEZZA AND EMILY HARDING

Elizabeth of East Hampton

Emma of 83rd Street

Anne of Avenue A

A NOVEL

**AUDREY BELLEZZA
AND EMILY HARDING**

GALLERY BOOKS

New York   Amsterdam/Antwerp   London
Toronto   Sydney/Melbourne   New Delhi

G

Gallery Books
An Imprint of Simon & Schuster, LLC
1230 Avenue of the Americas
New York, NY 10020

For more than 100 years, Simon & Schuster has championed authors and the stories they create. By respecting the copyright of an author's intellectual property, you enable Simon & Schuster and the author to continue publishing exceptional books for years to come. We thank you for supporting the author's copyright by purchasing an authorized edition of this book.

No amount of this book may be reproduced or stored in any format, nor may it be uploaded to any website, database, language-learning model, or other repository, retrieval, or artificial intelligence system without express permission. All rights reserved. Inquiries may be directed to Simon & Schuster, 1230 Avenue of the Americas, New York, NY 10020 or permissions@simonandschuster.com.

This book is a work of fiction. Any references to historical events, real people, or real places are used fictitiously. Other names, characters, places, and events are products of the author's imagination, and any resemblance to actual events or places or persons, living or dead, is entirely coincidental.

Copyright © 2025 by Audrey Bellezza and Emily Harding

All rights reserved, including the right to reproduce this book or portions thereof in any form whatsoever. For information, address Gallery Books Subsidiary Rights Department, 1230 Avenue of the Americas, New York, NY 10020.

First Gallery Books trade paperback edition October 2025

GALLERY BOOKS and colophon are registered trademarks of Simon & Schuster, LLC

Simon & Schuster strongly believes in freedom of expression and stands against censorship in all its forms. For more information, visit BooksBelong.com.

For information about special discounts for bulk purchases, please contact Simon & Schuster Special Sales at 1-866-506-1949 or business@simonandschuster.com.

The Simon & Schuster Speakers Bureau can bring authors to your live event. For more information or to book an event, contact the Simon & Schuster Speakers Bureau at 1-866-248-3049 or visit our website at www.simonspeakers.com.

Manufactured in the United States of America

10 9 8 7 6 5 4 3 2 1

Library of Congress Control Number: 2025938926

ISBN 978-1-6680-9765-6
ISBN 978-1-6680-9766-3 (ebook)

This one's for us.

Anne of Avenue A

PROLOGUE

Anne broke Freddie's heart on a Friday.

It wasn't something she planned to do. In fact, as she stood in the back room of the Half Pint, surrounded by a crowd of friends and acquaintances she barely recognized singing "Jingle Bell Rock" at the top of their lungs, it didn't even enter her mind. All she could really think about was how her cashmere cardigan didn't quite fit in with the apparent dress code of ugly Christmas sweaters and candy-cane-striped stockings, and how the cheering and yelling and singing clashed with the music blaring from the bar's ancient speakers, which were half-hidden by the tinsel hanging from the ceiling. And how, despite the chaos and the noise, she was actually enjoying herself.

Anne Elliot had always thought she hated parties. It wasn't so much that they were chaotic—though they were definitely that—but they were always so draining. Energy was required to meet the chaos, the yelled conversations and the press of the crowd, and it always left her feeling hollow. But even as the thought entered her head, a tall figure appeared through the doorway, two drinks in hand. A reminder that maybe she didn't hate parties that much. At least, not a Freddie Wentworth party.

"FREDDIE!" someone yelled across the bar. Everyone else turned to witness his return as well, cheering and raising their drinks toward him.

He raised his two glasses as well and nodded. Even in the dim glow of the neon signs, Anne could see his green eyes as they scanned the room, the messy brown hair in dire need of a trim poking out from under a red Santa hat, the lopsided grin barely concealed behind a comically bushy white fake beard. When his eyes met hers, it widened into a full smile.

Anne and Freddie had been together for two and a half years, yet when he looked at her like that, she still felt her heart struggle to operate, tripping and catching like a motor caught in the wrong gear. It was the same look he'd had on his face when they met, back when she was a nineteen-year-old sophomore darting between college classes at NYU, working so hard for no one to notice her and still shocked that somehow he had anyway.

Freddie started toward her, weaving his way through the festive crowd, saying hello and nodding as needed. He was the host, after all, and over the course of the past two years, he'd become something of a celebrity among the NYU crowd. Whether it was a Halloween bash on a sprawling rooftop in Brooklyn or a day drink in an empty office building in Midtown, his parties were infamous.

The music transitioned to "All I Want for Christmas Is You" when he stopped just in front of her. His usual uniform of a vintage T-shirt and baggy jeans had been replaced by an oversized Santa costume that hung awkwardly on his tall frame. But somehow, miraculously, he could pull it off. Such was the magic of Freddie Wentworth.

"What are you staring at?" he asked, narrowing his eyes. Despite the beard, Anne could still see that familiar easy grin tugging at the corner of his mouth, the crinkling at the corner of his eyes that made her feel like the most special person in the world.

She shrugged, feigning nonchalance. "Nothing."

"It's the beard. It's doing it for you, isn't it," he deadpanned.

"You're ridiculous." She rolled her eyes, barely curbing her smile.

"Ridiculously good-looking, right?"

Now it was impossible not to laugh. Anne let it bubble out of her, and he watched, his smile broadening, like he had unlocked his one achievement for the night.

"Which one of those is mine?" she asked, nodding to the drinks in his hands.

"Good question." He held up the two glasses. Under the glow of the nearby neon beer sign, they looked almost identical. "One of them is a Sprite and cranberry, and the other one is a cocktail called Christmas in Your Mouth."

She considered both, then grabbed the one in his right hand and took a deep sip. The bitter taste of pine and cranberry and orange assaulted her mouth, while some undefinable alcohol burned her tongue.

Freddie watched her gag and winced. "That bad?"

She nodded and reached for the other glass.

He gave it to her, then took the cocktail back and took a sip for himself. "Huh. I never thought Christmas would taste like cheap tequila and grenadine."

She laughed again. This time it sent the last remnants of alcohol up her nose, making her eyes water.

The crowd was just hitting the crescendo of their song as he took another sip and snaked his arm around her waist, bringing her back flush against his body.

"Merry Christmas, Annie," he whispered, his lips almost touching the shell of her ear.

She smiled. This is what she had missed over the past few weeks. The ease, the laughter, the constant touches and whispers. She had taken it for granted before, but now it suddenly felt like a rare, precious thing that needed attention.

Between managing the expectations of her parents and surviving her overloaded class schedule, Anne's senior year at NYU had become so hectic she barely had a moment to herself. Of course, Freddie would probably argue that it wasn't too different from the previous few years. She always pushed herself, relied on her lists and schedules to eke out as many hours in the day as possible.

But her senior year had brought a whole new sense of urgency. Anne was a year older than Freddie and a year above him at NYU, so while he was allowed to continue with his nonchalant attitude toward higher education, Anne was forced to buckle down and take her last remaining credits even more seriously. Slowly, their time together became more sporadic, squeezed in whenever she could find an afternoon or weekend. She had convinced herself it was fine, a temporary hiccup in a relationship that had always been so easy, so perfect. But then her mind wandered to next year . . .

Nope. No spiraling, she thought, and took a sip of her drink. She had time to tell him. All she had to do right now was relax, enjoy the party, and—

"All I want for Christmas IS YOU!" the crowd sang in unison, throwing their arms up.

The move sent someone stumbling into Freddie from behind, making him lurch forward and sending his drink splashing out of its glass and all over Anne.

"Shit," Freddie murmured.

The man responsible turned around, his drunken eyes barely

able to focus on Anne's now-sodden blond hair and navy blue sweater, then up at Freddie.

"Oh," he said. "Sorry, man."

Freddie shot him a sharp glare and handed him what was left of their drinks.

"Cool," the man replied. "Thanks."

Freddie ignored him as he took Anne's hand and gave it a tug.

"Let's go get you cleaned up before this requires a dry-cleaning bill," he whispered. They weaved their way through the throngs of people until they reached the door.

Outside, the sidewalk was still covered with snow from the day before, and Freddie threw his Santa coat around Anne's shoulders, revealing his Jets hoodie underneath, as they walked around the corner to a quieter section of Third Street. Once the sounds of the party had faded a bit, he stopped and turned her around to face him.

Under the faint light of the streetlamp, he leaned down and blotted a bit of still-dripping drink off her cheek with the edge of his sweatshirt. When he was done, he didn't look away, just studied her expression, her pale skin, her blond hair pulled back in a neat ponytail. She had grown to love that look of his, too—it was like she was a complex machine that he wanted to take apart and put back together again.

"What's the damage?" she asked, smoothing the side of her ponytail with her palm.

"Grotesque. Awful," he said, that wry grin still playing with his mouth. "But I love you anyway."

Anne smiled and reached up, pulling off his ridiculous beard. He took a step forward to bring his body flush with hers and press her back against the cool brick exterior of the building. His hand moved slowly up the line of her neck to her jaw. Since he started working on his hydroponics project last year, his hands had slowly become more calloused. She had always loved how he touched her, but now those same fingers felt rough as he cradled her face and slowly ran his thumb over her bottom lip. She loved that even more.

"I can't believe it's already Christmas," he murmured. "We have to make the next couple of weeks count before I lose you to school again."

The reminder opened up a pit in her stomach. She usually loved Christmas—the way it seemed to cover New York in a magical sheen, how the city almost felt like a village where everyone was happy to see everyone else and everything was perfect. For a couple of weeks, at least.

But this year the holiday felt looming, a warning that she and Freddie only had a few perfect days left before reality set in. She would have to tell him about next year, admit that she had applied to Columbia School of Business for her master's a few months ago, and that an email had arrived just a few days before with the news that she had been accepted.

Anne hadn't thought she would get in—that was half the reason she didn't tell him she'd applied. But the other half... She let out a long breath. Her parents had always pushed her to do something lucrative with her love of mathematics, and after four years of pursuing a degree in economics at NYU, she thought they would be appeased—she would be able to graduate and finally focus on what she wanted to do. Or, at least, figure out what that was, exactly.

What did she want to do? The question felt so broad, so undefinable. Where did she even begin? She had loved math since she learned how to hold a pencil—how logic and rules and numbers combined in an infinite number of ways to solve an infinite number of problems—but what did that even look like in the real world? She still had no idea. Every job seemed to want to reduce that love down to budget lines and algorithms. For the first time in her life, she found herself thinking that she had math entirely wrong. The world didn't want numbers viewed in vibrant three-dimensions like how she saw them, but in stark, flat two.

Maybe that was why she had been so receptive when her mother had started seeding her opinion last summer. An MBA was obvious, didn't she think? A degree Anne could apply to any number of fields, regardless of what she ultimately wanted to do.

It was a safe choice. And no doubt it would be lucrative. There was just one nagging issue: She didn't know how to tell Freddie.

We said no spiraling, she reminded herself. Not today. Besides, she had a plan and all she had to do was follow it. She would tell Freddie once classes started in January and their conversations inevitably went to the following year. While Anne was graduating this May, Freddie still had one more year left before he would leave with a degree in environmental engineering. He had talked about starting a nonprofit after, one that would focus on sustainable farming around the world, but the details were still unclear. With Freddie, they usually were. But in this case, it would work to her advantage. While he figured out his next steps, she would be getting her MBA.

She had planned for every contingency, every possible impediment. It would be fine.

"Hey," Freddie whispered, so close Anne could feel his breath against her lips. "What do you think about exchanging gifts now?"

She opened her eyes enough to look up at him quizzically. "I thought we were doing that next week at your parents' house."

He shrugged one shoulder. "I know, but I don't think I can wait that long."

Anne didn't know why she was surprised. While she had an almost obsessive need to plan, work out the details and systematically weigh the pros and cons to every decision, Freddie had a habit of being impulsive, regardless of what plans were already in place. She usually loved that about him, but right now, the suggestion struck a familiar annoyance deep down in her chest.

"I don't have your gift, though," she said. "If I had known you wanted to exchange now, I would have brought it with me, but—"

"I promise not to hold it against you," he replied with a wry grin. Then he pulled something from his pocket before putting both hands behind his back. "Pick a hand."

She threw him one last sardonic look before considering both, then nodded to the right.

His hand appeared, clasped in a fist. When he unfolded it, there was a piece of paper folded into a neat triangle waiting in his palm.

She smiled. It was a tradition established early in their relationship. Whether they had skipped class to go explore a new museum downtown or only saw each other long enough to share a coffee and a quick kiss, Freddie always slipped her handwritten notes, even if it meant he had to secretly stash it in her pocket or bag to inevitably find afterward. A perfect little paper triangle that contained a special, secret message just for her. She would always wait until she was alone to read it, then put it inside the box in her nightstand where she kept all the others.

"That's for later," he said solemnly, though there was still a glint of humor in his eyes.

She slid it into the back pocket of her jeans.

"Next," he said.

She laughed softly and nodded to where his left hand was still hidden behind him.

When he brought it forward, it held a small, wrapped box adorned with a red bow.

She slowly reached for it, examining its red-and-white striped paper before carefully tearing it off to reveal a nondescript maroon box. Inside, she found a silver link bracelet with a compass charm attached to its center.

"It only has the one charm now, but I thought we could start filling it up with all the places we go," he said.

"It's beautiful," she whispered. And it was, even as she tried to ignore the guilt that swelled in her chest again.

He smiled. "You like it?"

"I love it."

"Good. Because I thought we could start in Argentina." Then he pulled his phone from his back pocket, unlocking it before revealing what looked to be an email.

The screen was so bright, it took Anne a minute to read it. Then another to process the words. Argentine Airlines. Buenos Aires. One-way.

Her heart plummeted to the floor. "What is this?"

"Your Christmas present," he said softly. "I got accepted into the NYU Buenos Aires program for next year. And I want you to come with me."

"To Argentina?" she asked dumbly. Freddie had talked about NYU's program in Argentina for the past two years, but it was always with wistful longing. He could barely afford tuition as it was; there was never a chance he could shoulder the added cost of a year abroad. Or, at least, that's what she thought. She had missed a step, and she never missed a step. Now her brain was trying desperately to play catch-up.

"Not for the whole year, obviously," he replied. "That's why it's one way; you can decide how long you stay. But after graduation, I thought you could take some time and figure out what you wanted to do next while I—"

"But I thought it was too expensive."

"It is, but one of the professors in the environmental engineering department heard about the hydroponics unit I'm working on. He reached out and they want to give me a scholarship. I'll be able to work with the local community to . . . " He paused when he caught her confused expression. "What?"

A cold wind whipped down West Third Street, pulling strands of hair from her ponytail, but she barely noticed. She unconsciously pushed them from her face as her mind began to spin with every eventuality. "Have you considered the additional costs? Is there on-campus housing? What about insurance? And the trips back and forth. And your parents . . . "

"How about 'Congratulations, Freddie, that's amazing!'" He was still smiling, but there was a new line of concern between his eyebrows.

"It *is* amazing, there's just a lot to consider," she said, working to curb the panic in her voice.

"Not everything has to be dissected ad nauseum to weigh its merits, Annie."

But some things should, she wanted to say. Still, she couldn't have that conversation again. Freddie thrived on the big picture, following his gut. It was one of the things she loved most about him, even though she could in no way relate.

"You didn't even tell me you applied," she said. The words came out before she could realize her own hypocrisy. She hadn't told him about business school, either.

"I know, I'm sorry," he said with a sigh, stepping forward and enveloping her in a hug again. "But honestly, I didn't think I would get in, so I did it on a whim. And when the scholarship came through, I just thought, why not? You know I've always wanted to travel. I'm studying environmental engineering so I can do that and do some good for the world. And you always said you wanted to come with me."

A sharp ache ran down her chest. Over the past few months, they had talked about traveling the world together. Late-night discussions about all the places they'd visit someday, but it had always felt so far away, just one of a thousand different daydreams about what life would be like after college. An escape from the realities of the here and now.

"That was a possibility for the future, Freddie. Not a concrete plan."

His lips flattened to a grim line. It was an expression she rarely saw, one that didn't seem to fit his face. "Really? Well, that's news to me."

His white beard was still clutched in her hand as her mind raced. "A plan requires a defined goal, quantifiable steps to get there. I can't just take off to Argentina next year on a whim—"

"Why not?"

"Because . . . because . . ." She hated how she tripped over her words, but she also didn't know how to avoid it. She hadn't planned on having this conversation yet, so she hadn't had time to rehearse what to say, how to soften the surprise, so she just said it. "I'm going to Columbia Business School."

He blinked. "You want to apply to business school?"

Oh God.

Her mouth opened, but it was another moment before she found the words. "I already applied. And I got in. I start in August."

His brow furrowed while something dark and angry flashed across his face. "So let me get this straight. You can get mad at me for not telling you about Argentina, but you're allowed to apply to business school behind my back?"

"It wasn't behind your back," she countered. "I just wanted to wait to tell you until I knew that it was a real possibility."

"But why did you even apply?" he asked, genuinely confused.

"I weighed my options and decided that it would be a smart choice to get an MBA while I figure out what I want to do. You know I've been struggling with what to do after graduation, and after talking to my mom, I thought—"

"Right. Of course." Freddie scoffed. "I should have known this was your mom's idea."

Anne hated how his voice sounded so sharp, so different from the deep warmth she was used to. She also hated how they were back here, at the point where so many arguments ended up: her mother. While Anne's father, Walter Elliot, took little interest in her accomplishments, it was Bianca Russell who was always doling out opinions and advice. Freddie hated it. Yes, he had only met her once—and even that had been by accident—but he had heard enough stories about Bianca's influence over Anne's life to form his own opinion. Meanwhile, Bianca had her own thoughts about Freddie—his fantastical dreams about changing the world, his laissez-faire attitude toward planning for it, and how his mindset was so very different from Anne's.

"You both can't get what you want, you know," her mother had said when Anne told her about Freddie's dream to travel after graduation. "One of you will have to compromise for the other, and you don't want it to be you."

"What does that mean?" Anne had asked.

Bianca had just sighed, like she'd seen this movie before and knew how it ended. "I *mean*, you don't come back from resentment, Anne. Don't be afraid to be selfish."

"But I don't want to lose him if—"

"Trust me, if he really loves you so much, he'll stay."

Her mother spoke from personal experience—her marriage to Anne's father had dissolved a decade before and Bianca had had numerous affairs since then. But Anne always reminded herself that she was nothing like her mother, even as her words still echoed in Anne's head.

"It might have been her idea, but I'm not getting my MBA because my mother told me to," Anne replied, pulling the Santa coat tighter around her shoulders.

"Then why the hell are you?" Freddie asked.

Because that's what's expected, she wanted to say. *It's what's always been expected, and I don't know who I am away from that.*

"Because that's what people do. They grow up and do the hard things, like go to college and get degrees that are applicable to the real world."

"Who says we have to be like other people?" His expression had hardened, like he recognized the influence beneath Anne's words.

"We don't, but that doesn't mean we have to be irresponsible, either," she said, crossing her arms over her chest. "This is our future we're talking about. That deserves time and attention and—"

"A plan?" he cut in, his tone biting.

The word jostled a familiar nerve deep in her chest. The one that always twinged when she was reminded of how different they were, when he made it sound like her meticulous nature was some sort of flaw.

"Yes," she said. "Everything can't be an adventure all the time."

"Right," he said with a bitter laugh. "I know what those plans look like. Some big job down on Wall Street that your parents will be able to brag about. A 401(k) and paid time off while you wait to eventually retire." He shook his head. "That's everyone else's normal. But it doesn't have to be mine. Or yours, regardless of what your mom says."

Here we go again, she thought. She was working so hard to keep from screaming that her hands were fists at her side. Maybe that's why they always avoided talking about the future—they always ended up here, at an impasse that was never resolved.

"Don't punish me because you and I want different things," she replied, keeping her tone measured.

"That's the thing, Annie, I don't know what the hell you want," he bit back. "And neither do you."

It felt like a physical blow. So sharp and swift that it severed something, a vital line that was suddenly limp.

"That's why I'm going to Columbia in the fall," she said. She hated how her voice now sounded so small.

Freddie must have noticed the change, too, because his expression softened and his arms were suddenly around her, drawing her against his tall body.

"I'm sorry," he whispered into her hair. "It's just a lot. But we'll make this work, okay?"

"How?" she whispered.

"Well, if you're staying in New York, I will, too," he murmured.

She leaned back enough to meet his eyes. "What do you mean?"

"I'll turn down the Buenos Aires program and stay," he replied, his mouth quirking up in that crooked grin again.

It would have been so easy to dismiss his sentiment as a joke. Because there was no way he would walk away from an opportunity like this. Objectively, it was insane. But then she remembered that the same impetuousness that saw him apply could just as easily see him turn it down. It was Freddie's MO. And the worst part was that he would see it as a win, another adventure to traverse. For a little while at least, until he had time to contemplate what he'd given up. Then the resentment would set in.

"This isn't a decision you make on a whim, Freddie," she said, stepping back and out of his arms. "This is your future, and—"

"I know you like your plans, Annie," he cut her off. "But this is my decision. I want to spend next year with you."

He was still smiling even as a new seriousness settled in his eyes, and she could already see his stubbornness taking root. The decision was being made in real time and no matter how much she told him he needed to go, nothing was going to change his mind.

You both can't get what you want, you know, her mother whispered in her head.

This is what her mother had been talking about. They were at the crux of it, and one of them had to give to move them both forward.

Don't be afraid to be selfish.

The selfish thing to do right now would be to keep her mouth shut. Let him stay and get everything she wanted. Except Anne couldn't be selfish, not with him. He needed to go to Argentina, even if that meant she had to force him onto the plane herself. She was okay being the bad guy, as long as he didn't have to compromise his dreams for her.

That's when the realization hit her with awful crystal clarity. She needed to be the bad guy, cut him loose, and let him go.

She needed to break up with him.

It should have sounded crazy, a rash decision that would be laughable in the morning, and for anyone else it might. But Anne understood logic. Her brain knew how to attack a problem, and it had shifted this one into a beautifully simple calculation: Two equal forces will oppose each other until one of them bends, but only if both forces remain unchanged.

She simply had to take herself out of the equation.

"FREDDIE!" a voice called out from the front of the bar. "WHERE'D YOU GO, MAN?"

Freddie released a frustrated sigh. "Let's head back inside. We can talk about this later, okay?"

"You go ahead," Anne said, taking another step back. "I think I'm going to head home."

He stared down at her, like he could see how something had changed. How she was desperately trying to hide what was already floating in her head.

"Hey," Freddie said. "You okay?"

No. I have to let you go and I have no idea how, she thought. It was for the best; she knew that. But she could never tell him because that would only make him want to stay more. The irony was so sharp she wanted to scream.

But instead, she said, "I'm fine."

Maybe this was inevitable. That would explain why she had avoided the topic of their future for so long. Deep inside, she knew that when she did, there was no going back. This was it, for better or for worse. And living in purgatory was easier than taking that decisive action.

"Let me walk you to the subway," he said, taking a step toward her.

"No, it's okay. It's just a few blocks," she said, forcing herself to smile even as tears pricked her eyes. "Besides, the host can't leave his own party."

Somewhere in the bar, there were cheers, laughter. "FREDDIE! GET YOUR ASS IN HERE!"

Snow had started to fall again and the beginning chords of "Deck the Halls" floated in the air. Neither of them moved for a moment.

Anne knew what had to come next. But she couldn't quite muster the courage to say the words. Not yet. So she convinced herself she could wait. Until after Christmas, at least.

"I'll call you when I get home," she said. She began to take off the Santa coat he had draped over her shoulders, but he waved it away.

"I'll grab it next time I see you," he replied.

Another moment passed.

"I love you, Annie," he finally said.

"I love you, too."

His gaze traveled down her face, as if trying to read her mind. She held her breath, waiting for him to say it, to know like he had always known so much about her. But nothing came. He just turned and disappeared around the brick wall without another word.

It wasn't until she was home at her dad's apartment in the East Village that she remembered the small paper triangle in her back pocket. She read it in the privacy of her bedroom.

It's Friday, December 22nd. We're having our annual Christmas party at Half Pint with all our friends and you just walked in. You haven't seen me yet, and I'm going to let you look around for a minute so I can watch you. I don't get to watch you so much these days, and I miss it. You pierce my soul, Annie. That view fits a part of me and I never want to be without it. I love you so much, and I can't wait for our next adventure.

—Freddie

She tried not to cry as she folded it back into its original shape and carefully put it into the small box in her nightstand that held all the others.

You both can't get what you want, her mother's words echoed in her mind again.

She didn't want to believe it, but maybe this time, her mother was right.

CHAPTER 1

Eight Years Later

"You miserable, cocksucking tramp!"

The words reverberated off the walls of the cramped edit room, hitting a part of Anne's inner ear that made her cringe. Her editor was unfazed, though—David just paused the video and turned to stare up at her from his keyboard, the light from his monitor illuminating his apathy.

"Well?" he asked, his voice monotone.

"You have to bleep it." Anne tried not to sound too condescending, but after editing over fifty episodes of *Divorce Divas* together, she had assumed the answer was obvious.

"Which part?"

"The cocksucker part, David."

"Yeah, but like, the whole word? Or just the cock part, and leave the sucking?"

Anne blinked back at the screen. *Huh.*

As she stared at the suspended image of Denise Sinclair, one of the series' biggest stars, frozen mid-motion as she was about to throw a glass of champagne at her former best friend, Marsha Beaumont, two questions popped into her head. First, why was this the most mentally stimulating conversation she'd had in months? And second, was "cocksucker" one word or two?

The door to the edit room swung open before she could ponder an answer to either. The harsh fluorescent light of the hallway silhouetted Theo Travers's broad frame in the doorway. His usual easy smile had been replaced by a grimace as he swept a hand through his dark tousled hair.

Theo was the showrunner on *Divorce Divas* and was an objectively attractive man. A few years ago, Anne had even harbored a small crush on him, but it had fizzled almost as quickly as it started, more of a distraction from the monotony of life than any real affection. But she still appreciated how good he was at his job. A master flirt, he excelled in any negotiation, while his inflated ego meant it took a lot to rattle him. Which was why his look of concern right now was so unfamiliar.

"Anne. Can I grab you for a sec?" he asked.

Anne straightened. Thanks to years of her father's overspending, she had implemented a strict "time is money" policy at Kellynch Productions, which meant that edit sessions—and their expensive editors who were paid by the hour—were not to be interrupted unless the building was on fire.

"Is the building on fire?" she asked.

"No no no, nothing like that." Then he paused, considering. "Well, it's an emergency, but David can keep editing. I think."

Anne turned to relay the direction to David, but the editor's attention was already back on the screen in front of him as he offered her a limp salute.

Theo nodded to the hallway and Anne followed him, smoothing the front of her carefully pressed gingham button-down as she mentally prepared herself for whatever was coming. After working at her father's production company for the past five years, she had faced a litany of odd—and, at times, mildly salacious—reality TV emergencies. She was sure she could handle this one. No problem.

Near the end of the hall, Theo stopped, looking both ways to make sure no one was listening.

"You're working on that Sinclair fight, yeah?" he asked, almost whispering.

Which one? Anne wanted to ask. The entire series had been defined by the number of fights they could fit into twenty-two minutes, and over the past few years Denise Sinclair had become the top supplier. Whether it was threatening to kick her ex-husband off their private jet while flying at thirty thousand feet or screaming at her sister-in-law for sleeping with her boyfriend, her fights were always the most vicious. And the most popular.

Still, Anne knew the one Theo was talking about. The fight to end all fights. The entire production staff had been talking about it for the past week. Denise had thrown that glass of champagne at Marsha, one of the other stars, during a birthday dinner at an upscale restaurant on the Jersey Shore before lunging at her from across the table.

It had been shocking, but moreover, it had been violent. Denise had managed to pull out three of Marsha's hair extensions and give her a bloody nose before the crew could separate them.

"Yeah, we're trying to piece together the footage to make it look less . . . " Anne tried to find the right word. She wanted to say bloodthirsty, but instead said, "*intense*."

Theo nodded, even as he winced.

Anne paused. "What?"

"I just got a call that Marsha is pressing charges. All the footage is now evidence, so we have to send it over to the police. She's threatening to sue the network, too."

Anne let her head fall back as she groaned. She should have

anticipated this. Marsha had called the police from the floor of the restaurant with an ice pack on her nose, screaming about her new bald spot. Denise had threatened to quit the show if she pressed charges. But to be fair, that was the usual order of things for these fights. Once the cameras were gone, Denise never brought it up again, another one of her brushes with the law that was swept under the rug.

Apparently not this time.

"I know," Theo said. "And of course the network is losing their shit and micromanaging the entire thing, putting us on hiatus until—"

"Wait," Anne said, straightening again. "What do you mean, hiatus?"

"Well, the fight was the main story for our last three episodes, right? But we can't finish the episodes until we're allowed to touch the footage again, and that could be months."

The numbers began to add up in Anne's head. Kellynch was already running on minimal staff, but there was no way they could afford to keep everyone on while they went dark. Then there was the rent for the office, the editing equipment, her own income...

She reached up, smoothing her blond hair even though she knew it was still securely fastened in a ponytail. It was a nervous tic she had had since grade school. "Shit."

Theo nodded. "Yeah."

"*Divorce Divas* is the only show we have in production."

Theo leaned a shoulder against the wall. "Well, look on the bright side. Hiatus means vacation."

"Theo—"

"Imagine it. You, me, a beach in the Virgin Islands..."

If Anne wasn't so overwhelmed, she probably would have laughed. But right now, all she could think about was how to triage the situation. Her brain went into overdrive evaluating every possible plan, ready to start giving instructions to Theo, when her phone buzzed to life in her pocket. She pulled it out to see a picture of Bianca Russell on the screen.

"I have to take this," she said, offering Theo an apologetic smile.

He threw her one back as she ducked into an empty editing room and shut the door.

"Hi, Mom," she said as she collapsed into the lone chair in front of the empty desk.

"Hello, my love," Bianca answered. "How are you?" Her voice sounded even and upbeat, which should have been a good thing, but after Anne had witnessed her use the same tone to fire two different management companies when she was the co-op president of their building—one of whom was a six-foot-tall man named Guido with supposed ties to organized crime, who left her mother's office in tears—it only added a level of stress to every interaction.

"Fine," Anne replied. "At the office dealing with a few ... things."

Silence filled the other end of the line, and she could almost see her mother's pursed lips, the slight arch of her perfectly shaped eyebrow as she worked to stay quiet about the world's worst-kept secret.

Anne let herself collapse into a nearby chair. "How do you already know what's going on here?"

"A little birdie told me," Bianca mused. "Your father and I may have divorced years ago, but many of the players remain the same, don't they?"

Of course. Anne should have known. Bianca had helped Anne's father start Kellynch Productions decades ago, thanks to her family's money that got it off the ground. And even though her mother vowed to never touch television production again after the divorce, her name was still listed as an executive producer for *Divorce Divas*—and on the royalty checks, too.

"There's so much to do, I don't even know where to start," Anne sighed, rubbing her temples. "Maybe I should call her and see if I can't smooth things over a bit."

"Oh, please," Bianca said with a dry laugh. "You never liked her, anyway."

Anne frowned. It was true she'd never been Denise's biggest fan, but that seemed like the least of their worries now.

"Maybe, but this affects a lot more people than just her," she replied. "No one on the production staff gets paid when a show like this goes on hiatus."

"The show is on hiatus?" Her mother sounded genuinely surprised.

Anne paused. "Isn't that why you're calling?"

"No, but this is delicious. You know, I don't usually believe in karma, but—"

"Mom," Anne cut in. "If you're not calling about the show, then what are you calling about?"

"Well, I don't know the details, so I shouldn't say anything," Bianca replied in the same tone as before, the one that belied an impending apocalypse. "But if I were you, I'd go home and have a chat with your dad about his latest ex-wife." Then she let out another dry laugh.

∽

Anne heard yelling even before the elevator arrived on the eighth floor of the Uppercross.

"You cannot be serious!" her father proclaimed as she opened the front door of their apartment. Walter Elliot was pacing through the living room, his arms crossed over his silk paisley shirt. At one point in his life, he had been incredibly handsome—tall, with striking blond hair and a sharp profile—but years of trying desperately to hold on to his looks via a series of collagen injections and thread lifts had turned the sixty-year-old into a taut, somehow bloated version of the original.

Across from him, seated on the long red leather sofa her father had custom-made last year, Harold Vernon removed his reading glasses and pinched the bridge of his nose. He had been her father's lawyer for as long as Anne had been alive, and while that job alone proved that he had the patience of a saint, she could tell he was close to his breaking point.

"Walter," Mr. Vernon said, leaning forward. "I know this is difficult—"

"No, this is ridiculous!"

"No, this is divorce," the lawyer replied bluntly.

The sound of the front door closing behind Anne drew the attention of both men. Unfortunately, their reactions to seeing her could not have been more different. While Mr. Vernon looked relieved at her arrival, her father's desperate expression turned to a scowl.

"Did you know about this?" her father barked.

Anne blinked. "Know about what?"

Walt let out a wail while Mr. Vernon sighed deeply.

"The judge finally ruled on the divorce settlement," the lawyer replied.

"Stop using that word!" Her father stomped over to the black-and-gold bar in the corner to make a drink, blissfully ignorant that it was eleven a.m. on a Monday.

Here we go, Anne thought, bracing herself. She had known about the divorce for a while. If she was being honest, before the wedding itself, though she had been smart enough to keep that to herself for the past few years.

Walt had met his second wife at a cocktail party in Los Angeles. MacKenzie was an influencer looking to break into television and hadn't been bothered by the twenty-year age gap, especially when Walt promised to develop a series exclusively for her. But things began to fall apart quickly after their wedding in Tulum three years ago, and now there was no series, no money, and no MacKenzie. The last Anne heard, she was living in Ibiza with her new restaurant-tycoon boyfriend, and communicating about the divorce exclusively through her lawyer.

"And?" Anne asked.

Mr. Vernon put his reading glasses back on as he brought his attention back to the papers in his hand. "MacKenzie was awarded fifty percent of all shared assets. Including this apartment."

Walt let out another wail. With his monthly Botox injections, it should have been impossible for him to look haggard or stressed. Today proved to be the exception.

Anne shook her head. She hated that she was surprised. It was no secret that her father hadn't made MacKenzie sign a prenup. Still, it felt like the air had been knocked from her lungs.

"All right," Anne said, the numbers already running through her head. "So what does that mean, logistically?"

Mr. Vernon barely concealed a grimace. "Her lawyers have already written to the co-op board about her intention to sell."

Anne slowly sat down on the other end of the sofa. So that's how her mother had known. Bianca Russell had been the Uppercross co-op board president for a decade before she moved out following her own divorce from Walt. She had ruled all eight floors of the building with an iron fist and still stayed in touch with many of the board members.

"What am I going to *do*?" Walt lamented.

"As I see it, you've got two options," Mr. Vernon replied. "It's clear MacKenzie isn't interested in the apartment, just the financial incentives. With that being the case, you could buy her out of her half."

Even as he said it, the lawyer looked dubious, and Anne couldn't blame him. Walt Elliot's lack of fiscal responsibility was no secret. Even as a child she had suspected that his spending habits were out of control. But the true weight of it wasn't something she'd had to consider until after her parents' divorce. When she took over the day-to-day running of Kellynch, she had created a detailed personal budget for her father, in an effort to curb his spending and keep him from dipping into the company's profits to fund his whims. If he had followed it like he'd promised, not only should he have a healthy savings account, but his credit score probably improved, too.

If, she thought to herself.

"Buy her out?" Walt cried. "It's *my* apartment! Besides, I don't have that kind of money just lying around."

"You don't need the entire sum," Anne replied. "We can take whatever you have in your savings, then take out a mortgage to fill in the gap."

"You want me to take out *another* mortgage?"

Anne stilled. There had never been a mortgage on his apartment. Bianca Russell had come to their marriage with blue-blood family money, and Walt had received a healthy settlement for their seventeen years together. And while Bianca took her remaining fortune and spent her time traveling around the world with a steady stream of younger boyfriends on her arm, her father had gotten the apartment and then proceeded to spend his income on plastic surgery and vacations.

"What do you mean 'another' mortgage?" she asked.

Her father rolled his eyes. "Did I mortgage this apartment last year? Yes. But that was only to pay off a few outstanding personal loans."

"What about the savings account we set up for—"

"You have to spend money to make money, Anne! *Everybody* knows that."

Anne let out a long breath, hoping it would somehow dilute the mix of frustration and disappointment swirling in her chest. Why was she even surprised? This wasn't a new problem. Walt had been overspending for years without consequence. It was part of the reason her mother had left him. Yet Anne had naively thought that if she stayed close by, she might be able to curb it. That had been the main motivation behind living at home through college, then later for working at his company. Walt couldn't possibly put his livelihood in jeopardy under her watchful eye, right?

Right, she thought dryly, shaking her head.

This wasn't how it was supposed to go. When she graduated with honors from Columbia Business School six years ago, she almost immediately started working at a large hedge fund in Manhattan. The work had been exciting at first, with days spent working with numbers and projections, promises of promotions, and a defined track for success. But within a few months she couldn't ignore the moral gray area she was forced to work in. She quit unceremoniously one Tuesday afternoon after a meeting where her boss made a joke about foreclosing on people's homes, and she walked out the door feeling like a thousand-pound weight had been removed from her neck. Walt Elliot obviously hadn't seen it that way, though, berating her for the loss of her title and her salary. A few days later she happened to answer a call from her father's accountant and learned just how close Kellynch was to bankruptcy.

The solution seemed obvious: She had an MBA, why not use it to help save her father's business? The fact that she went on to spend the next five years digging his production company out of crippling debt over and over again had not been part of the equation, though. Walt rarely acknowledged it, either. He paid her close to nothing, but then he also didn't charge her rent, so perhaps the expectation was that she would ignore everything else going on in his life. Unfortunately for him, old habits die hard.

"Dad, we've been over this—"

"Don't take that tone with me," he hissed. "I have it all under control. Once we sign the contract for another season of *Divorce Divas*, the initial payment will cover—"

"There's no contract, Dad," Anne cut him off. She could already feel a headache coming on. "Not for a while, anyway."

Walt's face blanched. "What?"

"The network put us on hiatus."

"Why?"

"Remember that fight Denise got into with Marsha last month?"

Her father stared at her blankly.

Stupid question, she thought. It had been months since Walt even stepped foot in the Kellynch offices.

"Well, Denise attacked Marsha, and now Marsha, along with the restaurant, is pressing charges. We can't even finish the current season until the investigation and trial are over, which could take months."

"Why are you doing this to me?" Walter moaned, slumping back onto the red leather sofa as he cradled his glass to his chest.

Anne tried not to roll her eyes as she turned back to Mr. Vernon. "You said we had two options. What's the second?"

Mr. Vernon's expression turned grim. "Sell the apartment."

The words landed like a lead weight in Anne's brain.

"*Sell?*" her father said, frantically gesturing around the apartment with his free hand. "This is where I live!"

Where we *live,* Anne wanted to correct him.

But she kept her mouth shut. To her father, the only thing more embarrassing than having his daughter swooping in to save him from financial ruin was having that same daughter still living at home at almost thirty years old because he couldn't afford to pay her enough to move out.

"Do you have another idea?" Mr. Vernon asked.

Her father took a half second to consider. "I could sell my Max Betrug painting."

Anne had to close her eyes to school her frustration. "That's a print, Dad. Not an original painting."

"What about the Bentley?"

"You sold that two years ago."

Walt's head fell back as he wailed again.

"This is the best option, Walt," Mr. Vernon replied. "You can use your half of the sale to pay off some debt and rent someplace nearby. Maybe in Brooklyn."

"You want me to move to *Brooklyn?*" Walt exclaimed. "But my masseuse is here! I built these bookcases specifically to feature my Emmy!"

Her father continued his monologue, but Anne blocked it out. She was good at that. Instead, she turned and stared out the nearby window as she tried to curb the panic that was already clouding her analysis of the situation. The apartment was on the eighth floor, and she could see the treetops that canopied Tompkins Square Park just below. The leaves were starting to change from green to autumnal reds and yellows. In a few months they would be adorned in Christmas lights and covered with snow.

You can do this, she thought, forcing her heart rate under control. She just needed a plan, time to sit down and go over the situation rationally, work through the numbers systematically, and—

"Alexa!" her father called out without removing his arm, which was currently thrown over his face. A device lit up on the kitchen's marble countertop on the other side of the room. "Set a reminder to call Dr. Zgonc for a sound healing treatment today."

"*Reminder set*," Alexa replied happily.

"Now, considering this neighborhood and those... renovations, I'm sure we can sell this place quickly," Mr. Vernon said. "But we'll need to work fast to move things along. The president of the co-op board is a Realtor, correct? I'm sure he can—"

"Where's my ashwagandha?" Walt yelled without looking up. "My herbalist was supposed to deliver it this morning! I can't have this conversation without my ashwagandha!"

Anne was about to remind her father that perhaps his five-hundred-dollar-an-hour herbalist was one of the reasons he was in this mess, but at the same time, it felt futile. The full weight of eight years' worth of relentless work and sacrifice being washed away in one afternoon landed squarely on her chest and all she could do was stand up and walk back out the front door.

Her father was still berating Mr. Vernon as Anne turned down the hall and up the nearby stairs to the building's roof deck. The steel door slammed shut behind her as she stepped out into the almost blinding midday sunlight, and the laments from apartment 8A were replaced by the sounds of the city below.

She had grown up in this building. Her father called their apartment the penthouse, but really it was just the top floor of the Uppercross, one of the few taller apartment buildings along Avenue A in Manhattan's East Village. Her parents had bought their apartment when her mother found out she was pregnant. Walt's way of dealing with impending parenthood was to grasp at any thread of youth and relevance he could, so a newly remodeled, two-bedroom apartment in one of New York's most iconic—and edgy—neighborhoods was perfect. He had hoped to absorb some of the neighborhood's hip pedigree by osmosis, but he soon learned that he would much rather brag about his address than spend any time getting to know the neighborhood.

Not Anne, though. Some of her earliest memories were of wandering the hallways of this building, watching new people move in and familiar faces move out, of all the doormen that played cards with her during their shifts, and the anticipation of the changing seasonal décor—Halloween pumpkins, Christmas lights, summer potted roses and lilies out front. She remembered the new-paint smell from every time they remodeled the hallway columns, and all the hours she'd spent sitting on the same forest-green leather couches in the lobby before school started. The winding paths through Tompkins Square Park became her backyard playground, and the shops lining the road were filled with owners who knew her by name, let her do her homework next to them as they rang up customers, and watched her grow up.

Now she had to think about movers and showings. Packing up her life and going... where?

She closed her eyes, letting the wind pull wisps of her blond hair from her neat ponytail.

Even at her most dejected moments, she tried not to let herself look back, to regret decisions that there was no possibility of changing. But she gave in for a moment there on the roof, allowing herself to linger on all the choices and decisions that brought her to this point. Suddenly, the crystalline image of Freddie Wentworth landed in the center of her mind. His kind eyes staring down at her, crinkling at the corners, thanks to his lopsided smile.

Something deep in her chest ached. Thank God he wasn't here to see her now.

CHAPTER 2

Freddie walked out of his terminal at JFK Airport on Friday morning to find his driver there, waiting. The driver himself was different than the one who had been there last weekend, but the placard he held up was the same:

FREDERICK WENTWORTH

"Shit," Freddie mumbled to himself. He'd forgotten to tell his assistant to cancel the car reservation, that he'd just get a yellow cab into the city, maybe order an Uber. Anything that didn't make him feel like a visitor to his own town.

He gave the driver a tight smile and a nod, then followed him out the terminal's sliding glass doors. When they reached the curb and Freddie saw the gleaming Suburban waiting, he ran a frustrated hand through his hair. He had cropped it a few years ago, but that didn't mean the habit of pushing it out of his face was gone, especially when he was frustrated.

But the minute the driver opened the back door and Freddie slid into the car's plush interior, a bit of his annoyance dissolved.

After a cross-country red-eye flight, he was exhausted and needed to sink into the leather seat to relax—he had to admit that a yellow cab wouldn't have cut it.

The car pulled away from the curb, sliding into traffic as they joined the expressway headed toward Manhattan. It was elevated, cutting right across Queens, and Freddie studied the low buildings packed close together on a never-ending grid of streets below. Growing up, he hadn't been privy to this view—he only knew his old neighborhood through the lenses of subway stops and the passenger seat of his dad's plumbing van. Even then, it was side roads, back alleys. His first time on the expressway had been when he left the city eight years ago with only a couple of duffel bags and a one-way ticket to Buenos Aires. Now he was back, but this time in a chauffeured car and wearing a suit that cost more than his student loans.

Would that kid even recognize him now? Probably not, and the clothes wouldn't be the only reason why. New York was his hometown, and he never would have guessed he would stay away for so long, even if it was due to building his own business.

Still, regardless of how successful he was, how his budget travel had been upgraded to first class, the monotony of living out of a suitcase had become too much. So had the corporate meetings, the investor lunches, the suits and small talk. He needed some downtime to figure out what came next.

He needed New York.

The thought almost made him laugh—the idea that New York would offer a respite from the breakneck speed of the past few years showed how insane his life had become.

His phone pinged in his jacket pocket. He pulled it out and saw a text from his Realtor waiting.

BIRDIE CARRINGTON

> Two bedroom in the East Village with views of the river! What's not to love? Still on for noon today? This really is the one.

Freddie smiled to himself. Birdie had said that about the last thirty apartments they had viewed. After he sold his company and decided to move back to the city, his friend Will had introduced him to his aunt, Birdie Carrington, the owner of Carrington Realty. She had taken Freddie under her wing to ensure, as she put it, "he returned home to a true *home*." Meanwhile, he just wanted to find a place so his mom would stop guilt-tripping him to stay at their house in Queens.

FREDDIE

> I'll be there. I think Sophie will be too.

Three dots appeared on-screen, then vanished, only to pop back up again. Freddie could practically see his Realtor cringing at the mention of his sister.

BIRDIE CARRINGTON

> Great.

A moment later, she sent a link to the address. He clicked it and his smile abruptly faded. The building was on Avenue A across from Tompkins Square Park. He hadn't been down in that neighborhood for years.

Not that you were ever invited there to begin with, he reminded himself. He quickly closed out of his messages.

He had spent the past eight years avoiding all thoughts of Anne Elliot; he wasn't about to start down memory lane now that he was back. For the first time in years, he felt free, and he refused to let the past change that.

His phone pinged with another text.

He looked down, ready to see another message from Birdie, but saw one from his mother instead.

MOM

Your sister just called to tell me you two are looking at an apartment together today?

Then another ping.

MOM

YOU TOLD ME YOU WERE COMING IN TOMORROW

And another.

MOM

FREDERICK WENTWORTH, IF YOU EVEN THINK ABOUT STAYING IN A HOTEL TONIGHT I WILL PERSONALLY WRING YOUR NECK

Okay. Maybe not completely free, he thought, and let his head fall back onto the headrest.

Freddie saw his sister standing in the center of the apartment building's lobby before he even entered. She was hard to miss—

despite being just five feet tall, her bright, hot-pink bob made sure she stood out in any room. Or, in this case, from just outside one.

He stepped across the threshold, ready to give her a hard time about siccing their mother on him, but before he could open his mouth, the familiar voice of his Realtor rang through the air.

"Isn't it just *gorgeous?*" Birdie Carrington crooned, appearing around the far corner, her white hair perfectly curled at her shoulders and a Birkin thrown over one arm. She waltzed across the checkerboard floor toward Freddie, then leaned forward as if she would hug him—but a hug never came, only a brief kiss on either cheek. Behind her, Sophie rolled her eyes.

"And the neighborhood!" Birdie continued as her hand went to her chest, causing her collection of gold bracelets to clatter. "I'm so glad you could make time to see this one. You'll love it. Just *love* it."

"More than you loved the penthouse on Fifty-Second, apparently. And that condo on Fifth," Sophie added. "I arrived a few minutes early and heard *all* about it."

Birdie's lips pursed, as if she had forgotten that his sister was there. She probably wished she could. Sophie's running monologue during these showings had become the bane of Birdie's existence.

"Your brother has taste," Birdie said with a huff. "Who can fault him for being picky?"

Sophie raised her hand. "Me. I can fault him."

Birdie gave her a sharp smile, then turned on her heel and started toward the elevator.

Freddie shot Sophie a warning look before following.

The lobby was like so many in Manhattan—clean and modern and hollow. Ivory tiles with a beige runner led down the long room to a tall mahogany desk at the back, while on the wall to his right were rows of mailboxes and an unassuming abstract painting. None of it would have bothered Freddie except for the fact that remnants of what had been replaced were still evident if you looked hard enough. There was still turn-of-the-century marble wainscotting on the walls, and the mailboxes—each with its own small brass door—looked original to the building.

Birdie ignored all of it as she made her way to the open elevator. Freddie held the elevator door for his sister, then stepped in himself.

"The entire building was redone a few years ago, including a fabulous roof deck with 360-degree views of the city," Birdie said, sliding into the elevator and pressing eight. The gears above them groaned as the car began its journey up. "Most of the apartments have also been remodeled with luxury amenities."

"Most?" Sophie asked.

"Well, it's impossible to accommodate *all* the apartments. You can't just evict longtime residents, what with rent control and grandfathered leases. This is New York," Birdie replied, as if they should have known the intricacies of the city's housing ordinances. "But there's only a few of those in the building. For the most part, your neighbors would only be the best of the best. And yes, it's a co-op, but the board is supposedly *very* motivated. We should have no problems greasing the wheels."

The comment irked Freddie, but he kept his mouth shut.

"Eighth floor!" Birdie announced as the elevator doors opened. He waited, allowing Birdie and Sophie to exit first, then followed them into a short hallway. "Up those stairs is a door that leads to the roof deck. Apparently, everyone in the building has access, but for you it's right outside *your* door." Birdie waved down to the other end of the hallway as she turned left and stopped at a massive door. "And inside is a dream. Twelve-foot-high ceilings, parquet de Versailles floors, marble en suite bathrooms, and a French scagliola fireplace."

Sophie let out a loud, melodramatic gasp. "Scagliola?"

Birdie didn't pick up on the sarcasm, just nodded proudly as she unlocked the dead bolt and waltzed inside.

Sophie started forward, too, pausing just long enough to whisper to Freddie, "What the hell is scagliola?"

He chuckled to himself and waved her ahead.

Morning light streamed in from all directions as they stepped into the apartment. The main living room was massive and sat in the corner of the building, so two walls featured tall windows that were open, letting in the breeze. Birdie wasn't lying—the parquet floors were beautiful, as was the crown molding and, from what he could see from across the room, the marble countertops in the kitchen that opened up on the other end of the apartment. But all of it was overshadowed by everything inside. Freddie had seen enough apartments now to know when personal adornments—photographs, awards, even kitchen magnets—had been removed in hopes of a quick sale, and this one was no exception. But in this case it didn't help matters, because now there was nothing to distract from the interior design: the matching red leather sofas that were in the shape of an S. The blown-glass sculpture in the corner. A life-size porcelain tiger by the bar.

He walked past it all, down a hallway on his left where he found two bedrooms. One of them was huge, with an en suite bathroom, while the smaller one at the end of the hall barely had enough room for its queen-size bed. But it did have the best views. Like the living room, it sat in the corner of the building, but on the northwest side, with one of the windows facing uptown and the other the East River.

After a few minutes, Freddie wandered back to the living room. Birdie was standing by the bookcase, eyeing a sculpture on the shelf, while Sophie was near the kitchen, seated on a stool, leaning an elbow on the marble countertop.

"Well, what do you think?" Birdie asked, her expression lighting up when she saw him emerge from the hallway. He opened his mouth to speak, but she barreled on. "I know the interior design may not be your cup of tea, but the owners are taking everything when they move out at the end of the month, so just try to look past it. *Visualize*." She held up her arms, framing the room like it would somehow help with the exercise, when something in her bag began to vibrate.

"Your Birkin is buzzing," Sophie said, her tone bored.

Birdie reached inside and pulled out her phone.

"Oh! That's the listing agent. He lives in the building and wanted to stop by," she said, her attention on the screen as she headed toward the door. "Keep looking around. I'll be back in just a few."

A flurry of movement, a parting wink, and she was gone.

"Well?" Sophie said, draping her arm over the marble countertop as she mimicked Birdie's affected tone. "Are you *visualizing*?"

Freddie sighed, running a hand through his cropped hair. "Are you here to mock Birdie or help me decide on an apartment?"

"Oh, come on, this has to be the fiftieth place we've seen," she whined, sitting up straight as she made a face at the bright orange canvas on the wall beside her. "How many apartments do you need to look at?"

He hated to admit that she was right. Over the past three months, they had seen more than enough apartments. Birdie had described each one the same way, too—some variation of gorgeous, luxurious, or chic. After the first dozen, Freddie realized she wasn't being disingenuous. They were all gorgeous, luxurious, *and* chic, but they were also exactly the same. New and modern, atop some high-rise in Midtown.

None of them ticked that one box that even he hadn't quite

defined yet. The one that would ease that annoying bit of lingering self-doubt and stop him from feeling like he still needed to prove himself. Where the hell had that come from, anyway? He had left this city eight years ago, and in that time he had founded his own company, Wentworth Hydroponics. His modular farms were being used around the world, his company had just been acquired by one of the largest agriculture corporations to ever exist. He should be returning to New York like a conquering hero.

Maybe it was imposter syndrome. Or maybe it was just that same feeling everyone grappled with when returning home years after moving away: Regardless of how old you are, you still somehow regressed back to who you were when you left.

"We're not kids anymore, Soph," he replied. "I don't need my big sister's help to find a place to live."

"Maybe not, but I need a distraction from watching all my dreams crash and burn," she said, plastering on a painfully fake smile as she motioned to the window. "I'm serious, I can practically see the flower shop from here. It's two blocks away."

He glanced over at the view. Shit, she was right. The storefront that would have been her and her husband's floral shop was just a few blocks away.

Sophie's divorce wasn't new. She and her soon-to-be ex, Jimmy Bruno, had been hammering out the details for months. But it was still taking some time to get used to. They had been high school sweethearts, falling in love freshman year and never leaving each other's side for over a decade. Jimmy had been the first person to help Freddie with Bertha, the make-shift hydroponics system he built in his parents' basement in college, and had talked Freddie's father off a ledge when he eventually found out about it. Freddie and Jimmy had gone to Yankees games together, even had a few double dates with Sophie and Anne. But the cracks between Sophie and Jimmy started to form a few years ago, when they decided to open a floral shop together. Jimmy had argued that they lived in Queens, so that's where the shop should be, but Sophie wanted to think bigger. Soon, they had signed a lease for a storefront in the East Village. Freddie was sure there had been problems before that, but the business only accentuated them. So much so that Sophie filed for divorce before Bruno's Blooms even opened its doors. Now Sophie had a storefront, all the equipment, and no idea what to do with it.

"You'll be fine, Soph," Freddie said, softening his tone slightly. "The shop can still happen. You just need to hire someone to handle the business side of things."

"Right. Between contractors and vendors and helping my brother find a place to live, I'll make sure to pencil that in," she murmured.

"We've been over this. I don't need your help to find an apartment."

"And leave you to your own devices?" His sister rolled her eyes. "Yeah, right. If you end up in another apartment with a twenty-four-hour concierge, Mom is going to keel over."

Freddie shook his head, even as he laughed. Sophie knew as well as he did that he never took advantage of the always-available concierge at his apartment in Los Angeles. In fact, he hadn't even known about the service until he was moving out.

But that hadn't stopped his sister or the rest of the family from giving him shit about it, as if he had somehow forgotten where he came from. Impossible for numerous reasons, not least of which was that his parents still lived in the small house in Queens where he grew up.

"Besides," Sophie continued, getting down from the counter stool and wandering into the center of the room. "I think this is the best one we've seen. I mean, the view is awful, obviously." She gestured back to the window framing where her shop should be. "But the apartment itself is kind of gorgeous."

Freddie nodded absently, giving the living room another glance.

"Anne used to live around here, didn't she?"

"Who?" he asked, pretending to find the purple acrylic dining table interesting.

With anyone else, his feigned ignorance would have worked, but not his sister. Sophie turned, giving him a look similar to the one he had thrown her way just a moment before. The same one they had inherited from their mother.

"Oh, I'm sorry. Is there another Anne who lived in the East Village and broke your heart that I should know about?"

He scoffed. "You missed your calling. You should have been a stand-up comedian."

"Doubly funny since I wasn't kidding," she replied, glancing out the window again. "So? Did she?"

He pretended to think about it as he walked forward toward the kitchen. "Yeah, I think so."

"You think so?"

"Well, I was never invited over, was I?"

Sophie's mouth made a small O, as if she was just recalling that small detail. As if he hadn't spent almost his entire collegiate life talking about Anne Elliot. Sophie knew every detail, including how he'd never seen her family home even once during their almost three-year relationship, how he still wasn't sure if it was because she was embarrassed of her family or of him.

A long moment passed before Sophie continued, "What's she doing these days?"

He shot her another look.

"What?" His sister's eyes went wide, like she had no idea what she was doing.

"You know I haven't talked to her in years, Soph."

"Yeah, not right after the breakup, but you two must have connected on social media or something. It's been seven years."

"Eight," he said before he could stop himself.

To her credit, she didn't call him out on it. "I'm just saying, Freddie. You two were a big part of each other's lives. Now you don't even know where she is?"

"No. I don't." His voice sounded cold. Final. It was out of character enough that Sophie blinked, the only tell that she was surprised.

Shit. It was rude, but he didn't have the patience to apologize and invite the conversation to continue. He had spent years separating himself from Anne Elliot, both mentally and physically. It was easier when he wasn't in New York, but now that he was back, he didn't want to fall into old patterns.

He had moved on. And maybe reclaiming this one last bit of his city would be the final step he needed.

That last thought was punctuated by the front door swinging open again. Birdie waltzed back in with a smile, followed by a man about Freddie's age. He was slightly shorter, though, with black hair and wearing a pair of trendy wire-rim glasses.

"Frederick! This is Ellis Rowley. He's the listing agent for this utopia," she said, motioning between them.

Ellis let out a chuckle and shook Freddie's hand. "Nice to meet you. My husband James and I live on a lower level of utopia. Apartment 5A. I'm also the co-op board president, so don't let the application deter you. I can move it along quickly."

"But you still have to move *fast*," Birdie added, her singsong voice almost hitting shrill levels. "Something like this won't stay on the market long."

Freddie turned to look around the apartment again.

The windows were open, allowing in the crisp autumn air. Temperatures had only just started to cool and the leaves outside were beginning to change color, leaving an earthy tinge to the breeze that billowed the curtains. The living room sat at the northeast corner of the building, so he could hear the sounds of traffic below, along with children's laughter from what Freddie could only assume was Tompkins Square across the street. It was all just far enough away that it added life to the apartment while maintaining a level of serenity that even the red leather sofas couldn't ruin.

He smiled. Birdie was right. Without the ridiculous furniture, the bad art, those awful curtains, it was good. Better than good. It was perfect. Natural light streaming in from all directions, tall ceilings lined with original crown molding. It had character and charm. The perfect place to start fresh. He could already picture the housewarming party he would throw, a huge gathering of all his favorite people to welcome him back to the city he had missed so much.

Was it too impulsive to decide on a place after just one viewing? Maybe. But being impulsive hadn't steered him wrong yet. Why start now?

He turned back to Birdie and threw her an easy smile. "Then let's start the paperwork."

CHAPTER 3

The next month was a blur. Between temporarily shuttering Kellynch Productions—and breaking the news to its staff—getting the apartment ready for showings, and trying to figure out where she was supposed to go herself, Anne barely had time to come up for air. When she finally did, it was October, and an offer to buy the apartment was on the table. In just a few weeks, someone else would be living there.

She tried not to think about that nagging detail, which was easier thanks to her father. He had insisted that the sale be done anonymously—as if having names attached would send a bulletin out across the city about his financial straits—so information about the potential buyer was sparse. And that was okay. Better, actually. Anne didn't want a name. It was bad enough thinking about some stranger walking around her kitchen, her bedroom . . .

It was never really hers, though, was it? Despite how much time she had spent there, how much it had shaped her life, apartment 8A wasn't hers. It never had been. It was her father's. He owned everything while Anne barely had a savings account.

Yes, but you have a plan, she thought. And that was always the first step to solving any problem, right? Sure, her current plan only had two steps—find a job and a place to live—but she could build off that. Just as soon as she finished coordinating the move for her father. And wrapped up all payroll at Kellynch. And—

No spiraling, she reminded herself.

Right. She couldn't think about any of that, not until she got through this co-op board meeting and ensured they approved the sale of the apartment. That's if they ever actually got to that item on the agenda.

"This is censorship!" Beverly Santenello bellowed.

A collective groan rose from the group assembled in the rows of metal folding chairs currently set up in Ellis Rowley's living room on the fifth floor.

"Bev, we voted on this last month," Ellis replied patiently from where he stood in front of them, even as his expression looked increasingly pained. The tie he had been wearing at the beginning of the meeting was loosened, and his new wire-rim glasses were already askew.

"To clarify, that vote was regarding Labor Day decorations," Glen Rinnard of 2B interjected from the front row. His day job as a tax lawyer meant such clarifications were just about his only contribution to these meetings.

"Right," Beverly agreed from where she stood in the second row. All eyes were on her and her short gray hair sticking out in all directions. "And I only put Dennis out for Halloween."

Anne sat in the back row, biting back a smile. Beverly had lived in the building since the late sixties, and had been propping up Dennis, her life-size Satan dummy with glowing eyes, in the window of her fourth-floor apartment every October for almost as long. Apparently, it had never been an issue until the building was renovated a decade ago, attracting a new echelon of tenants, and now every autumn the same battle was waged in the Uppercross co-op meeting.

Ellis readjusted his glasses. "Regardless of the technicalities, there have been complaints—"

"What complaints?" Beverly snapped.

"Well, there's been some concerns about it appearing demonic and lowbrow—"

"From who?"

"They were submitted anonymously," Ellis said, shifting his weight.

"So, it was Wendy," Beverly replied, shooting a death glare across the room.

"It's distasteful!" A shrill voice rose up from that direction. Anne knew it was Wendy Graham, a fairly new tenant who had moved from the Upper West Side and spent her weekends in Connecticut. "And scary!"

Beverly scoffed. "You want to talk scary? I went on a date with Lou Reed in 1968. *That* was scary."

A dozen different conversations suddenly broke out across the room. The Uppercross only had sixteen units, so despite Ellis's efforts as co-op board president to restrict the monthly board meetings to just the board members, everyone inevitably showed up, attracted by the need to air their grievances as well as partake in the charcuterie boards that Ellis's husband, James, laid out in the kitchen.

Over the din of conversation, Ellis found Anne and looked at her pleadingly. He may have been the board president for the past five years, but Anne came from co-op board royalty. Her mother had run these meetings so efficiently during her tenure as president that no one could fill her shoes, though the rest of the building regularly looked to Anne to try. Whether it was negotiating with plumbers or talking through tenant disputes, Anne was inevitably brought in to help.

"Why doesn't Beverly just close her curtains at night, like last year?" she offered.

Ellis's eyes lit up. "Right! That's right. Thank you, Anne. Why don't we agree to have you close your curtains at night, Bev?"

Beverly considered for a moment. "Fine." Then she sat down.

"Great! Fantastic. Moving on." Ellis cleared his throat as he looked down at the tablet in front of him. "Next item of business is the proposed sale of apartment 8A."

There was an uncomfortable shift through the room as a few eyes darted Anne's way. She was used to it—she could barely traverse the lobby these days without a look of pity from one of her neighbors.

"Now, under normal circumstances, we wouldn't put a time limit on the vetting process for applications," Ellis continued. "But I think we can agree to fast-track this one—"

"Objection," Beverly blurted out as she stood up again.

Glen raised his hand. "She means point of order."

"Point of order," Beverly continued, her tone flat. "Does anyone else think it's funny that our president here is trying to push through this sale while he's also conveniently the listing agent?"

Conversation erupted again as tenants talked and debated with one another, all while Ellis stood in front of them looking defeated. Anne was tempted to go up and try to help but stopped herself. That wasn't her role here anymore, was it?

The thought sent a jolt of anxiety through her bloodstream. She stood up and slid out of her row, then headed for the kitchen's swinging door.

The usual array of food was laid out on the countertops: glasses and plates and about five vastly different charcuterie boards. After James and Ellis were married a few years ago, James had thrown himself into his role as first husband of the Uppercross, and as such, made sure to have each board meeting include the finest catering platters that the gourmet grocery store around the corner had to offer. But Anne ignored all of it and went straight to the selection of wine bottles lined up along the terra-cotta backsplash.

Anne had never been a big drinker. Those times Freddie had convinced her to go out with his friends in college, it was routine for her to order a drink, have a sip or two, and then stealthily slip it to him to finish before anyone noticed. If she had more than that, she would spend more time worrying about the inevitable hangover than enjoying the evening itself.

Not now, though. Anne took a deep sip of her wine, ignoring how it burned down her throat as she straightened her shoulders and smoothed out the front of her fitted cardigan.

This is fine, she reminded herself. *It's all under control. You can handle this.*

A moment later, the kitchen door swung open behind her and James walked in.

"It's like watching a car crash in slow motion," he said as he reached for a bottle of red. His array of rings clattered against it as he poured himself a glass. "I'm serious, Anne. I will pay you a million dollars not to move out and leave us with those people."

"Do you have a million dollars, James?"

It was rhetorical. James was the first to admit that being the first husband of the Uppercross was wildly underpaid.

"No, but I will find it, because if you leave, Ellis will have to deal with these psychos on his own. That means I'll never see him, and he'll be stressed, and then we'll get a divorce."

Anne smiled. "You're not getting divorced."

"I know. That's why I need a million dollars," he whined. Then he paused, eyes wide.

"Oh! What about the basement? There's an apartment down there, right? You could move in down there!"

Anne's brow furrowed. "You mean the laundry room?"

"It has a window," he added, as if that helped.

The door to the small kitchen swung open before Anne could reply, and Cricket entered, mouth slack and eyes crossed like she was about to drop dead of boredom. The expression did nothing to spoil her features, though. Her lips only looked more perfectly full, and the tilt of her head somehow made her long mane of curly brown hair frame her high cheekbones perfectly.

Cricket lived in 4B, the apartment across from Bev, and she also happened to be Ellis's younger sister. This fact was the source of the building's last great political drama two years ago when the former tenant of 4B moved out and Cricket, who wanted to move to New York to be an actress, moved in. Bev was the first to note that the apartment, which also happened to be one of the few remaining ones in the building with rent control, had never been officially listed. By the time Cricket had moved in and Ellis hired her to work part-time at his real estate office while she auditioned for roles, half the building was ready to revolt.

But then something incredible happened: Cricket and Bev became friends. Or, at least, Cricket thought they did. Once she learned that the woman across the hall had slapped a police officer at the Stonewall Riots and slept with Iggy Pop, Cricket was enamored. Soon, all objections were dropped, and Bev hadn't been able to shake Cricket since.

"Everything all right?" Anne asked, her voice low so it wouldn't carry to the next room.

"It's just so *boring*," Cricket said. "All they're talking about is, like, reserve funds? Credit scores? Who even cares."

"You know you don't have to come to these things, Cricks," James said. "It's a board meeting, not a resident meeting."

"Tell that to your husband. He said I have to, so I understand 'equity capital.' As if that's even a thing. Meanwhile, I'm missing rehearsal! The play opens next month, and I still haven't learned the choreography for the cybernetic fairy number!"

James's head cocked to the side, like he was choosing his words carefully. "I thought you said it was a Shakespeare retelling."

"It is," Cricket replied, as if that was obvious.

Anne cleared her throat to mask her laugh, while James looked at Cricket with a mix of bewilderment and awe.

Then the kitchen door swung open again and Beverly shuffled in.

"Somebody needs to remove whatever climbed up Wendy's ass and died," she murmured.

James put a finger on his nose. "Not it."

Anne smiled and poured Beverly a glass of red wine, handing it to her as they all shifted to accommodate the latest arrival.

"How's it going out there?" Anne asked.

"Looks like the sale is going through." Beverly took a big gulp, then nodded to James. "Watch out. Ellis sounds smitten with the buyer."

"He paid cash, so I don't blame him," James said with a sigh. "Though I don't have visual confirmation of hotness yet."

"I do," Cricket replied. Her tone was innocent, but her smile was decidedly not.

Three sets of eyes snapped to her.

"You met him?" Anne asked, genuinely curious.

Cricket nodded. "He came by Ellis's office the other day to go over some paperwork."

"And?" James asked, leaning over the sliced melon to make sure he got every word.

"I *may* have introduced myself," Cricket replied with a playful shrug. "And I *may* have taken the keys so he has to stop by my apartment to pick them up after the closing."

"Oh my God, you're going to sleep with someone in the building," James's mouth was agape. "That's so messy. I love it."

Cricket smiled, then seemed to catch herself. "Don't tell Ellis or I'll kill you."

James promptly zipped his mouth shut.

"Did you get his name?" Anne asked. She hated being nosy, but she also couldn't help it.

"Oh, I'm so bad at names," Cricket replied, her eyebrows pinched together like she was concentrating hard. "I do remember that it's sexy, though. Super old-fashioned. Freddie... something? It sounded like one of those guys who returns from sea after years away and—"

Bev groaned. "I knew you were watching *Poldark* again. I can hear it through the walls."

"Captain Freddie," James whispered, low and seductively.

Cricket laughed as Anne's heart stuttered. Obviously, it wasn't *her* Freddie. Statistically, that would be almost impossible. The last time she had googled him a few months ago, it looked like he was living in Los Angeles. Still, the name triggered her pulse, sending it careening through every vein so quickly that all she could do was stare at the bottle of pinot noir still in her hand.

"Well, that was very unfair of you, Cricks," James chided her as he leaned over and grabbed an olive from a nearby bowl. "Anne should have had first dibs, since he's technically taking her apartment. Give her an opportunity to move back in."

"If she leaves at all," Bev said, turning a pointed glare at Anne. "Squatters have rights in New York, you know."

Anne let out a nervous laugh, expecting the others to join her, but everyone else in the kitchen looked like they were weighing it as a viable option, too.

"I'm not going to squat," Anne said to the group.

"Of course not, sweetie," James said, his tone placating as he patted her hand.

An uncomfortable silence fell on the kitchen.

"So . . . where are you going?" Cricket finally asked.

"I sent out a few emails this morning," Anne said with a tight smile, avoiding their gazes as she smoothed down the side of her neat ponytail. "There was one listing out on Staten Island that looked promising, so hopefully they get back to me."

James blanched. "Oh, Anne. Not Staten Island."

She was about to defend the city's most maligned borough when Cricket let out a squeal. "Wait! I have an idea!"

Bev shot her a glare. "Oh God. What is it?"

"Chloe got mono!" Cricket replied, practically bouncing in her seat.

It took a moment for Anne to remember who Cricket was talking about, and even then, she wasn't sure she could recall a face to go with the name. All she knew was that Cricket had a friend who had moved into her spare room over the summer. It only occurred to Anne at that moment that she hadn't seen the woman in weeks.

"Remember?" Cricket continued. "She wouldn't get out of bed for ages and she thought she had seasonal affective disorder, but it turns out she has mono! She ended up moving back home for a few months so she could focus on getting better and catching up on *Love Island*. You can have her bedroom until she comes back!"

"Actually, this is kind of brilliant," James said, looking at Cricket like he was impressed.

"It's also illegal," Bev murmured. "You can't sublet a rent-controlled apartment."

Cricket laughed as if Bev were joking. "It's not an illegal *sublet*. It's a real estate opportunity!"

Bev snorted, then took another deep sip of her wine.

Anne opened her mouth, not even sure what she was going to say. Her first instinct was to politely decline, assure all of them that she had this covered, but the reality was, she wasn't so sure. Then the kitchen door opened again, and Ellis's head popped in, his expression pained.

"Why does it feel like there are more people in here than at the actual board meeting?" he asked. "I'm out there fighting for my life against Wendy and Glen."

"Sweetie, how do you feel about sublets in the building?" James asked.

Ellis paused, his eyes darting to Cricket, already suspicious. "Why?"

Cricket squealed again. "Because Anne is moving in with me! We get to keep her!"

"It would just be for a couple of months," Anne added. "Until I find something more permanent. Once the show ramps back up—"

"We'll be roomies!" Cricket clapped in celebration.

"Wait. That's a really good idea," Ellis replied, eyes wide. "Then you'll still be here to oversee the plumbing work next month. And follow up with the elevator guy about that permit issue."

"It's perfect!" James squealed.

It should have been good news. A light at the end of a very long tunnel. And maybe it was, Anne reminded herself. Yes, Cricket was a few years younger than her, but they were friendly. There was no doubt the rent would be cheap, too. She could stay in the building and focus on finding a job. Then she could begin to look for something else, an apartment of her own... the plan started to come together in Anne's mind, calming her anxiety enough to smile.

"Yeah," she said. "Perfect."

CHAPTER 4

Apartment 4B was not perfect.

In fact, as Anne stood in the middle of Cricket's living room, covered in sweat and dust after spending the day packing up her now-empty bedroom upstairs and clinging to a cardboard box filled with her most prized possessions, she couldn't think of any possible way this scenario could be worse.

"Welcome home!" Cricket exclaimed. "Don't worry about the smell. It's patchouli, I promise!"

I stand corrected, Anne thought.

Cricket had spent the past week extolling the virtues of her apartment, and Anne had patiently listened, keeping her questions about Cricket's collection of K-pop memorabilia to herself. And even though Anne had been too busy to stop by and see it until the very last minute, i.e., the morning she needed to be out of her old apartment to make way for the new tenant's painters, she knew the layout thanks to the units above and below it. The front door opened to the living room—flanked here by two beanbags and a litany of tapestries that Anne was fairly sure were against fire code—and a small kitchen to the left. A stick of incense burned on the countertop, framed by a few burn marks on the Formica from where the ash had fallen during previous uses. It sat dangerously close to a pile of posters for Cricket's play, each one featuring a half-naked woman covered in silver body paint and perched precariously close to a man's crotch.

To be fair, Cricket hadn't lied. The apartment was lovely and bright despite the BTS posters and foam furniture throughout. She just hadn't mentioned how much stuff she had, and how haphazardly it was strewn across every available surface. Anne was already mentally cataloging how to organize it, a game plan to tackle at least the living room. A beautiful vision of plastic bins and labels danced in her head, and for a minute, she almost felt better.

"Help yourself to whatever you see in the fridge," Cricket said as they passed the kitchen. "And don't worry about glasses, I usually just use the Solo cups above the fridge. I hate doing dishes, you know?"

Oh God.

They continued forward, down the short hallway and past the bathroom to an open doorway.

"Ta-da!" Cricket said, waving jazz hands toward the waiting room. "What do you think?"

Anne tried not to cringe as she surveyed the fairy lights that hung from the ceiling, the remnants of stickers along the walls. But at least there was a bed! And a dresser! That was a plus, right? Of course, the dresser was missing its bottom drawer. And the room appeared to be missing a window, too.

"It's great," Anne said.

Okay, maybe not great, but it could work. It had to. She couldn't start looking for an apartment until she had a job, even though she technically *had* a job—it was just on hiatus at the moment. But once the show came back, she would still be stuck looking for a new place to live with a minuscule salary, and—

Nope, no spiraling today. She had somewhere to live; that's all that mattered right now. The first item on her plan could be ticked off. Tomorrow she would unpack her things and organize, then she could focus on finding a job—something to tide her over until the show came back, anyway. It was all under control.

"I'm just across the hall if you need anything, so . . . " Cricket turned and caught Anne's expression. "Something wrong?"

Just my hopes. My dreams. My life.

Anne pushed the thought away and forced a smile. "Just thinking about all the unpacking I have to do."

Cricket's expression lit up again. "So exciting! I would love to help, but I have to get ready for rehearsal. Then I need to go and hang up those posters around the neighborhood. Oh, you're coming to the play, right? We're opening in a few weeks, and I really need the energy of the crowd behind me, you know? So I can really feel my character."

"I thought you were an understudy?" Anne asked.

"I am, but you never know when you'll be called upon. That's theater. Speaking of which, do you have any body glitter? All the understudies have to bring their own."

Anne narrowed her eyes at her, trying to judge if she was serious. "I'm all out."

Cricket sighed as she turned toward her room. "That's okay. I'll pick some up when I head out."

Anne waited until she heard Cricket's door shut, then she fell back onto the mattress. The springs let out a low, anguished wheeze just as the first chords of Taylor Swift's "Anti-Hero" blared out from behind Cricket's bedroom door. It was so loud Anne almost missed the sharp knock at the front door, followed by Bev's voice bellowing, "TURN IT DOWN."

This is fine, Anne told herself as a kernel of panic lodged in her chest. After all, it was temporary. She just needed some earplugs. Maybe a few candles. That could help with the smell, too—which was definitely patchouli and not weed, right? Right. Once she got out of these old sweats and jumped in the shower, she would feel better. It was amazing what a conditioning mask could do.

She almost believed it.

Her phone let out a ping in her hand and she looked down to see her father's message on the screen.

DAD

> Is it asking too much to get an update or do I have to drive back to the city to find out where my furniture is?

And just like that, her tenuous morale deflated to nothing.

It would be easy to ignore the text, but she had learned from years of managing her father's company that the longer you ignored Walter Elliot, the more attention he demanded until it became impossible to get anything done. This would only be compounded by the fact that he was currently without his personal belongings while trying to acclimate to his new loft apartment in Brooklyn.

ANNE

> They picked up the furniture from storage at 9am.

> They should be in Brooklyn by noon.

DAD
> So I'm just supposed to wait around all day??

ANNE
> If they're not there by noon, we can call.

DAD
> By that point my furniture could be floating in New York Harbor!

An array of responses flew through Anne's mind, but in the end she just put her phone on silent and leaned back into the mattress again. She knew she should get in the shower, but at that moment, all she could do was lie there and stare up at where someone had put a collection of glow-in-the-dark star stickers on the ceiling, and wonder what else could possibly go wrong.

Another sharp knock echoed down the hallway from the front door. Anne almost called out to Cricket to tell her Bev was getting angry, but then she remembered that this was her home now—at least for a little while. Surely, she could answer the door.

She stood, using her forearm to push some of her blond hair from her sweaty face, then headed down the short hallway and swung the door open.

"I'm sorry, Bev. I—"

But it wasn't Bev.

There was a man there waiting, his head bent down to look at his phone. Tall, in a well-tailored suit, with brown hair that was slightly mussed. Then he turned to face her, revealing a smile she hadn't seen in eight years.

Freddie Wentworth.

For a split second, she forgot she was covered in sweat and dust. Or that her hair was unwashed and sticking to her forehead, or that her sweatpants were awkwardly riding up her ankles. For that split second, she was twenty-two again and life wasn't really that bad because Freddie was there, his green eyes crinkling at the corners, an easy smile turning up his lips.

But it was only a split second.

That's how long it seemed to take him to recognize her. That's when his smile faded, and suddenly the reality of the here and now crashed into her with mortifying clarity. Her hair, her clothes, the way his eyes traveled across it all and seemed to critique every detail.

"Hi," she said.

"Hi," he replied slowly, his brow furrowed.

She had never seen him in a suit before, and her pulse tripped at the altered view, how it sharpened the lines of his now-broad shoulders and accentuated his height. His dark hair was shorter now, so she could see the stern line of his brow.

She opened her mouth to say something, but it just hung there gaping for a long moment.

"Hi," she repeated. It sounded almost offhand, like the word was a reflex while her brain tried to make sense of the last thirty seconds. "What are you doing here?"

"I live here," he replied.

Somewhere in her brain, she recognized that voice—she had dreamed about it over the past eight years—but now it was missing some key component. The warmth, the light tinge that made it sound like he was always just a few moments away from laughter.

A thousand different questions swirled in her head. Her brain desperately grasped at them, trying to formulate at least one into a coherent string of words. Maybe then she could think of what else to say, ask what he meant, and why—

"Is that Freddie?" Cricket's voice called down the hall. Anne could hear her bounding toward them until Cricket's body slid in beside her own in the doorway. "Freddie! I totally forgot you were stopping by today."

From the lip gloss to the low-cut leotard Cricket was now wearing, Anne doubted very much that she had forgotten. But whether Freddie knew that or not didn't seem to matter.

Cricket sighed and leaned against the doorframe. "How are you?"

Freddie's gaze bounced between Cricket and Anne, his confusion creating a deep crease between his eyebrows.

"Oh my gosh, I'm so rude!" Cricket let out a bubbly laugh. "Freddie, this is my roommate, Anne."

His gaze snapped to Anne again. She was ready to offer a yet-to-be-conceived excuse as to why she was living with a twenty-two-year-old wearing a leotard at noon on a Tuesday, but then Cricket continued.

"Anne, this is Freddie. He's the one who bought your dad's apartment."

No. No no no. This wasn't happening.

A heavy silence swallowed them up as Freddie stared at her.

Anne's mouth fell open again. But to say what? There was no way he knew that he had just bought her old apartment. How could he? She'd never had the courage to invite him over; all she had told him during the course of their relationship was that she lived on Avenue A. Even if he had suspected—which she highly doubted, considering the expression on his face right now—he couldn't possibly have assumed she would still be here. Eight years was a long time, and when they last spoke, she had big plans that should have left this place far behind.

Should have. God, that was becoming the mantra of her life.

"Good to see you, Freddie," she finally said.

He nodded, his jaw tight. "You, too."

"Wait." Cricket's lips made a bow. "Do you two know each other?"

"We were at NYU together," Anne replied quickly. She was working hard to maintain a smile, but it felt thin across her face as she met Freddie's gaze again.

"Right," he replied. His expression was unreadable.

"Oh my gosh, that's insane!" Cricket said, batting a hand against Anne's arm. "And to think, you literally *just* moved the last of your things out of there. How crazy that you both didn't know!"

"So crazy," he said, his tone flat.

Anne wanted to crawl under a piece of furniture and die.

Cricket laughed for a little too long. "You're so funny!"

"I try," he said, flashing her a tight smile. "Well, I have painters arriving soon, so about those keys..."

"Oh! Right." Cricket turned and grabbed a manila envelope off the entry table along with a set of keys, then handed both to him. "There's the key to the apartment, and the key card for the roof."

"Thanks," he said, taking it.

"I also put my number in there, in case you have any problems. Or you need someone to take you around the neighborhood. I can show you where to get the best cup of coffee." Cricket shrugged, as if the idea had just come to her.

Anne averted her eyes, but they only ended up landing on Freddie again. He wasn't looking at her anymore, but somehow that was worse. Like he wouldn't acknowledge her at all.

"We should let him go, Cricket," Anne cut in, her hand gripping the doorknob so tightly she thought she might break it. "I'm sure he's anxious to go up and get settled."

"Right!" Cricket said with a satisfied sigh. "Well, welcome to the building, Freddie! And call if you need anything!"

He nodded to her before he looked at Anne again.

A million different words ran through Anne's mind, along with a million different ways to put them together. She could ask how he was, what he had been doing, tell him how much she had wondered about him over the past eight years. But in the end, none of that mattered, did it? Because, from the way he was glaring at her, she knew he didn't care either way.

"It was really good to see you, Freddie," she said, forcing yet another smile. One that would mask how her heart sank with the realization.

Then she closed the door.

CHAPTER 5

*F*uuuuuuuuuuuck.

Freddie was dreaming. Or hallucinating. Maybe both.

But as he stared at the dull gray paint of the front door to apartment 4B, he didn't wake up. And if Anne had looked out the peephole right then, she would have seen him standing there, waiting for his brain to reboot. He wasn't even sure if it did, only that he eventually found his way back into the elevator and pressed up.

The doors closed and when they opened again, he half expected to wake up in a cold sweat and realize this was all a dream. That the last ten minutes hadn't actually happened at all.

He didn't, though. When the elevator arrived on the eighth floor, he was left staring out into the hallway, still trying to process it all.

He hadn't recognized Anne at first. When the apartment door had swung open, it hadn't even registered. Her clothes were different from anything he had seen Anne in before—the carefully pressed shirts and pristine sweaters had been replaced by a baggy sweatshirt, and her blond hair was in a messy bun instead of blown out and pulled back, like she used to wear it. But then he saw her eyes. Those blue eyes were the same, clear and large and locked on him.

There hadn't been any time to figure out how it was possible, why she was standing in a doorway of his new building. Ellis's assistant had interrupted before he'd had an opportunity to say more than hello. Then she shut the door before he could say goodbye.

The elevator dinged, warning that the doors were about to close again, and he finally stepped out. The keys were still in his hand, and he was only half-aware of sliding them into the lock, turning them until he heard the dead bolt echo in the empty apartment beyond. Then he swung it open and stepped inside the hollow foyer of his ex-girlfriend's childhood apartment.

What. The. Fuck.

Was this some kind of twisted joke? He didn't believe in the universe sending him signs, but this was too close to some kind of karmic revenge. A chill ran through his spine as he felt his mental walls crumbling into a pile of dust.

He ran a hand down his face. Had he somehow known that this was the place Anne avoided taking him to for so long? He only knew about an old building in the East Village—she never mentioned the Uppercross by name—but now here he was, the owner of her former home.

He slowly walked through each room, looking for any details he might have missed before. But it was empty. Even worse, the painters would be arriving any minute to apply a clean coat of eggshell white. He had organized her erasure without even realizing it.

Wouldn't you have done that anyway? a voice mused somewhere in his head. *She did.*

That's right. She had.

We were at NYU together. That's how she had described their relationship. Reduced to its most basic form. And suddenly the tinder of long-neglected pain had flared alive in Freddie's chest. There was no reason the words should have hurt as much as they did. It was the truth. But a truncated version of it, one that left out the fine details, the messy, bleeding heart of it.

His wallet suddenly felt heavy in the pocket of his jacket. He let a moment pass before he reached for it, waited even longer to swallow his pride and open it to look inside.

There it was, slotted between his credit cards and a couple of twenties: the very first note to Anne, written on a flimsy bar napkin and folded into a triangle. He had scribbled it down after meeting her for the first time. It was during his first semester freshman year and he'd seen her from across the bar at the Half Pint. Once he built up the courage to introduce himself, they'd talked for hours, only pausing when the bartender announced last call. After he walked her outside to make sure she got a cab, he went back in, grabbed a napkin from the bar, and wrote her a note.

But he'd never given it to her. The plan had been that he would eventually, so he put it in his wallet for safekeeping, waiting until the time was right.

Obviously, it never was. He'd given up that dream years ago. But he never had the nerve to get rid of it. Instead, he'd carried it with him to Argentina, all while ignoring and denying what she had meant to him, painting over the cracks that Anne Elliot had left in her wake.

And now he was about to do it in the most literal sense with Benjamin Moore's eggshell white. Except instead of feeling cathartic, he felt robbed of something. He had never seen this place, never known this side of her, and now it was gone.

But she's not, that same voice whispered.

He ignored that, too. He couldn't start down that road again. His heart had been broken before; he had no interest in it happening again.

No, right now he needed to clear his head.

He shoved his wallet back in his pocket and pulled out his phone, swiping open his contacts and pressing "call."

As soon as it connected, Freddie sighed. "Feel like blowing off work this afternoon?"

~

"So you moved in with your ex-girlfriend?"

Freddie paused in his backswing to glare at his friend George Knightley. The towering nets surrounding the driving range at Chelsea Piers wafted in the wind, enclosing the long stretch of grass ahead of where they stood on the third level. Sweeping views of the Hudson River and New Jersey lay just beyond, while golf balls flew out from the stalls below them.

"I didn't move in with her." Freddie finally swung his golf club, sending his white ball careening ahead. "I moved into her old apartment."

"But she still lives downstairs," George said, leaning his weight on his nine iron. "With that woman who's interested in you."

"Cranefly," a deep voice piped in from behind them.

They both turned to where Will Darcy was sitting on the bench along the wall of the building. His blond head was bent down as he stared at his phone, and there was a half-finished beer at his side. They had been here for a half hour, and the man hadn't even taken his suit jacket off yet.

"Cricket," Freddie corrected him. "And she's not interested. She's just . . . a very aggressive flirt."

"That's not helping your case, Freddie," George replied with a smile.

Freddie shook his head. He had known George for years through his brother, Ben, though they hadn't become friends until recently. In college, Ben's restaurant bought the microgreens Freddie harvested from the hydroponics system in his parents' basement. George found him a few years later, after Freddie had moved to Argentina permanently. Freddie had applied for a few patents, and George was just getting his venture capital firm off the ground. He saw the potential in Freddie's work, and after a few video calls, decided to be the first investor in Wentworth Hydroponics. And now, a good friend. George had been Freddie's sounding board as he debated whether to sell his company, and he had introduced him to Will, whose mergers and acquisitions firm negotiated the deal. And even though all the documents were signed last year and the sale was old news, the friendship between the three of them remained strong.

Except for moments like this, when he wanted to throttle both of them.

"Did you guys come here to hit balls or give me shit?" Freddie asked the two men.

"Neither," Will replied, his tone bored. "I came for a drink."

George chuckled as he walked toward the tee. "Come on, Freddie. You have to admit, if this had happened to either of us, you would be first in line to give us endless shit."

Freddie frowned. George was right, but he sure as hell wasn't going to admit that.

"Shut up and hit the ball," he murmured.

George smiled, then swung his club through the air and sent the ball flying. "So what are you going to do?"

"I'm not sure what I can do."

"You could sell the apartment," Will replied, as if it was obvious.

Freddie threw him a dubious look. "I just signed the papers. I've got furniture being delivered in a couple of days."

He also didn't want to sell. He had loved it even before he'd known it was Anne's, and now that he'd learned the truth, he felt even more responsibility for it. But he also didn't know how to be there without thinking of her. He dreaded having to learn.

George leaned down and set up another ball. "What happened between you two?"

"What do you mean?" he asked, feigning ignorance.

"You and Anne. Why did you break up?"

How many nights had Freddie lain awake wondering the same thing? Over the past eight years, he had his stable of working theories, but no definitive answer. After he gave her the charm bracelet at the Half Pint all those Christmases ago, it felt like something broke, and he had no idea how to fix it. Anne hadn't even tried. Over the next few weeks, she forced more and more distance between them until she finally called and laid out the simple truth: They wanted different things. But even though she was going to Columbia, and he should go to Argentina, she still wanted to be friends. Then she had said the words that had hurt more than anything else anyone had ever said to him.

"I wish you the best."

Like their relationship had been a sidenote in her life. Something that could be summed up in a greeting card.

He was so confused and hurt that all he could do was block her number.

There were times when he was tempted to look her up, to unblock her and send a text. The anger maintained his resolve, though, and over the years the pain had crystallized. It wasn't just that Anne had broken his heart—she had found fault with a fundamental part of him that always aimed for the big picture and figured out the details later.

It was what drove him to the engineering program in Buenos Aires in the first place. He wanted to do it, so he did. The hows and the whens would work themselves out; they always eventually did. That's how he lived his life: Zero in on a goal and go for it. He acted on instinct and dumb luck, and it served him well.

He had always assumed Anne loved that about him, but in the end, maybe that was the ultimate problem.

"I went to Argentina. She stayed," he replied simply.

"And then?"

Freddie shrugged. "And then nothing. I haven't talked to her since."

George winced, while Will let out a loaded sigh behind them.

"Be careful," he murmured, his attention still on his phone.

"Of what?" Freddie asked.

"Getting back together with her. If it goes south, you can't exactly pick up and move out of the country again."

Freddie forced out a dry laugh. "Not going to happen."

George turned around, frowning. "Then what are we doing here?"

"I just need something to do," Freddie said, running a hand down his face. "Half my problem right now is that I have too much free time to think about all this shit."

"And convince your friends to blow off work to listen to you work through it out loud," Will murmured, sending him a wry grin before taking a sip of his beer.

"Let's be honest. It didn't take much convincing," George said, lining up another shot.

Freddie let out a long breath as he shook his head. "What's funny is I actually *miss* work."

George paused. "I thought you were looking forward to some time off?"

Freddie scratched his jaw as his gaze wandered out to the far nets and the boats drifting by on the Hudson just beyond them. That's right, he had said that. He had meant it, too. After spending almost a decade building Wentworth Hydroponics, and working so hard to use his technology to help people who needed it most, he had been almost relieved to sell and have some time to himself. But now, the long stretch of idleness felt daunting, and he had no previous experience to help him through it.

"I was," he finally replied. "But I think I suck at relaxing."

Will scoffed. "I could have told you that."

Freddie couldn't help but laugh.

"Well, if you're looking for something to do, Mark Segel over at AirSoil is still asking to talk to you," George said.

Freddie paused. "Who?"

George frowned. "Do you read any of my emails?"

"No."

Behind them, Will chuckled.

"Mark Segel," George repeated. "He founded this green energy start-up last year, AirSoil. They're one of our companies who just had their Series B funding round and look pretty solid. Mark wants to build out a sustainable farming division and was asking if you'd be up for a meeting."

"Is this a job interview?" Will asked suspiciously.

"No," George replied. "Just a meeting. But you never know what it could grow into."

Freddie considered for a moment, then nodded. "All right. Let's set something up." Then he turned to notice Will's dubious expression. "What?"

"Nothing," Will said, bringing his attention to his phone

again. "I just thought you weren't interested in becoming a cog in corporate America."

It was a line Freddie had used when he first met Will, when they were working out the details of selling his company and the possibility of Freddie staying on as CEO. Freddie had dismissed it—he had always hated the idea of working for someone else. Even worse if that work required him to wear a suit and go into an office every day. But just a few months later, Freddie found himself doing just that, attending all the sales pitches and board meetings required for the sale. It had been tedious, yes, but he could handle it. And if this new company was investing in sustainable farming initiatives, the very thing he had once wanted to start a nonprofit to do, would it be so bad to talk?

"It's just a meeting, Will," he replied.

His friend didn't look convinced.

"Okay, enough work talk." George lined up another shot, then sent his driver slicing through the air. "Now, what about the housewarming party? Is that still on, or has it been canceled due to the current situation at home?"

Shit. The housewarming party. Freddie had almost forgotten about that. He had sent out a text inviting all his friends in the city before his run-in with Anne. Now the impending party felt more like an obligation. "It's still on."

"Good. I was worried I'd have to break the news to Emma that you canceled it. She would have never forgiven you," George said, the corner of his mouth ticking up like it always did when he mentioned his girlfriend.

Will hummed behind them. "But if you *need* to cancel, we understand."

Freddie's brows creased together. "What?"

George laughed, sliding his club back in the stand. "What Will's trying to say is please cancel the party, because Emma and Lizzy are using it as an excuse to take us to karaoke afterward."

"No, you're going to karaoke," Will said, glaring at George from under his brow. "I'm going to observe."

Freddie almost wanted to laugh. When he first met Will and George, the three of them had decidedly been bachelors. It was a fact he had almost taken for granted, until George finally admitted to being in love with his neighbor and best friend Emma. As if that wasn't bad enough, Will went and fell in love with a Hamptons local the following summer. Freddie was the last man standing and, thanks to past experience, happy to stay that way.

"The party is happening." Freddie said it like he was issuing an edict. "I'm back in New York and I want to celebrate. One ex-girlfriend isn't going to derail that."

He forced the words out, but they still felt sour on his tongue.

"Fine," Will said with a disappointed sigh. He took his phone back out of his jacket and began typing, only to pause and shoot them both an expectant look. "Are you two playing golf or what?"

CHAPTER 6

The offices for Kellynch Productions were empty and dark when Anne walked in Friday morning. Thank God.

She arrived early, bundling up in her peacoat and knit hat to face the first below-freezing temperatures of the year on her trek from the Uppercross. She told herself it was because there was work to do—the network needed to see past contracts and she needed to make sure all the footage had been sent over as promised. The fact that it had given her a convenient reason to avoid another run-in with Freddie Wentworth was just an added benefit. At least that's what she told herself.

The office was on Fifth Street and Third Avenue, just a few blocks from Tompkins Square Park. The rent was eye-wateringly high, which was made worse by the fact that there was no strategic reason to be there other than her father being able to brag about the address. When she had first come on board to save the company, she had begged him to relocate, but he was adamant about staying. So the cuts came from other departments, and she had picked up the slack. Honestly, she hadn't minded. She needed a distraction to keep herself from pondering just how far her life had veered off course.

Such as going to your closed-down office to pick up a few documents rather than risk running into your ex? a voice murmured in her head. She frowned. Apparently, old habits die hard.

Bianca Russell used to say Anne's brain was a perpetual motion machine. Since she was little, she would lose herself in a task, be so absorbed that the world would almost fall away. Anne never had the heart to tell her mother that the skill was born out of necessity, to avoid her parents' screaming matches, another attempt at finding control in a world where she felt like she had none. It was also what helped her deal with being an introvert in a beautifully extroverted city. When she got into NYU, it was as thrilling as it was terrifying. There was no question she would live at home—the apartment was just a few blocks from campus—but it only made it harder to make friends, to find her place. So she threw herself into school, taking on extra classes, volunteering for study groups. It worked for a while, too.

Then she met Freddie.

He made it impossible to hide. She didn't even want to. They were like two puzzle pieces that fit so perfectly, they didn't have to worry about anything else. Then, when they finally did, it was too late.

The weeks after he gave her that ticket to Buenos Aires, she had tried to pull away slowly, hoping it would ease the conversation she knew they eventually had to have. The one she'd practiced for days, had taken careful notes on so he didn't think she'd come to the conclusion to break up lightly. She didn't mention the fact that she was doing it so he wouldn't turn down the opportunity to go to Argentina—forcing him to live with that would have been just as bad as letting him stay. Instead, she'd only asked to stay friends.

And then he blocked Anne's number.

She hadn't realized at first. But after not hearing from him for a week, then two, she had tried to call him. The phone rang and rang, and it wasn't until the eighth ring that she realized why it wasn't going to voicemail: He had blocked her.

The confusion was followed by anger, and then pain, then such a heady mix of both that there was nothing to do but fall back on that need for control again. She threw herself into school, and then her job at the hedge fund, not taking time to celebrate her graduation or even move out of her father's apartment. That was the point. She had needed to stay in motion, to keep her brain engaged so it wouldn't linger on what she'd lost along the way.

Except it didn't work. Diving headfirst into her job only made her notice every detail that she hated, the lists of numbers that were only that. Flat and binary.

She had tried hard to ignore that, too. But it only lasted so long before she knew she needed to quit.

That was the first time she had looked up Freddie. The day after she walked out of that office building on Wall Street for the last time, she'd caved and pulled out her phone. She opened Instagram and typed out his name.

And there he was. Speaking Spanish.

It had been an odd reintroduction. Did Freddie speak Spanish? Apparently so. He was also still in Argentina, implementing the same hydroponics system he had perfected at his parents' house, in a village near Patagonia. Over the next few years she would occasionally check in, but the posts became less frequent, until finally they began to redirect to another account: Wentworth Hydroponics. Those photos were more polished, and the ones that featured Freddie became less and less until they stopped altogether.

In some of her more desperate moments, she had allowed herself to wonder what it would be like to run into Freddie again. In her imagination, it was always somewhere familiar, like they both had been struck by the need to visit their favorite bench on the High Line again and found themselves there at the exact same moment. Or maybe they would bump into each other while Christmas shopping near Union Square, maybe even at Fishs Eddy where they used to go. They'd reach for the same mug, then laugh, and it would be like old times again.

But in all her daydreams, she hadn't anticipated the version of Freddie she met yesterday. Serious. Impassive. Like he didn't know her at all.

It was the worst kind of irony. She had broken her own heart—and his—so he wouldn't have to compromise himself or his dreams. Change who he was or what he wanted. Yet, from the looks of it, he had gone ahead and done that anyway.

Good job, Freddie, Anne thought bitterly, then pushed all thoughts of Freddie Wentworth away. She was good at that.

She pulled off her knit hat and flipped on the overhead lights, illuminating the empty office. It was an open plan, with a glass wall office for her father in the corner. She couldn't remember a time when he had ever actually used it, but it was there, still waiting. Her desk was in the other corner, tucked into one of the tall windows facing the Hudson. She knew what she had to grab—a few hard copies of contracts and budgets, her three succulents from the sill, and maybe a few packs of Post-it notes and labels for—

"Anne Elliot."

The sound of her name sent Anne's heart into a tailspin. She spun around, half expecting to see Freddie himself stepping off the nearby elevator. But instead, she found Theo Travers.

"Theo! Hi," she replied, the relief sending a smile to her lips. "Sorry, you startled me. I didn't think anyone would be here."

He smiled, too. "Ditto."

Silence fell as they stared at each other. He looked good—better than he had in recent months, when the stress of the series was weighing heavily on them both. Or maybe it was the fact that he was in jeans and a Yankees baseball cap, instead of his usual work attire of slacks and a button-down.

The air in the empty office suddenly felt heavy. Had she ever been alone with Theo before? In all their years of working together, she couldn't recall a moment that hadn't involved an editor nearby or a production assistant waiting around the corner.

"So . . . " She swallowed. "What are you doing here?"

"Just had to pick up a few things. Didn't think it would be so long before we'd be back in the office."

A pang of guilt hit her chest. Amid the show's hiatus, the sale of the apartment, and the return of Freddie Wentworth, Anne had totally overlooked the fact that her life wasn't the only one turned upside down recently.

"God, I'm so sorry. I should have checked in."

"No, you shouldn't. I'm sure you've had enough to deal with," he replied with a wince.

She smiled. It was true—Theo had witnessed enough of Walt Elliot's behavior to sympathize.

"So, what have you been up to?" she asked, pushing her blond hair away from her face. God only knew what it looked like after she took off her hat.

"Funny you should ask," he said, looking slightly guilty. "I was going to give you a call but I was still figuring out how to tell you . . . "

"Tell me about what?"

He seemed to consider, hand cupping the back of his neck as his brow furrowed. "I'm thinking of breaking off and starting my own production company."

She blinked. She didn't know why she was surprised. Yes, Theo had worked on *Divorce Divas* for years, but his fealty wasn't required. He could go work on any show, for any network—that's how television usually worked.

"Theo, that's great!" she said. And she meant it.

"Yeah?" he asked, venturing a small smile. "I thought you might have an issue, since this is your dad's company and all. But I had a call with a network exec last week and soft-pitched a show. He seemed really into the idea, so it might have legs."

"Congratulations," she said. "To be honest, I'm relieved. I've been worried about what everyone was going to do."

"Well, they haven't greenlit it yet." He shrugged. "I have a meeting in a few weeks to pitch the higher-ups, and they want to see a prospective budget, how it would need to be staffed up. So I've been working on that and . . . it's a lot."

Anne almost laughed. She was the one that dealt with all the logistics and paperwork at Kellynch, so she knew his sentiment was the understatement of the year.

"Is there anything I can do to help?" she asked.

His expression turned sheepish. "Is it bad that I was hoping you'd ask that?"

"Of course not," she said. "I've done so many of those, I see them in my sleep."

"Good," he said with a relieved sigh. "Well, I've tried to create one, but it's a bit of a mess. Could I send it to you and get your thoughts?"

"Sure."

He smiled again. "Anne Elliot. Always coming to the rescue."

"I try." She forced a laugh. "Just email them to me when you're ready."

"Okay." Then his head cocked to the side. "You know, if all goes well and this gets the greenlight, I'd love to bring you on board," he said after another moment. "What do you think? Theo and Anne, running their own show. Could be fun. That is, if you're ready to leave this place."

Anne paused. It could be a good opportunity, especially right now when it felt like she had none. But it also felt odd, like trying on a sweater that you'd outgrown. She never wanted to work in television—she hadn't even really enjoyed it. Still, at almost thirty, it was the only long-term job experience she had.

"Let's get your pitch in good shape, then we can go from there. All right?" she offered.

"All right."

His voice was deep, and the words seemed to hang in the air expectantly. It was enough to make Anne's pulse trip.

"What are you doing right now?" Theo asked after a moment. "Feel like grabbing a drink? We can exchange war stories."

She laughed, pushing her hair away from her face again, a nervous motion. "How about a coffee after I go over that budget for you?"

He smiled again, but this time it felt so loaded that Anne couldn't help but blush. "It's a date."

CHAPTER 7

The next two weeks passed without a single sighting of Freddie Wentworth. Anne would have almost thought their entire encounter outside Cricket's door had been a fever dream except for the array of delivery trucks that seemed to be perpetually parked on the curb, with furniture and boxes addressed to F. Wentworth in apartment 8A.

Still, she was doing a good job of ignoring it. Between reviewing Theo's production documents and responding to her father's barrage of texts demanding an update on three boxes missing from his move, she barely had a moment to unpack her own things, let alone acknowledge her ex living just a few floors above. Thankfully, Cricket was in her final week of rehearsals, so Anne had the entire apartment to herself, and she could finally get around to making the windowless bedroom her own. She hung her mounted print of Ada Lovelace above the bed and alphabetized her favorite books along the top of the dresser—*A History of Pi* by Petr Beckmann lined up ahead of a book by Edward Tufte about visualizing data, which sat ahead of Hawking's *A Brief History of Time*—then fixed the dresser's bottom drawer and printed out labels for its contents.

Of course, cleaning and organizing her room had slowly transitioned to cleaning the bathroom, which had spiraled into giving the kitchen a complete scrub-down, organizing the cabinets and pantry, filing the mail piled on the dining table, and systematically re-alphabetizing Cricket's bookshelf full of movie scripts. Four hours later, Anne collapsed onto her bed with a groan. She was exhausted and smelled vaguely like disinfectant, but she didn't care. She was officially moved in.

There hadn't been many triumphs over the past few weeks, so she took a moment to admire her work. The cobwebs that had clung to the corners were gone and the fairy lights were neatly coiled up in the hallway closet. There were now shelves mounted above the dresser, each featuring color-coded bins labeled with their contents. She even found space for a small nightstand where she placed her coveted tower of Post-its and a vanilla soy candle. She'd call that a win.

And a win deserved a celebration, didn't it? Or at least some takeout.

She placed an order for dumplings and orange chicken from her favorite Chinese restaurant on Fifth Street, then took a quick shower. Once she was dried off and feeling vaguely more human, she slid on a pair of black leggings and a sweater and pulled her still-wet hair into a ponytail. Then she grabbed her laptop and sat on her newly washed duvet to watch an episode of *Gilmore Girls* while she unpacked a nearby box labeled *MISC*. It was mostly books and pens, things that had been in her nightstand upstairs, so she simply started filling its drawers with it now. It was mindless work, and she was only half paying attention when her hands lifted out a small plastic storage box.

Her heart faltered. For a moment, she could only stare at it while Lorelei Gilmore ranted somewhere nearby. She should just stash it in the back of her bottom drawer. Better yet, put it back into the cardboard packing box and forget it forever. But instead, she slowly removed the lid.

Dozens and dozens of paper triangles sat waiting inside. Some were from lined notebook paper, others from blue stationery, a cacophony of random yellows and whites and creams. And all of them were from Freddie Wentworth. Each and every note he had ever written to her. In her more masochistic moments, she would read them, but as the years went by, the pain somehow compounded so she couldn't even unfold one. But she could never get rid of them, either.

Her phone began to buzz, startling her back to reality. She quickly closed the box and shoved it in the bottom drawer of her nightstand before looking to see her mother's name on the screen.

"Hi, Mom," she answered.

"Hello, darling!" Bianca Russell's voice sang through the line. "You sound awful."

Anne smiled, leaning back against the wall. "That's because I'm exhausted."

"How's the new apartment? Please tell me it has a doorman. You need a doorman."

Anne rolled her eyes, but only because she was safe from her mother seeing her do so. Bianca Russell had been born into privilege and a trust fund, so the idea that life could be curtailed by a lack of funds or job prospects was entirely foreign. Still, Anne couldn't entirely hold her at fault—she had always been careful to avoid telling her mother how much she was doing for her father, and how little he was paying her for it. She always thought it was a means of saving them both from embarrassment, but now it only seemed to feed into further untruths, like the one where Bianca assumed that Anne could somehow afford a palatial loft apartment downtown.

"Actually, I'm still in the Uppercross, just staying with a friend."

A pause. "Like, a roommate?"

"Just until I find a job. No one is going to approve me for an apartment until I have a steady income."

"Oh, don't worry about that. I can just transfer you some money so you—"

"No, Mom," Anne replied, suddenly feeling like she was fifteen years old again. They had been over this numerous times over the years, and no matter how many times Anne reiterated that she was uncomfortable with taking handouts, her mother never failed to offer it. "I don't need money. I'll be fine once the show comes back."

"But who knows how long that will take," her mother replied. Then she hummed to herself, the way she always did when she was pretending to just come up with an opinion that had actually been marinating in her head for ages. "Listen, I know you think you didn't enjoy finance, but I'm sure that's only because you jumped right in after Columbia. You were burned out! If you went back now, you would feel differently."

Anne closed her eyes and let her head fall forward. She had always assumed that at some point, her mother would stop sharing unsolicited advice, but that moment never seemed to come.

"To be honest, Mom, I'm feeling a little burned-out now."

"Then you should come stay with me in Paris," her mother said. "The food is amazing, and the men are *gorgeous*."

Anne wanted to laugh. The only thing that could make her feel more pathetic right now was going to see the City of Love for the first time with her mother. "How are things with François?" she asked, deftly diverting the conversation to safer topics.

For the next few minutes, she listened patiently to tales of her mother's latest conquest, her subpar dinner the night before, and her continual health scares with her dogs, who had a habit of eating objects off the sidewalk that inevitably almost killed them. It was all so predictable that Anne let her mind wander and was almost surprised when her mother asked: "So, who moved into the old apartment?"

A pit yawned open in Anne's stomach. She had been hoping to avoid this topic.

"I'm sorry?" she asked, as if she hadn't heard the question.

"Your father's apartment. If you're still in the building, I'm sure you've gotten a look at them. Is it a New Yorker or some rich European who's never there?"

"No, not European," Anne replied, trying to feign innocence. "You know him, actually."

"I do?"

"I went to NYU with him. Freddie Wentworth?"

Anne wasn't sure why her voice went up like a question. Her mother knew exactly who he was.

Silence filled the line, a signature Bianca Russell move, as if she had been caught off guard and was reassessing her next move.

"Freddie Wentworth?"

Anne took a deep breath to keep her frustration from bleeding into her tone. "You know Freddie Wentworth, Mom."

Bianca tutted. "I wouldn't say I *know* him. I only met him once. Remember?"

Anne's frustration deflated quickly, replaced by a decade-old embarrassment. How could she forget?

Bianca Russell's only encounter with Freddie had been a mistake, but one that wasn't entirely Anne's fault. While she had actively worked to ensure that Freddie never met her father—she still cringed with embarrassment even contemplating how Walt would behave during such an encounter—she never really had the same worry with regards to Bianca. It was only that her mother was so rarely in the city. After her parents separated when Anne was in fifth grade, her mother began to travel the world rather than settle permanently in the city. By the time Anne was in high school, Bianca barely spent more than a few weeks in New York throughout the year.

Anne still talked to her mother regularly, though, and in college, many of those conversations had been about Freddie. She told Bianca everything about his dreams for his nonprofit and yet-to-be-defined career, and about his lack of concrete plans to make it happen. And to her mother's credit, she never prodded too much, even though she shared her opinions freely. As a woman who collected relationships like other women collect shoes, Bianca was only too happy to use her experience to steer her daughter's love life.

"Put yourself first, Anne. You have too much going for you to follow a man around the world while he figures himself out," her mother would say whenever Anne told her about Freddie's plans to travel after college. "Your future is in New York, and if he loves you, he'll stay and figure it out. I know you love him, but you have to be selfish."

That had been Bianca Russell's mantra since her divorce: Be selfish. Put yourself first. And as much as Anne would love to try, the idea felt diametrically opposed to every instinct she had.

But the thought still never left her head, either. And instead of trying to reconcile it, she just relied on the fact that those two worlds would never meet. After all, Bianca only ever spent time in the city over Christmas, and even then, it was usually spent at expensive lunches uptown. The probability of a chance encounter with Freddie, one where she might share her uncensored thoughts with him, was negligible.

Unfortunately, Anne's luck never seemed to follow the rules of probability.

It all came to a head the week before Christmas her junior year of college. Freddie had skipped a seminar class and insisted on taking Anne to lunch at Bergdorf Goodman with the first check he'd received for selling microgreens from his basement hydroponics system. The check was minimal, and he hadn't even known that the iconic department store had a restaurant until that morning, but when he asked Anne for her favorite place for lunch in the city, that was her answer, so he'd hailed a cab and away they went.

They ordered a bottle of wine from a region of France that neither of them could pronounce and laughed until they cried over something on the menu called lobster napoleon, which Freddie assumed was served with an accent and inferiority complex. It was like so many days spent together—afternoons on the High Line, evenings wandering the West Village—simple and perfect.

So perfect that Anne hadn't considered that this was her mother's favorite restaurant, too. Or that Bianca had arrived in town for Christmas just a few days before. Even if Anne had, what were the chances she would be having lunch there at the same time?

It wasn't until Bianca stopped in front of their table, waiting for their laughter to subside, that Anne realized her lapse in judgment.

"Mom." It was all Anne thought to say. A long moment followed before she continued. "Freddie, this is my mom, Bianca Russell. Mom, this is my . . . friend, Freddie Wentworth."

My friend. The words had left her mouth before she could stop them. Freddie's attention snapped to her, his brow furrowed. She didn't turn to look at him, though.

"Ah yes," Bianca had mused. Another moment passed before she finally brought her attention to him. "I believe you've mentioned him. The dreamer, right?"

Oh God. Anne had wanted to curl up under the table.

Freddie smiled, but it wasn't his usual warm grin. This one looked artificial and sharp. Anne hated it. "That's me."

The small talk lasted a few painful minutes, then her mother made up some excuse to leave. Anne knew it was a lie from the final stare Bianca gave her as she walked away, but she held out hope that Freddie didn't see it. That he had been spared that last embarrassment. God knew Anne hadn't.

Bianca let out a heavy sigh on the other end of the line, drawing Anne's attention back to their conversation. "So, how did he get on down there in . . . where did he go again? Peru?"

"Argentina, Mom."

"Yes, how did he get on once you cut him loose so he could go to Argentina?"

Anne closed her eyes, trying to mine her patience. Even after explaining the rationale behind breaking up with Freddie to her a thousand times, her mother had never fully grasped the decision, probably because breaking up was the antithesis of her advice. He had been ready and willing to compromise for her, sacrifice his lofty dreams and stay in New York. Anne had won. What was the issue? And while Anne appreciated her mother's staunch devotion to her daughter's selfishness, there was still a pang of regret that it also showed how little her mother knew her at all.

"He just bought Dad's apartment, so I'm assuming he did all right," Anne countered.

"And didn't have to compromise a thing," Bianca mused to herself.

Anne was tempted to tell her just how much it appeared Freddie had compromised, from his expensive suit to his trendy haircut, but she let that bitter pill stay on her tongue.

"It's fine, Mom," she said. "I should only be here for another month or two. I'm sure I can avoid—"

"Hold on, room service is at the door," Bianca's voice sang, and Anne could hear the knocking in the background.

Anne tried to temper her annoyance as she waited, listening to her mother's affected French in the background, the exchange of "mercis" before the door closed again.

"All right, I'm back," Bianca announced a moment later. "I was dying for some sorbet. What were we talking about?"

"Nothing," Anne said, forcing a bit of levity into her voice. "It's not important."

"Exactly the attitude to adopt with an ex." Her mother clicked her tongue. "Now tell me, what are your plans for Thanksgiving?"

Before Anne could admit the mortifying truth—she had no plans—the buzzer by her front door went off.

"I have to go. My dinner just got here," she said.

"All right, sweetie. Call me later!"

Anne hung up, then threw on her sheepskin boots to head down to the elevator.

She hadn't bothered to look in a mirror before running out to catch the elevator, so for the next four stories she was forced to stare at her reflection in its metal doors. Regardless of what was happening in her life, she always prided herself on looking put together. That hadn't changed in the past eight years. Yet she couldn't ignore the new circles under her eyes, the gauntness of her cheeks. She looked tired, her usually meticulous veneer worn down to reveal just how thin she was stretched. She hated it.

She heard the din of conversation even before the doors opened onto the lobby, but she was still surprised by the wall of people waiting when she emerged from the elevator. Before she had time to even process it, they began to press forward so quickly that she had to raise her hand and say firmly, "Getting off!" like she did on the subway during rush hour.

She had just made it past the doors when she caught sight of the deliveryman by the front desk with a white plastic bag from Jiang's Kitchen in his hands.

Anne started making her way over, skirting the edge of the crowd by following the wall and picking up bits of conversation as she passed.

"Freddie said it was gorgeous . . ."

"No, he's back from LA permanently . . ."

"How much did he sell his company for again?"

Oh God. It was a Freddie Wentworth party.

This is fine, she thought as she continued forward. Better than fine. If he was having a party, that meant he was upstairs and there was no chance she would run into him. Yes, there might be some old friends in the crowd, but as the reflection in the elevator so kindly reminded her, she didn't look exactly like she did back in college. All she had to do was avoid eye contact with anyone and there was a good chance she could grab her food and escape upstairs unnoticed. She was almost there, steps away from the deliveryman and her orange chicken, when a familiar voice rose up nearby.

"Anne?" Then, a moment later, more assuredly, "Anne!"

Anne barely had time to turn around, to register where she knew that voice from, when a woman with hot-pink hair emerged from the crowd.

"Oh my God, it is you!" she squealed. The minute Anne recognized Sophie Wentworth was the moment Freddie's sister's arms were around her. The hug was all-encompassing, and Anne's shock was quickly overshadowed by an aching nostalgia. Oh, she had missed this. How had she forgotten how well the Wentworth family hugged? Full-bodied and unfiltered. It was like each one was the fulfillment of a lifelong wish. Anne hadn't even realized how much she'd missed them until Sophie finally released her. "I can't believe Freddie didn't tell me he invited you!"

"Oh, he didn't—"

"How long has it been? Eight years?" Sophie barreled on, as if she hadn't expected Anne to answer anyway. "How is that even possible?"

Anne let out a nervous laugh. "I know."

A loud ding rang through the lobby as the elevator arrived again, and everyone began to move forward.

"I can't wait to hear *everything*," Sophie said, hooking her arm with Anne's as she ushered them both to the front of the crowd. "How did Freddie keep this a secret?! And here I thought I wasn't going to know anybody at this thing!"

"Oh, no, I can't . . . " A shot of panic hit her chest as she slowed her steps, trying to muster a polite excuse to extricate herself from the moment, but it was too late. Sophie pulled her inside the elevator just as the doors closed.

CHAPTER 8

For the first time in his entire life, Freddie was ready for the party to be over.

The music—a new album from an electronic duo that he used to love—was awful. His newly painted apartment was lit up with carefully placed lights along the walls, full of strangers whose names he wouldn't remember in an hour all mingling and laughing as waiters passed around platters of hors d'oeuvres. Back in college he used to be the life of the party, but now he was counting down the minutes until he could sit down and enjoy some silence.

When had that happened? When he was younger, he made anything and everything into an excuse for a party, mostly because it had felt like there was so much worth celebrating. The future held nothing but limitless opportunity, and all they had to do was grab it. The excitement had been so pure and so naive he almost wanted to laugh.

"So what do you think?" George asked.

The sound of his friend's voice pulled Freddie from his thoughts. The room was bursting with people and lights and music, but the two men had created their own little bubble in the center of it.

It was the only thing keeping Freddie from retreating back to his room and shutting the door.

"About what?" Freddie replied.

His friend's brow furrowed. "The meeting with Mark from AirSoil. He emailed you about sitting down over lunch sometime soon, right?"

"Right." Freddie nodded as if he had been following. He vaguely remembered the email, but it was like so many he had seen before—full of platitudes and false sincerity, all under the guise of making him feel important—that he hadn't even really bothered to absorb the details. "Yeah, I think it's set."

"You think?"

Freddie turned to his friend and flashed him a crooked grin. "Don't worry, George. I'll make you look good."

His friend didn't look convinced, but before he could press Freddie further, the front door opened again and more people poured into the apartment, followed by squeals and laughter and greetings.

And Anne Elliot.

Freddie's heart stumbled. *Shit.* What was she doing here? He hadn't invited her. He could have—for a split second he even considered it, but he had wanted to avoid this feeling more—the tension in his muscles, the ache in his chest as his gaze found her striking profile held high as she glanced around the room, her blond hair pulled back in that neat ponytail he remembered so well, her bow lips puckered just slightly . . .

Then his gaze slid to his sister at Anne's side.

Double shit.

He turned so his back was to them and took a deep sip of his drink.

George frowned. "What's wrong?"

"Nothing."

George turned to see what Freddie had been looking at.

"Your sister's here," he said.

"I know."

George considered. "The pink isn't *that* bad."

Freddie was about to tell him to shut up when Sophie burst through the crowd with Anne in tow.

"Freddie! Why didn't you tell me you invited Anne?!" she exclaimed.

Freddie opened his mouth to speak, not even sure what the hell he was going to say, but just like that day when he picked up his keys, Anne had an answer ready first.

"He didn't," she said, a painfully forced smile on her face. "I just live downstairs."

Sophie's eyes grew wide. "In the *building*?"

Anne nodded, then stole a quick look at Freddie. "Hi, Freddie."

"Hi," he said. His tone was even and clipped.

"I can't believe I didn't know this," Sophie said, turning her shocked expression to her brother. "Did you know this?"

"We ran into each other a couple of weeks ago downstairs," he replied, then took another sip of his drink.

"Shut. Up." Sophie's mouth hung open. "That is nuts!"

"What's nuts?" George asked, his brow furrowed.

"These two dated in college and hadn't seen each other in eight years and now they live in the same building!" Sophie replied so loudly that a few people standing nearby turned.

George paused, then his eyebrows did a slight bob, like he had just connected two salacious dots.

Freddie shot him a look that he hoped communicated a demand for his friend to keep his mouth shut.

"It's purely a coincidence," Anne added, waving a hand between them as if batting away whatever cobwebs were left there. For a brief moment, her eyes darted around the room again at the walls now a clean eggshell white, over the black-and-white photographs that had replaced the modern art. Was she critiquing what he had done to her old home? Silently judging how thoroughly she had been erased?

If she was, she didn't say anything, and Freddie was almost ashamed by the relief that shot through his system. The last thing he needed was his sister learning that his apartment had been Anne's.

"It's fate! It's kismet!" Sophie exclaimed with a flourish of her hand.

"No, it's the New York real estate market," Freddie murmured.

His sister shot him a sharp glare, then turned back to Anne.

"What have you been up to? Where are you working? You went to business school, right?" Sophie asked, the words coming out in such quick succession that Anne looked almost panicked. "No wonder you can afford this building, it's gorgeous! Are you working downtown at some investment bank or—"

"Pace yourself, Sophie," Freddie interrupted. "You just walked in the door."

His sister rolled her eyes. "Oh, I'm sorry. I didn't realize I wasn't allowed to be excited to see someone after eight years."

Freddie frowned and glanced over at George. His friend was watching the scene with mild amusement.

Sophie turned to Anne again. "Ignore him. Ever since he sold his company, he thinks he's God's gift to business. He traded in his cargo shorts and hoodie for a closet full of designer suits."

"I don't think anyone misses the cargo shorts," Freddie said, throwing her a sardonic glare.

Sophie kept her attention on Anne as she nodded over to him. "Do you want to guess how much that suit cost? And I bet he still paid a fortune to have it altered within an inch of its life."

"So altered I barely recognized him," Anne said, that small, familiar smile on her lips.

The words snagged on something uncomfortable inside him. Freddie knew that smile, how it held back a wave of opinions, allowing only the smallest, least offensive through. He had always been the one she would dissect and probe those opinions with later. But now he was square in its sights.

That was it, the thing poking at his chest. It felt like she was judging him. After years of telling him how important it was to have a plan, to grow up and be an adult, she was judging him for doing just that.

Sophie cackled, her head falling back as she clapped. "Right? Exactly."

"And what about you?" Freddie asked, masking his annoyance with a placid smile as he nodded to Anne. "You were in the Columbia Business School to C-suite pipeline. How'd all those big plans work out for you?"

The words sounded sharp even though the question was genuine. He was desperate for any information about where she had been these past eight years, what she had done. But he had also seen her apartment downstairs. Met her roommate. Things clearly hadn't worked out for Anne the way she'd planned, and he was almost embarrassed at his need to point that out.

She stared at him, eyes slightly narrowed.

"Great," she replied. "Everything's great."

Their eyes stayed locked for another moment. Then Freddie looked away.

George cleared his throat, breaking the tension. "Can I get you ladies a drink?"

"Oh my God, yes. I need vodka," Sophie said, as if she had completely forgotten her one goal of the night. "Anne, do you want a drink?"

She doesn't drink hard liquor, Freddie almost said. The words were on his tongue so fast that it surprised him, a small detail he had worked so hard to bury for the last eight years yet reappeared like it had just been waiting for the right opportunity to emerge.

"No, that's okay." Anne shook her head. "I should actually be going."

"No way! Here, give me your phone," Sophie said, not even waiting for Anne to comply before taking it from her hands and typing away. "I'm going to text myself so I have your number, and we can meet up for a coffee and catch up without the running commentary and bad music."

POP.

A champagne cork flew across the room and someone screamed, only for the room to erupt in laughter and cheers. Freddie looked to see the source of the commotion, and when he turned back, Anne was already making her way across the room, disappearing back through the front door.

~

The last of the guests left before midnight. A few years ago, it would have almost been embarrassing for a party to end so early, but now Freddie only felt relief as he collapsed into one of his plush new armchairs and took a long sip of his beer.

That had been a fucking disaster. Sure, he hadn't thrown one of his parties in years, but it never entered his mind that he wouldn't enjoy it. Yet, even before Anne walked in the door he was ready to disappear back into his bedroom. And then after she did...

Freddie pushed the memory aside, taking another sip of his beer. His starched shirt felt itchy and restraining, but he didn't have the energy to get up and change, so he just unbuttoned the top few buttons and rolled up the sleeves, then let out a long-withheld sigh.

"I think that was the last of it," Sophie called out from the kitchen. "I put all the wineglasses here on the counter and the plates in the sink."

"You don't have to do that, Soph," Freddie said. "The cleaning people are coming in the morning to handle all of it."

Sophie snorted out a laugh as she grabbed a bottle of water from the refrigerator. "Just when I think you've said the bougiest thing possible, you go and say something that completely tops it."

"Thanks?" he replied with a wry smile.

She shuffled toward him and landed in the deep armchair across from him. They sat in silence for a long moment, looking out the window at the skyline glowing against the dark sky.

"So," Sophie finally said. "Are we going to talk about it?"

Freddie's body tensed even as he maintained his calm expression. He knew this was coming. "Talk about what?"

Sophie snorted again. "Okay."

He frowned, leaning over and putting his beer on the coffee table. "Soph—"

"Did you know Anne Elliot lived in the building when you bought this place?"

He ran a hand through his hair. Sophie didn't know the half of it, and he was in no mood to tell her.

"No, I didn't. But it's fine. She's an old friend who I haven't seen in a while. That's it."

Sophie rolled her eyes. "My darling brother, that's like saying the ocean is a little damp."

"Come on, it's not like we were about to run off and get married or something," Freddie said. "We were practically kids when we were together."

"Right. I distinctly remember a conversation about rings, though."

Freddie took another sip of his beer.

"What even happened between you two?" she asked. "One minute you were looking for a place to live in Buenos Aires with her, and then she just never came up again. Did she cheat on you or something?"

"Jesus, no," he murmured. "Nothing like that."

"Then what?"

"We broke up."

"Okay, but *why*?"

His head fell back on the cushions. He didn't want to turn over those last few weeks, especially with his sister. How Anne had pulled back, forcing distance between them until she ended it. How, even after her practiced speech, none of it got to the core issue, the reason that drove her to decide to do any of it.

Anne said she wanted to break up because they "wanted different things." As if either of them knew what the hell they wanted back then. He didn't even know now. And by the looks of it, she was struggling, too. The future had been such an amorphous, intangible thing between them that he hadn't really thought about it before she ended their relationship. Then after, he put all his energy into the future in a desperate attempt to erase the past.

"It was eight years ago," he replied. "I'm over it. You should be, too."

"Right." She let out a bitter laugh.

He opened his mouth, ready to reiterate his point in the hopes that she would let it lie, but then he caught the hurt that flashed across his sister's face.

Sophie had always been his fiercest ally. Even when they were little, and their parents would catch him playing video games at three a.m., she would be the one to argue why he didn't deserve a punishment. She was also the one who convinced their father not to dismantle Bertha after he found out Freddie had raided his plumbing van to build it. And once Anne started spending time at their home in Queens—enjoying his mom's homemade dinners and indulging in his dad's obsessive ranting about the Mets—Sophie was more than happy to adopt Anne as the little sister she'd always wanted. Tonight had been a quick flash of that, enough for him to realize his sister had lost something eight years ago, too.

"Sorry, Soph," he murmured.

"It's fine." She waved him off, the Wentworth signal to move on. "You're coming out to Mom and Dad's next weekend, right?"

Shit. He vaguely remembered a text from his mom earlier in the week, something about Christmas decorations in the basement, but it was one message among a flurry of others, and he had completely forgotten.

"Do I need to?"

He felt like an ass the minute he saw his sister's glare.

"Are you serious?" she asked. "You know Dad's back won't let him lift those boxes up the basement stairs. And if you don't do it, Mom will try and end up with a broken pelvis or something."

Freddie winced. "Thanks for the guilt trip."

She just shrugged. "Jimmy's not around for the literal heavy lifting anymore, so you need to step up."

"All right, all right. I'll be there."

They finished their drinks before he called her a car to take her back to Queens, then walked with her downstairs to make sure she got in safely. After that Freddie went straight to bed before he spent any more time thinking about how far his life had veered from where he thought he would be eight years ago.

CHAPTER 9

FROM: Theo Travers
TO: Anne Elliot
SUBJECT: Production Docs

Hey, Anne—Thanks for your thoughts on the budget! I added some info re: equipment rental—would you mind plugging some numbers in? And maybe you can look over a few other changes I made? See attached. Also, I would love to get your eyes on the production schedule—that's attached, too. Thanks, partner!

Theo

Anne read over the email again, looking for some point she might have missed. Then she went back to the documents Theo had sent. Maybe he had made a mistake? The budget spreadsheet had only a few more lines filled in than when she sent it earlier in the week, and even those were just links to different equipment rental houses around the city. Did he expect her to call and get quotes herself? Meanwhile the supposed eight-week schedule was largely blank, with only blocks set aside for pre-production, shooting, and post. There was no information about the size of the crew, the location—even what this mystery show was about.

"This is fine," Anne murmured to herself. She had trudged across Tompkins Square Park to Monkford Café a half hour ago, hoping to get a few minutes to herself—and away from the sounds of Taylor Swift echoing through her bedroom wall—to scour job listings, but apparently, now she would be spending her time single-handedly orchestrating another television show.

She picked up the mug next to her laptop and downed the remains of her latte like it was a shot. This shouldn't have been so hard. Theo knew what was required for most shoots. He could handle this on his own.

Maybe he has a lot on his plate, the rational part of her brain whispered.

That was true. Starting a production company from scratch was no easy task, and if he needed her to do a bit more legwork with these documents to ensure that she was a part of it, so be it. After all, she didn't exactly have any other option.

She needed a job. She could barely afford her small room in apartment 4B without one. And as much as she disliked the idea of another job in television, she had been over her bank statements, she had systematically worked through the list of pros and cons. Partnering with Theo was the best option, not to mention the only one.

Her gaze drifted back to the half-empty spreadsheet in front of her, the hours and hours of work she knew lay ahead. Suddenly Freddie's words from the party echoed in her head.

You were in the Columbia Business School to C-suite pipeline. How'd all those big plans work out for you?

Anne glared at the computer screen in front of her.

"Not great," she murmured under her breath.

She slammed her laptop shut. There was no way she'd be able to focus now.

Anne knew she shouldn't have followed Sophie up to that party. But no matter how many times she replayed the moment in her head, she couldn't find any way around it. She had been so shocked to see Freddie's sister she hadn't had a chance to think of an excuse in time to avoid the elevator up to the eighth floor, and then she was there, in her old apartment, except a new version of it. The view was so disconcerting that she barely had time to get her bearings before she turned around and there he was, standing in the middle of the room in a starched white shirt and navy blazer, like he was always meant to be there.

But it wasn't really him, was it?

Her Freddie had been passionate, alive with empathy and frustration and humor. Now there were only glimpses of that, faint whispers behind a stark mask that was as alien as it was apathetic.

Suddenly, the catalyst behind so much of her old hurt and confusion began to make sense.

She had always tried to equate the person she knew in college with the one who had so quickly blocked her number, the man who'd chosen to cut her out of his life completely instead of remaining friends. It was something she never would have expected from the old Freddie, but this new version . . . it wasn't so hard to believe.

He had treated her like a stranger. No, worse than a stranger. She had felt insignificant, like her decision to give him up wasn't the one reason he had this shiny new life in the first place.

Yeah, but he doesn't exactly know any of that, does he? the voice in her head chided.

Anne glowered at her empty coffee mug. Sometimes she really hated being so rational.

A ping from her phone broke her train of thought. She reached into her bag, expecting to find another text from Theo on the screen, following up on his email.

But when Anne pulled out her phone, it wasn't a text from Theo but from Sophie Wentworth.

SOPHIE

> HEY! So good seeing you last weekend! I'm in the neighborhood today—want to grab coffee?

Anne's heart did an odd stumble. She had almost forgotten that she had exchanged numbers with Sophie at Freddie's party. She had been so anxious to get out of there, the steps in between had fallen through the cracks in her memory.

She unlocked her phone and opened the message, ready to reply, but her fingers hovered over the screen.

Was it wrong to renew her friendship with Sophie? She had spent so much time distancing herself from that part of her life that it felt dangerous to contemplate revisiting it. But it had been eight years, right? Surely if Sophie was reaching out, she felt comfortable getting together. Anne should, too.

ANNE

> You too! I'm actually at a coffee shop nearby now. Monkford Café? It's right off Tompkins Square Park.

SOPHIE

> STOP IT! I'm literally just one block over. Will be there in like 5 seconds!

Anne smiled as she slipped her phone in her bag. The fact that Sophie genuinely wanted to catch up felt like a lifeline she didn't know she needed. Over the past few years, Anne had been so busy working to keep Kellynch alive, she hadn't kept any friends close, even though she desperately wished she had. Now, if there was a possibility she could rekindle her friendship with Sophie, it felt almost unfair to deny herself a second chance at it.

A minute later, the bell above the cafe door rang out, and Anne looked up in time to see Sophie swing through it, her shock of pink hair almost glowing under the lights and her quilted coat a blur of color as she moved toward Anne's table.

"I'm telling you, it's kismet!" Sophie announced, leaning forward and enveloping Anne in another one of her signature hugs. "What are the odds that you'd be here at the exact same time I'm in the neighborhood!"

Anne considered pointing out that the odds were actually quite high, considering she lived just across the park, but instead she smiled.

"Do you live nearby, too?" she asked.

"No," Sophie said with a rueful sigh. "Still out in Queens. But my floral shop is off Twelfth Street and First."

A warm sense of pride grew in Anne's chest. The first time she met Freddie's family, she quickly learned that their mother Jean passed her green thumb down to both her children. Jean Wentworth had a vegetable and herb garden that had taken over their entire backyard. Freddie helped take care of it—in fact, ensuring the plants survived a particularly harsh winter was what drove him to create his hydroponics farm in their basement. Their father helped, too, thanks to his plumbing business and extensive knowledge about irrigation. But Sophie's love had gone the other way. She loved flowers the way that Anne loved math: not for any utilitarian function, but because of the beauty in the details. They bonded over finding the mathematical Fibonacci sequence in dahlias and applying the golden ratio to bouquets. Sophie had voiced a dream of opening a shop in the city one day, too, and even though her fiancé, Jimmy, was supportive—he offered to manage the future shop's finances—Anne had always worried about the lack of a concrete plan in place. It was a Wentworth family trait.

"That's great, Sophie!" she said. "When did you open?"

Sophie let out a dry laugh. "Not open yet. The rate I'm going, I'm not sure I ever will be. I can create an amazing wedding bouquet, but apparently organizing invoices is my kryptonite."

Anne's smile faltered. "Isn't Jimmy handling all of that?"

Her friend shrugged, pretending like the sudden flash of sadness in her eyes wasn't there. "We broke up."

The news was so shocking that Anne was struck dumb. Jimmy Bruno had been Sophie's childhood sweetheart. He had been at the Wentworth house for every Sunday dinner. Anne had even attended their engagement party. "Oh, Sophie. When?"

"Six months ago," Sophie replied. "But things hadn't been good for a while. I stupidly thought the flower shop would help fix things. Jimmy had been there while I dreamed the whole thing up and he got a degree in business management, so it made sense that he would take over that side of things while I focused on the creative. But it just led to more fights until we were barely even speaking."

"I'm so sorry," Anne said, reaching across the table to squeeze her friend's hands.

"It's okay," Sophie said with a sigh. "I'm just glad the whole thing is over. The divorce was awful, dividing everything up. I had to move back in with my parents, but I got the shop, which is great. Or at least I thought it was great. We're supposed to open next month, and I have no idea how to actually run it."

The waiter appeared beside their table to take their order—an oat milk matcha flat white for Sophie and another skim latte for Anne. When he left, Sophie leaned both elbows on the table and smiled.

"Enough about me. What about you?" she asked. "The last I heard you got into Columbia Business School. What are you doing now? I always pictured you running a hedge fund and breaking men's balls for a living. And, honestly, if that's what you're doing, I'm so jealous."

Anne nearly laughed. It was almost funny hearing the impression she had left on Sophie eight years ago. She might not have known what the hell she was doing with her life, but at least she had looked like she did. It was a mantle Anne was still carrying.

"I tried the finance thing for a while, but it wasn't for me. Then my dad's TV production company ran into some budgeting issues, so I took over the finances for a while."

"How long is a while?"

"Five years." The words came out so quickly that it was only when Anne heard them aloud that she processed them. Had it really been five years? How depressing.

Sophie watched her expression as the realization struck. "It's crazy how fast the time goes, huh?"

Anne let out a long breath. "Yeah."

The waiter returned with their drinks, and the conversation

moved on. But no matter what topic came up, there seemed to be an unspoken understanding that Freddie would not be one of them. Anne was relieved, even as the temptation to ask about him grew.

The bill finally came, and they split it, still talking as they gathered their things and started toward the door.

"What are you doing for the rest of the day?" Sophie asked as they walked out onto the sidewalk.

"I have to finish going over some production documents for a friend," she said, working to not roll her eyes as she buttoned her peacoat to ward off the new chill in the air. "Then I promised to help my roommate hang up some posters for her play. What about you?"

Sophie gave the bloated canvas bag over her shoulder a pat. "These invoices and bills need to be paid and I have to figure out a way to keep track of the fact that I paid them. Then, according to an accounting video I saw on YouTube, I should use them to project my outgoings for next year. Then I need to look into green business incentives, since I installed this gray water recycling system . . . " She sighed. "So, yeah, I'll probably spend the next week drinking and crying."

Anne smiled. "Do you need help?"

"With the drinking?"

"No, the accounting," she replied with a laugh.

Sophie's eyes widened. "Are you serious?"

Anne nodded. Sure, she had a mountain of work ahead of her with Theo's production budget and schedule, but none of it triggered the same curiosity and excitement that had been stoked alive by Sophie's shop.

"I know it sounds overwhelming, but once you set up a system to keep track of everything, it's easy. Then you can use that to feed projected cash flow."

"I don't know. That feels like a lot to ask . . . " Her friend's eyebrows knitted together.

"Let me help, Sophie. I want to," Anne said, surprised by the giddiness already growing in her chest.

"Okay," Sophie said, though she still looked unsure. "You have to let me pay you, though."

"We'll cross that bridge when we come to it," Anne said. Then she held out her hand. "Deal?"

Sophie narrowed her eyes, as if considering. After a moment, she took Anne's hand and shook. "Deal."

Anne smiled, more excited about the projected budget for Sophie's floral shop than she had been about anything in months.

CHAPTER 10

"What are you, blind!" a voice bellowed over the blaring sound of the Jets game as Freddie walked through his parents' front door.

He had taken the subway, out of nostalgia as much as convenience, and when he walked up the steps onto Queens Boulevard, he suddenly felt eighteen years old again, coming back to his parents' house after class at NYU. He walked the three blocks to their house, too lost in the memory to notice how the temperature had dropped, until he stepped inside and paused on the threshold, his nose numb, even as he smelled the garlic and onions wafting down from the kitchen. It was a moment that could have been bottled from his childhood.

"Hey! I'm here," he called out, closing the door behind him.

His father's head popped around the corner from the living room, his brow furrowed like he was still in doubt of who had just walked into the house.

"Jets are down fourteen. Can you believe it?"

Freddie smiled. "Dad, they're one in five. I can believe it."

His father sighed. Not only was Fred Wentworth Sr. a carbon

copy of his son, just thirty years in the future; he had also passed down his eternal—and oftentimes heartbreaking—love of the New York Jets.

"Freddie!" His mother's five-foot frame appeared in the doorway of the kitchen. She hurried down the hall as he hung up his coat, and enveloped him into a warm embrace only to pull back a moment later and glare at him with a critical eye. "You look tired. What's wrong?"

"My mom made me come out to Queens on a Sunday to get her Christmas decorations up from the basement," he said, feigning his best martyred expression.

Jean Wentworth rolled her eyes. "I can't with you."

"I haven't even had breakfast, Mom. I'm so weak . . ."

She waved a hand at him as she turned and headed back into the kitchen. Freddie followed, while somewhere in the living room, he heard his dad's deep chuckle.

The kitchen had always been the heart of the Wentworth house, with food always readily available, while even more was in the process of being cooked. Today was no exception. A covered pot was simmering on the stovetop while the oven light revealed a loaf of bread baking. The standard fare was on the kitchen table: a bowl of grapes, a bag of fennel taralli, and, in the wild card spot, one lone banana.

"The tree is in the basement by the boiler, but check the box because it might have gotten wet when we had that big storm in June. And I still can't find that light-up Santa that goes on the roof, so keep an eye out."

Freddie nodded as he grabbed a few grapes from the bowl and popped one in his mouth. That Santa was terrifying and had given him nightmares since he was five, so he would not keep an eye out.

Fred Sr. appeared in the doorway then, slowly making his way over to the refrigerator and grabbing a beer. Freddie was tempted to tell him that he could have gotten that for him and saved his father the trip, but he stayed quiet. Since Fred Sr.'s operation last summer for a herniated disk, he didn't move as quickly as he used to, but he'd be damned if anyone reminded him of that.

"Is it me, or do we keep getting the Christmas decorations out earlier and earlier every year?" he asked, twisting the cap off his bottle.

Jean ignored the question as she took the lid off the pot and gave it a stir. "We can keep everything in the dining room for now and wait until next weekend to put up the tree, don't you think?"

Fred Sr. turned to his son. "I'll pay you twenty bucks to leave the tree down there."

His wife smacked his arm. Fred Sr. chuckled again and grabbed his apron-clad wife around the waist to pull her in for a quick kiss before she turned away with a coy grin. Freddie had watched this scene play out his entire life. It was truly disgusting.

At least, that's what he and his sister thought when they were little. There had been nothing more embarrassing than the fact that their parents actually liked each other. But now that he was older, he couldn't help but smile to himself.

The front door opened again, then slammed shut, followed by the sound of his sister's voice. "Where is everybody?"

"In the kitchen," their father called back.

A moment later, she appeared, her pink hair shooting out in all directions like she had just taken off a hat. "It's like a party in here."

Freddie popped another grape in his mouth. "If that's true, I worry about your social life."

She made a face at him, the same scrunched-up, cross-eyed one from when she was six.

"Hey," her mother smacked her arm. It was the height of Jean Wentworth's discipline. "Be nice."

"If I were an only child, I would be," Sophie answered sweetly, then collapsed into one of the chairs at the table.

"Where have you been?" their father asked her. He was halfway out the doorway, as if he hadn't quite decided whether to stay for the conversation or go back to the Jets.

"I was at the shop, picking up some stuff from the back office that I need to organize," Sophie said. "And then I had coffee with Anne Elliot."

Shit. Freddie's head fell forward. *Here we go.*

Jean's wooden spoon clattered onto the top of the stove. "What?"

"Oh, didn't Freddie tell you? She lives in his new building," Sophie said, a devious smile curling her lips. She was enjoying this too much. Meanwhile, their father winced and turned back to the living room.

Smart man, Freddie thought.

"Freddie!" his mother shrieked. "Why didn't you tell me?"

"Because we broke up eight years ago, Mom," he replied.

"But it's Anne!" Their mother turned back to Sophie. "How is she? What is she doing? I bet she's a high-powered businesswoman. Like Melanie Griffith in *Working Girl*."

Freddie let out a deep sigh. For his mom, nothing equated professional success more than a corner office and shoulder pads. Even after he sold his company for a small fortune last year, she still couldn't move past the idea that he was now unemployed. She had no frame of reference for a career that didn't require long hours in the city and a 401(k).

"She's good. Working at her dad's production company. Or she used to? Anyway, she offered to help me with all the bookkeeping for the shop," Sophie said, reaching for the grapes.

Freddie slid them out of her reach. "Excuse me?"

Sophie reached over and grabbed the bowl, setting it in her lap. "She's got some downtime and offered to organize the shop's finances so I'm not having a panic attack every day."

Their mother let out a wistful sigh. "She was always so smart. And helpful. And *so* beautiful."

Freddie ignored her, keeping his attention on his sister. She was still wearing the same shit-eating grin, but he couldn't decipher whether it was entirely due to telling their mom about Anne, or whether she was actually serious about accepting Anne's help.

"What happened to hiring someone?" he asked.

"I will, eventually. But for now, she offered, and I think she would be perfect."

"I don't think it's a good idea, Soph."

His sister turned to him with a frown. "Why not?"

He didn't even know. There was an odd panic clawing at his chest that he couldn't quite pinpoint. All he knew was that his need to keep Anne at a distance would be futile with Sophie Wentworth in the mix.

"I'm glad she's going to organize things for you, but who's going to be doing that on a daily basis when you open?" Freddie replied, trying his best to appear nonchalant. "There's receipts, budgets, taxes. It's a lot, and you can't handle it on your own."

By trying to keep his voice even, he sounded condescending, and both Sophie and their mother narrowed their eyes at him.

"Wow," his sister deadpanned. "Thanks for that vote of confidence."

"I just mean . . ." Freddie paused, trying to regain control of the narrative. "I still think you need to bring someone on full-time. Opening a business is hard enough—you have to actually run it, too. Who's going to do all that work six months from now?"

"I think you're just pissed that I have an excuse to spend more time with your ex-girlfriend than you do."

"Oh!" Their mother jumped again, as if a life-altering thought had just entered her brain. "Freddie, you should ask Anne out for coffee!"

"We broke up eight years ago, Mom," he reminded her again.

"That doesn't mean you can't be *friends*," she replied, like she was almost offended.

His gaze went up, hoping somehow the popcorn ceiling would give him patience. "Well, I can't. I'm busy."

Sophie snorted out a laugh at the obvious lie. "Doing what?"

Leave it to his sister to call him out.

"I'm meeting with the CEO of a new green tech company in about a week," he said, grasping at the first thing that popped into his head. "They're starting to explore sustainable farming and wanted to talk to me."

His mother turned around, her eyes hopeful. "A job interview?"

It took every ounce of his self-restraint not to roll his eyes. He already knew what she was imagining: her son in a double-breasted suit, walking down Madison Avenue like Don Draper.

"It's not a job interview," he replied. "We're just grabbing lunch."

His mother sighed, as if relieved. "Thank God. It's a job interview!"

He threw up his hands. "Sure. Fine. A job interview."

Sophie didn't look as thrilled. "I thought you sold your company so you could have some downtime."

He sighed. "And?"

"We need to be encouraging, Sophie," their mother scolded. "Your brother hasn't had a real job in years."

His sister threw her an incredulous look. "Mom, he sold his company last year for a stupid amount of money."

Jean Wentworth wasn't listening, though. She began stirring again, a smug smile on her face. "This is wonderful. I can't wait to tell Father Keenan to take you out of Sunday's prayer requests."

Freddie's head fell back as he groaned.

He tried to blend into the background after that, listening patiently as his mother detailed the guest list for Thanksgiving and the ever-changing menu. When the Jets game was over, his dad brought him down to the basement, past his old hydroponics system, to where the Christmas decorations were piled in the corner. Each box was supernaturally heavy and about to fall apart, but when he finally left two hours later, exhausted and still covered with a dusting of glitter from his mother's manger set, he was surprised to find he had enjoyed himself.

Freddie took the M train home and walked up to the front door of the Uppercross an hour later. He hadn't run into Anne since the party, and over the course of the week he had let his guard down so much that he hadn't expected to see her in the lobby when he walked in.

He froze in the doorway.

She was seated on one of the long leather benches against the wall across from the mailboxes, her blond hair tucked behind her ears and a stack of posters in her lap, listening to an older woman in a Ramones T-shirt who was gathering up her mail. She couldn't see him at this angle, and he couldn't help staring at her profile, the long delicate line that ran down her nose and over her bow lips . . .

What the hell are you doing? a voice chided in his head.

Shit, what *was* he doing?

He cleared his throat, starting forward again as if he hadn't seen her at all.

She looked up as he entered. Her eyes went wide and she stood up, sending the posters shooting across the floor and into his path.

"Crap," she murmured.

He looked down. For a moment, his brain didn't register the image on the paper, but then the silver limbs began to make sense. The bare torsos, the curve of a breast. Was that a nipple?

"They're not mine," Anne blurted out. "I'm helping Cricket hang posters for her play and... they look like that."

He brought his gaze up to hers, ready to make a joke, before he remembered that wasn't something they did anymore. It was a muscle memory he hadn't unlearned yet.

So instead, he bent down and picked them up, then handed them back to her.

"Thanks," she said. Her cheeks were flushed, but even that didn't diminish her sense of composure. She had always been like that, someone who had a quiet sense of control, regardless of the situation.

His mother's voice rang in his head: *And so beautiful.*

Damn it. He hated when she was right.

He cleared his throat again, trying to think of the right thing to say, when the older woman joined them, mail in hand. She was eyeing her ConEd bill when she finally noticed Freddie standing in front of her.

"Who are you?" she asked.

He smiled. "Fred Wentworth. I just moved in upstairs—8A."

The woman eyed him for a long moment, then she turned back to Anne. "Squatters' rights."

His brow furrowed, but before he could ask what she meant, the elevator arrived with a ding.

"Okay, Anne, I've got the tape and also the best news!" Cricket announced as she skipped out of the elevator and into the lobby. Then her gaze found Freddie. "Freddie! Oh, I'm so glad you're here for this, too! You'll never believe it."

The three of them stared at her, waiting.

Cricket smiled, rolling her shoulders back. "Thanks to an antibiotic-resistant UTI, Hannah had to drop out of the play! You're looking at the new Fairy Wench #2!"

She bowed dramatically before anyone could figure out an appropriate response, then continued. "Obviously, I'll set aside tickets for everyone to attend my debut. Anne, you already promised to come, so you're all set. And James and Ellis committed, too, so maybe you can all head over together! Like a party!"

The older woman glared at her a moment longer, then turned and started toward the elevator.

"Do you want me to leave your ticket at will call, Bev?" Cricket yelled after her.

"I'd rather eat glass, Cricket," the woman replied as she disappeared inside and the doors slid closed.

Cricket was apparently oblivious to the sarcasm. Her smile widened as she turned back to Freddie.

"What about you?" Cricket asked, taking a step toward him. Her voice had lowered to a suggestive whisper. "Can I interest you in a contemporary take on Shakespeare and an incredibly revealing fairy costume?"

Freddie's mind raced for a plausible excuse. He didn't enjoy live theater even when it was good, so he could only imagine what was waiting for him on that stage. But then his gaze snagged on Anne.

She was watching him from the corner of her eye with that same look she had given him at the party. The one that made him feel like she had already made up her mind about him, already knew exactly what he was going to do—offer a polite excuse and walk away.

It was all the motivation he needed to turn his attention back to Cricket and offer her one of his signature grins. "I'll be there."

CHAPTER 11

For a moment, Anne debated missing Cricket's opening night. Her rationale was solid: She had promised to attend the play, but she hadn't explicitly said which night. Anne reasoned that she could attend any show that week and still fulfill her obligation. And really, how could she even consider a night out when she still had to finish up all that paperwork for Theo, and start to go through everything needed for Sophie's shop?

No doubt about it, her logic was sound. But on Saturday, Cricket was almost in tears after learning that Hannah's UTI had cleared up and she would be returning to the play in just a few days. Cricket was desperate for Anne's assurance that she would be there to see her first—and possibly only—turn as Fairy Wench #2.

So, that Sunday evening, Anne put on her nicest outfit—a black cap-sleeve shift dress her mother had bought her at Bergdorf Goodman a few years before and a pair of heels she had barely broken in—grabbed her coat, and headed for the subway. She wasn't in a rush, and when the train was held at Fourteenth Street for an extended period of time, she was almost relieved. Yes, she was going to be late, but at least now she could sneak into the theater unseen, quietly support her friend. Maybe she could even leave early.

When she finally arrived at the off-off-Broadway playhouse where Cricket had instructed her to go, the houselights were down and the half-naked usher dressed in silver fairy wings gave her a disappointed look as he took her ticket and guided her down the dim row of seats toward the stage in the center.

Anne did not expect the space to be this intimate. There were only twenty or so seats set close to the performance space; it almost felt like the guests were part of the show. She had a sudden panic that this might have interactive elements. There was one vacancy available in the back of the three rows where she could blend into the shadows, and the usher motioned for her to take it. Her eyes tried to adjust to the darkness as she stumbled forward, almost falling into the small seat.

There was an actor onstage giving a monologue while she tried to shrug off her coat and scarf.

"Sorry," she whispered when her leg accidentally bumped into the man next to her.

"You're good," he murmured back. The deep timbre was familiar, and she froze.

Oh God. She knew that voice.

Suddenly the lights went up onstage and she looked over to where Freddie Wentworth was seated beside her.

You should say something, she thought. But her mouth stayed shut and her gaze darted away, toward the stage. No amount of avoidance could change how closely they were packed together, though. If she moved even an inch, her shin would be pressed up against Freddie's knee.

A loud gong suddenly clanged, and the stage was flooded with half-naked fairies battling a robot across an apocalyptic landscape.

"If I be waspish, best beware my fucking sting!" one yelled in a thick Long Island accent, then bared her breasts.

Anne winced. This was going to be awful.

As the lead fairy continued to pontificate, and more scantily clad actors covered in metallic paint took posed positions onstage, Anne's expectations dipped even lower. While the play was called *Get Shrewed*—a gritty reimagining of Shakespeare's *The Taming of the Shrew*, ending in bloodshed and fornication—she couldn't quite figure out why so many characters from *A Midsummer Night's Dream* had been incorporated. Then Freddie shifted so his leg brushed hers, and she suddenly couldn't focus on anything except where his hand now rested on his knee, dangerously close to her thigh. As the play wore on and the intimate theater crowded with more and more fairies, all dressed in cybernetic wings, the air she shared with Freddie felt so charged she thought she might suffocate.

She shut her eyes to calm her beating heart, but they were pried open by another booming clang of the gong as Cricket entered the stage with a crowd of other fairies and what appeared to be a robot nun. Her metallic bodysuit had pieces strategically cut out so there was more bare skin showing than crushed lamé, while the fairy wings flapped wildly behind her.

More chaos ensued, but Anne tried to keep her focus on her roommate. Despite the fact that her silver leotard was two sizes too small, and her glittery fairy wings were already falling apart by the end of the scene, Cricket did surprisingly well, and she was the one cast member who didn't off their top or reveal some kind of appendage—papier-mâché or otherwise. Everyone else, though...

"Fucking kiss me, Kate," Petruchio implored, and then promptly unzipped his pants.

Definitely papier-mâché, Anne thought, and she could have sworn she heard Freddie stifle a laugh.

The play dragged on, and when they mercifully neared the final act—fairies strewn across the stage in a show of bloodshed that smelled suspiciously like ketchup—Anne tried to pinpoint one redeeming element that she could mention to Cricket later. Then Freddie shifted again. It was slight, just a resettling into the small seat, but suddenly her shoulder was pressed into his arm. She could hear the soft cadence of his breath, smell the scent of his aftershave . . .

Oh. She remembered that smell. His clothes might have changed, his hair, too, but that distinct mix of sandalwood and citrus, that hint of cinnamon as well, hadn't changed.

She stole a brief glance down to where his hand was still splayed on his knee. She remembered that hand, too, the way his long fingers intertwined with hers in countless movies, endless walks. The way he held her . . .

Suddenly the entire theater went black. A moment later the stage lights came on again and there was a smattering of applause as the cast trotted back to the center of the stage, doing their bows before exiting as the houselights came up.

The audience stood in silence, looking at one another like they needed to confirm a shared hallucination. Meanwhile Anne avoided looking at Freddie at all, desperate to grab her coat and leave. That's when James and Ellis appeared from further down the row.

"Well, that was interesting," Ellis murmured.

"Question," James said, holding up his hand. "Was the donkey character supposed to be a robot or a fairy?"

"There was a donkey?" Anne and Freddie asked in unison.

Oh God. She could already feel her cheeks flush.

"Ha!" James pointed at the two of them with glee. "Jinx!"

Freddie shook his head and smiled. It looked so much like that smile Anne remembered from college that she had to look away.

Thankfully, Cricket picked that moment to appear back onstage.

"Cast party at the Black Door Pub across the street! Everyone's invited!" she announced to the dwindling crowd.

Damn it. All Anne wanted to do was go home where she had her pajamas and Netflix login waiting. Instead, she followed everyone else toward the exit to the street.

The Black Door Pub was already crowded when they arrived, full of cast members who had chosen to wear their costumes out to celebrate. After finally getting a soda water from the beleaguered bartender, Anne settled into a spot at the end of the bar with Ellis and James. She lost track of Freddie as soon as they came in, and finally released the breath she felt like she had been holding for hours. Everyone was laughing and chatting, as if nipples and synthetic phalluses were commonplace.

"There she is!" James suddenly yelled.

Anne turned just as Cricket rounded the corner of the bar. She was still in her costume, and her fairy wings hit almost every person sitting at the bar as she made her way toward them. Freddie appeared a moment later holding two drinks, a beer and something blue garnished with an olive.

Cricket smiled when she arrived at their end of the bar, giving each of them a hug before sitting on the vacant stool next to Anne, angling herself to where Freddie stopped nearby. A breathy *thank you* fell from her lips as she relieved him of her cocktail, then she addressed the small group of five.

"Thank you so so so much for coming," she said. She touched her hand to her heart before adding, "Seriously. It means the world. Even if I *did* flub a line."

"I didn't even notice," Anne assured her. Technically, it wasn't a lie—she hadn't noticed. She had barely followed the plot.

"At least your character didn't require nudity," James said, sipping his martini through a small cocktail straw. "I saw more breasts tonight than I have in my entire life."

"Oh, I usually do," Cricket said offhandedly. "But after I told the director that my brother was going to be in the audience tonight, they gave me a special exemption."

Ellis frowned.

Cricket turned to Freddie and offered him a beaming smile. "Do you think anyone noticed I messed up?"

"Not a chance. You were great," Freddie replied reassuringly.

The words hit Anne like a ton of bricks. She knew that tone, how it could make you feel seen and cared for. Like you were someone special. She used to be the recipient.

Suddenly, a glass of wine didn't sound like such a bad idea.

"I was just so caught up in the moment," Cricket said, letting her gaze shift as she stared off into the distance. "It's really important for me to embody the *essence* of my character, you know?"

"The essence of a cybernetic fairy living in a postapocalyptic Detroit?" Ellis quipped.

"Don't mind him. That performance was *art*," James said, giving a wave to his husband before bringing his attention to Freddie. "Speaking of beautiful things. I want to talk to our new neighbor."

Oh God. Anne turned to the bar, hoping to catch the bartender's eye and grab that wine.

"Yes!" Cricket said, clapping her hands and leaning a bit further toward Freddie. "We're making it all about me and I want to know about *you*."

Freddie let a small grin tug at his lips. "Okay. What do you want to know?"

"Well, I know you went to NYU with Anne," Cricket replied, counting off the facts on her fingers. James shot Anne a conspiratorial look then. Apparently, he and Cricket had discussed this before. "And I know you sold your own company recently and moved back to the city. But where were you in between?"

"Argentina, mostly," he answered. His voice was so deep, it was audible below the music. "Though I was traveling around a lot over the last couple of years."

"Argentina," James repeated wistfully.

Next to him, Ellis seemed intrigued, too. "What were you doing there?"

"I worked to integrate a sustainable farming system into local communities around Buenos Aires. It was based off this hydroponics idea I had in college."

He even built the prototype in his basement to help his mother grow herbs and microgreens, and named it Bertha, Anne wanted to add.

She didn't, though.

Meanwhile, Ellis looked impressed. Across from him, Cricket looked confused. "What's hydroponics?"

"Essentially, it's growing plants without soil by using a water-based solution packed with nutrients," Freddie replied.

"I've never been to Argentina, but I've always wanted to go," Ellis said.

James gasped. "We should go!"

"You should," Freddie said, nodding. "I'm a big proponent of travel. It helps you figure out who you are and what you want."

And become everything you promised you never wanted to be, too, she thought.

He didn't owe her anything. He could do whatever he wanted with his life. That's what the rational side of her brain said, anyway. But in her chest, the frustration and disappointment couldn't let her forget how he used to rail against conformity, how he swore over and over again that he would never put on a suit or show up to a nine-to-five job. She suddenly wanted to shed her meticulous exterior just to remind him, to let everyone know exactly what she thought of this new version of Freddie Wentworth.

Instead, she just took a deep sip of her soda water and started looking for the bartender again.

Cricket leaned into Freddie's side. "And did you figure out what you want?"

Freddie smiled again. "Well, I got to watch my dreams become a reality on a scale I never thought possible, so I think that's pretty close."

You're welcome, Anne thought. Yes, it was petty—he still didn't know she broke up with him so he wouldn't lose that opportunity to begin with—but after eight years and a blocked number, she was allowed a moment of petty.

Cricket exchanged a blatant look with James, and they both smiled.

"Okay, why don't we give Freddie a break," Ellis interrupted, giving his sister a critical glare like he knew exactly what she was up to.

"Fine," James said, and exhaled a long sigh. "Cricks, tell everyone about this fabulous costume. How did you get that body paint all over you?"

There was another coy smile on her lips as she responded, her body angled to favor Freddie's. Anne forced a smile, trying to listen as her friend launched into the detailed history of her silver body glitter, and how she brought her character into the modern world.

Other actors came by and there was more small talk about the play, and Anne did her best to listen and be present. But she couldn't stop counting down the minutes until she could politely excuse herself and go home.

"Another round?" James announced a half hour later, waving at the bartender.

"Absolutely not," Ellis said, pulling James's arm down. "Some of us have to get up early for work. And you had that Pilates class you wanted to try tomorrow. Remember?"

"Oh, right," James acquiesced with a loud sigh. "Pilates."

"I should head home, too," Anne said, already reaching for her coat and bag. She was surprised when she heard Freddie's voice.

"Me, too," he said.

"But the theater never sleeps!" Cricket exclaimed with a giggle, holding her arms out wide and almost spilling her drink over two castmates standing nearby.

"Yeah!" James exclaimed, looking around like he expected the rest of the bar to join in his enthusiasm.

Freddie chuckled to himself. "But unfortunately, I need to. I have a work meeting tomorrow."

James's expression fell. "Well, that's fucking boring."

"Okay. Time to go," Ellis said, taking the drink from his husband's hand and putting it on the bar.

The cold night air felt good against Anne's flushed cheeks as they stepped out onto the sidewalk. She inhaled deeply, letting the others continue their conversation.

You're almost there, she thought to herself. *Just remember: In less than twenty minutes, you'll be in bed watching season three of Gilmore Girls.*

"I'll get us a couple of cars," Freddie said, pulling his phone from his coat pocket.

"No way." Cricket scoffed, looping her arm with his as she turned toward the Avenue. "We're New Yorkers! We should take the subway! It isn't that far, come on!"

She was already marching forward with Freddie in tow before anyone could argue.

"Oh God, please tell me we're not going to Penn Station. Last time I was there I had night terrors for a week," James moaned, falling in step behind them.

"We're not going to Penn Station," Ellis assured him. Then he turned to Anne. "You're coming, right?"

Anne nodded and tried to smile, ignoring the effort it took to keep it there. Freddie was walking ahead with Cricket still by his side. She was chatting away, one arm flailing out animatedly while the other stayed looped through his. Anne tried to avoid looking, instead letting her gaze travel up the dark buildings, across the street to where a party was pouring out of a small bar. But always, from the corner of her eye, she was aware of them. It was like a physical manifestation of the past eight years—no matter what she did to ignore the memory of Freddie Wentworth, no matter how much she stayed busy to keep her mind from finding its way back to him, he was still there. A tall, looming figure on the periphery, present no matter what she might tell herself.

The subway entrance appeared a block later. One by one, they descended the concrete staircase, with Cricket taking two steps at a time while attempting not to let go of Freddie's arm as she skipped. The subway vestibule was quiet, with just one turnstile and a MetroCard machine off to the side. They missed the E train by seconds, the low hum of the engine trailing off into the distance. The track was now empty as the five of them stopped outside the gate.

"Come on, let's go!" Cricket pulled Freddie toward the turnstile, her large wings shaking and leaving a trail of glitter behind.

"I just need to get my phone out," Freddie said, fishing for it in his pocket.

Cricket rolled her eyes. "Why?"

Anne already had her app open, ready to flash on the turnstile. "Because you need to pay the fare, Cricket."

"James, where's my app?" Ellis asked, poking his phone's screen. "It was right here."

James glared down at it, then poked it, too.

"Pay? There's no one even here!" Cricket waved around the vestibule to prove her point. "Come on. I do this all the time!"

Then she placed her hands on the steel sides of the gate and attempted to vault over it.

"Wait, don't—" Freddie bolted toward her, but not before her foot caught mid-jump, her fairy wings tangled in the turnstile, and she landed on her back on the subway platform.

Right in the path of an approaching police officer.

CHAPTER 12

For a brief moment, Freddie thought it would all be fine. After a night of live theater and tragically placed Lycra, he thought the universe would cut him a break and the police officer would ignore them. Maybe even laugh at the fact that a literal fairy had just vaulted the subway stall to land at his feet. Crazier things had happened.

But then the officer reached down and took hold of Cricket's arm, pulling her to her feet. Cricket looked up at him, her lip curled, and cried, "Let go of me, you fascist!"

Suddenly, it was chaos. Another officer appeared on the platform as Cricket flailed, trying to free herself. Her shrill protests echoed off the tiled walls of the subway station while Ellis cried out for her to stay calm. He was desperately trying to get his phone app to work and also had one arm around James, who was in tears. Freddie was already moving to give Ellis his phone, let him use his app to get past the turnstile, when Cricket screamed again.

"You ripped my costume!"

Then she reared around, squirming one arm free to slap one of the officers across the face.

Shiiiiiiiit.

To his credit, the officer almost looked put out as he pulled the handcuffs from his belt, as if this wasn't how he wanted his night to go, either.

"You can't *arrest* her!" Ellis yelled. He still had his arm around James's waist while trying to work his phone. Freddie started toward him, phone ready, when Anne walked past him, sliding through the turnstile and calmly walking up to the officers while Cricket flailed.

"Can you tell me what specific charges she's being arrested for?" she asked, discreetly holding her phone out as she looked to take notes.

The chaos continued around them, but Anne remained composed as she listened to the first officer while the other recited the Miranda rights to Cricket.

"And what precinct do you plan to take her to?" Anne asked.

On the periphery, Freddie could see that a few other people had arrived at the station, trying to make sense of the scene. But all he could focus on was Anne, how she deftly navigated her questions, maintaining her composure even as Cricket started screaming, "PIGS!"

Her shouting was drowned out by another train entering the station, screeching to a halt, and releasing a few more people onto the platform. By the time it departed, the officers were escorting Cricket through the emergency door and up the stairs to the street. Anne followed them, while Freddie, Ellis, and James followed close behind. They reached the sidewalk just in time to see Cricket disappear into the back seat of a police cruiser. Then they pulled away.

"What's *happening*!" James cried, leaning into Ellis at his side. "Where are they taking her?"

"The officer said they'd book her at the Midtown precinct on

Thirty-Fifth," Anne said, hugging her peacoat around her body. "I can head over and—"

"No, I'll go," Ellis said with a decisive nod.

"What if she goes to *prison*?" James sobbed to no one in particular. "She can't go to Rikers! She won't go anywhere above Forty-Fifth Street!"

Ellis patted his shoulder and turned back to Anne. "Do you have the address?"

Anne pulled out her phone again and a moment later, Ellis's pinged. "I also sent you the arresting officer's name and badge number."

Freddie wanted to say something. Anything. But he had no idea what. Why the hell did he feel so paralyzed? He should have helped Anne down there, or calmed James, or at least gotten Ellis's app to work. It had all happened so quickly; his brain hadn't had time to engage.

"You might be able to get her released tonight, but I would call a lawyer to make sure it's all handled properly," Anne added.

At this, Freddie perked up.

"I have an attorney," he said, finally snapping out of his stupor and stepping forward. "I can give him a call if you need—"

Ellis shook his head. "It's okay. We know somebody."

"We do?" James asked, throwing his hands in the air like the question was rhetorical.

Ellis frowned. "Yeah. Glen in 2B. He's on the co-op board."

"But he's a tax attorney!"

Anne cleared her throat. "James, why don't you come home with me and—"

"No," James cut her off, shaking his head defiantly. "I will not abandon her. What if they hurt her? What if they make her wear orange?"

"It's fine," Ellis said, nodding to Anne and Freddie. "You two should head home. We'll grab a cab and head to the police station to see if we can't get her released tonight."

James was still lamenting every possible fate that could befall someone in an NYPD holding cell as Ellis guided him to the curb and waved down a passing taxi.

"We'll text you when we know what's going on!" Ellis yelled just before they climbed in the back seat. Then the car jolted forward, and turned at the corner.

Just as quickly as the chaos descended, it was gone, replaced by an eerie silence that seemed to swallow up their small section of the sidewalk. Freddie turned to look at Anne just as she brought her gaze up to his, and for a moment they just stared at each other. From the nearby subway stairs he could hear a train approaching on the platform—brakes screeching, doors sliding open, an announcement to stand clear of the closing doors.

"I should head down there. Grab the next train," she said.

Freddie let out a long breath. All the tension had left his body, and now his muscles felt like rubber. He was exhausted. "Want to share a cab? I've had enough of public transport for one night."

"That's okay. I don't mind waiting for a train and—"

"Come on. You'll be home in half the time. It's my treat," he cut in.

She hesitated, then finally nodded. There was a hotel across the street and a few cabs waiting along the block. Freddie nodded to one of the drivers who was idling, then opened the back door of the car for Anne.

She slid in, sinking into the seat. Just as Freddie sat down in the other, a low moan escaped her lips.

He froze. He remembered that moan, and for a split second

he hated his brain for conjuring up why, those moments so many years ago when he had been the one to elicit them.

"You all right?" he asked.

"I don't normally wear heels." She sighed, reaching down to slip her heel from her shoe. "And now I remember why." She wiggled her other heel free and let out another moan. Then she leaned back and closed her eyes, her neck arching up and lips parting slightly the way they used to when he—

He turned away abruptly. Maybe this was a bad idea.

"Where to?" the cabbie asked.

"Avenue A and Ninth Street," Freddie replied.

The cabbie nodded and turned left, heading downtown.

The sound of the passing traffic filled the taxi, but in the back seat there was only a heavy silence. Freddie tried to ignore it, watching the city blocks dissolve into one another, but it felt unnatural. He and Anne had never sat in silence like this before. From the first moment they met, it was like they had known each other over a lifetime. Stories and jokes and observations were shared easily and nothing felt forced.

Of course, that was before. Now he just had to get used to the after.

The sound of his phone's ringtone cut through the silence. He pulled it from his jacket pocket and saw his mother's picture on the screen.

Shit.

He discreetly sent the call to voicemail.

Just as he was putting it back in his pocket, it began ringing again, his mother's face still on the screen.

He let out a long breath and answered. "Hi, Mom."

"Did you just send me to your voicemail?" His mother's voice was loud, and he had absolutely no doubt Anne could hear every word from the next seat.

"Mom—"

"I know you did. Sophie told me you can tell when there's a click at the end of the ring."

He squeezed his eyes closed, hoping for some patience. "I'm sorry I sent you to voicemail. I was busy."

"Are you on a date?"

"No, Mom," he said through gritted teeth.

"Who are you with?"

"It doesn't—"

"Is it Anne?"

Shit.

His eyes snapped open and darted to where she was seated next to him, eyes wide. Oh, yeah, she could definitely hear everything.

"If it's Anne, tell her we said hello!" his mother continued, then her voice became a yell. "The Wentworths say hello!"

He was going to kill her. Or at least, never help with Christmas decorations again. "Okay. Will do. Now, why are you calling?"

"To wish you luck on your job interview tomorrow! Don't be nervous, you'll do great."

He sighed. "It's just a meeting, Mom."

"What are you going to wear?"

"Sweatpants. Flip-flops. Maybe Sophie's Eras Tour T-shirt."

Anne turned back to the window. He could just make out the slight shake of her shoulders, like she was laughing.

"I don't know why I bother." His mother let out an exasperated sigh before moving on. "All right, what time are you coming out on Thanksgiving?"

"It's almost two weeks away. I haven't thought about it."

"Well, I need to know because if it's before noon, I need you to pick up the antipasti from Aunt Susan's. She can't carry that thing herself."

"Then I'll be there before noon."

"Okay, I'll let her know. I'm going to bed now," his mother said, as if he had been the one to call her. "Remember to tell Anne we said hello when you see her."

"I will, Mom."

They said their goodbyes and he let the screen go dark, staring down at his reflection as he tried to regain some semblance of dignity. He could pretend the call didn't happen and sit through the rest of the cab ride in silence. But even he wasn't that petty.

"My parents say hello," he murmured.

Anne nodded, barely biting back the small smile on her lips. "How are they?"

"Good." He leaned back and sighed. "Happy their son is finally back in the city to pick up platters of cured meats and cheeses."

She laughed, the sound so light and familiar that it almost hurt.

"I'm surprised they didn't convince you to move back home to Queens," she said.

"They tried," he said, focusing on where his fingers were laced together in his lap. He should have left it at that, let the silence return, but in the periphery, he could see her waiting for him to continue. She used to do that, as if more information was guaranteed if she gave him time. And after a moment, he found himself obliging. "I used to stay with them when I was in town. In the beginning it was once a year, if they were lucky. I told myself it was for them to make up for the fact that I left. But it was for me, too. Then, when I was looking for a place, I was there almost every weekend and I just . . . "

"You just?" she asked.

He let out a frustrated sigh. Why was he telling her this? They hadn't had a conversation in years. She probably didn't even care. But it still felt like a heavy weight around his neck, this thing he just needed to offload. "It felt like they were trying to freeze time. Yeah, I had been trying to freeze a bit of my life there, too, but it was like they almost resented who I am now and wanted me to fall back into that old version of myself from before I left. Like who I am now doesn't matter as much as that twenty-year-old meddling with Dad's toolbox in the basement."

Her gaze flitted down his suit, but her expression had lost a bit of the judgmental edge he had come to expect in recent weeks. In fact, she looked almost contrite.

"That doesn't sound like such a bad problem to have," she said.

He threw her a wry grin. "It is when you come in on the red-eye and the first thing your mom needs you to do is stir the Bolognese for three hours."

She laughed again, but this time she turned to the window as if it could hide her smile.

Another memory hit him, the way she used to turn away from him to hide her smile. How he had always used it as an opportunity to lean down and steal a kiss. He hadn't let himself recall that in years, and even though he tried not to linger on it now, the image still took up residency in his brain and refused to budge.

But it was still just a memory, he reminded himself.

"So," he said, clearing his throat. "How'd you know how to handle all that back there? With the police."

"Oh." She rolled her eyes. "It's a long story."

He nodded to the traffic ahead. "It's a long cab ride."

"Well, I've been working at my dad's TV production company for the past few years. He really only has one show, *Divorce Divas*, and one of the stars can be . . . confrontational."

Freddie remembered her father's company and the show,

mostly because Anne had always talked about how ridiculous it was. He wanted to ask what had changed, about the steps between business school and reality TV, but it felt too intimate, trespassing on territory that wasn't his anymore. So instead, he asked, "How so?"

"She's been arrested eleven times."

He blinked. "Eleven?"

"Wait. Twelve," she said, eyebrows stitched together. "I forgot about New Orleans during Mardi Gras."

He cocked an eyebrow, waiting.

"Disturbing the peace," she answered his unvoiced question.

"Isn't that the point of Mardi Gras?"

"It was ten a.m. on Bourbon Street, and she flashed a cop car for some beads. When they told her they didn't have any, she threw a beer bottle at their windshield."

He let out a low whistle. "That's amazing."

Anne laughed softly. "And expensive when you have a production schedule and a very limited budget."

"Right." He smiled, averting his eyes down to where his hand played with the corners of his phone. "I was sure you were going to end up in finance or something."

Her expression had dimmed a little. "I tried. After I graduated from Columbia, I got a job at a hedge fund. Then I quit five months later."

"Why?"

She let out a dry laugh. "I may love numbers, but you and I both know I was never going to love finance."

A sharp ache hit his chest, one he hadn't felt in years. Maybe it was the familiarity—she had the courage to acknowledge their shared history, while he had been so eager to ignore it over the past few weeks.

The stillness was broken by a hard knock against the cab's plexiglass partition.

"FDR okay?" the cabbie asked.

Freddie frowned. "Excuse me?"

"Cutting down FDR Drive. Second Avenue is backed up."

Anne leaned forward. "That's fine, thank you."

The cabbie nodded and cut the steering wheel to the right.

Freddie turned, ready to continue with his line of questions, but Anne beat him to it.

"That's great news about your company."

"Sorry?"

"At the bar," she said. "You mentioned you sold your company last year. Congratulations."

That's right. He had said that. At the time, it felt good, a way of signaling that he had won, that he was doing better than anyone expected, but now it made him want to cringe. "Yeah. Thanks."

"And you have a job interview tomorrow?"

"It's just a meeting," he said. "There's this company looking to do something similar to what I did with Wentworth Hydroponics. I promised a friend I would talk to their CEO. You can't tell my mom that, though. She assumes since I don't have my company anymore, that I'm unemployed and one ConEd bill away from moving home to my childhood bedroom."

Anne smiled. "They must be really proud of you."

"Yeah. I hope so."

A long moment passed, then the cab came to a stop and there was another tap on the plexiglass. "Ninth Street at Avenue A."

Anne reached into her bag as if she was going to try to pay, but Freddie shook his head. "I already told you, my treat."

"But—"

"You took care of Cricket. Let me get the cab."

She hesitated, then nodded and stepped out onto the sidewalk while he pulled out his wallet. His pulse stuttered when he opened it. The flimsy paper corners of his first note to Anne were poking out from behind his credit cards. He cleared his throat, working to ignore it as he removed his AmEx to tap on the nearby payment screen.

Tompkins Square Park was dark and loomed across the street as he exited the cab. The Uppercross was right there on the corner, but the rest of the city seemed far away, like the darkness had hidden them away in their own secret corner. A long moment passed, then he turned to her.

Anne was just a few feet away, head back and blond hair falling down the back of her peacoat as she stared up at the dark sky. The glow from the streetlights was delicate on her skin, on where her eyebrows pinched together as she waited for him to continue. Suddenly everything he had been battling with for the past forty blocks dissolved, and all he could do was stare at her. At a face that, in this light, looked as if it hadn't really changed in eight years. Like she had been frozen, too.

"No clouds," she said, almost to herself.

"What?" he asked.

She tilted her head to look at him. "There's no clouds tonight."

He glanced up. He hadn't even noticed.

"I bet you could see Saturn from the roof deck," she said.

"I haven't been up there yet."

She turned to look at him. "Really?"

"Nope." Another moment passed. Then he shot her a lopsided grin. "Want to show me?"

∽

The lobby was empty as they walked to the elevator and Anne pressed the up button. The doors opened almost instantly, and they both stepped inside. He leaned back against the wall, trying to keep his posture casual, even as his pulse felt like it was kicking through his veins. The space was too small; he couldn't escape the sound of her short breaths, the smell of her perfume—vanilla and jasmine and peppermint. It reminded him so much of the Anne he used to know, the one who would sneak out at night to meet him at the High Line in the West Village or a jazz bar in Midtown.

He couldn't tell if it was the memory driving him crazy or the fact that it felt so far away, but before he could figure it out, the doors opened again on the eighth floor.

Anne hesitated for a moment, then stepped out. He half expected her to turn around, point to the stairs at the end of the short hall that led to the roof, and tell him to have a good night. Thankfully, she continued forward.

"I can't believe you haven't been out here yet," she said, producing a key card from her purse and tapping it against the door lock.

"I've been busy," he replied with a shrug.

"I thought you were unemployed?"

He smiled. "Just open the door."

She smiled too, ducking her head as if she could hide it. The motion caused her hair to fall in front of her face, and he had the urge to tuck it behind her ear.

"Here we are," she said, pushing the door open to walk outside into the cool night air.

He followed, and stepped out into a small oasis. Bistro lights were strung overhead, casting a soft twinkle across the roof deck's wooden floor. There was a long table in the center and what looked like someone's personal garden off to the side. Large pots held a place for summer flowers and matching wood pergolas with shade canopies stretched over long couches and tables. He peered out across the rooftops of the East Village and at the city skyline of lower Manhattan just beyond it. The views were incredible out to the water—looking uptown he could see the Empire State building glowing with orange and red lights for the fall. He turned around to find Anne standing a few feet away, the lights that lined the cables of the Williamsburg Bridge shining bright enough to make her silhouette glow.

"It's beautiful," he said softly.

"I know," she said. Then she let out a deep sigh and looked up. "When I was little, an astronomy professor from Hunter College lived on the third floor. He used to bring his telescope up here. He'd set it up right in the center and sit for hours. On really clear nights he would let me look through it. I saw Saturn and Jupiter. Even caught a couple of shooting stars once."

"What happened to him?"

"He moved to Midtown. Right near the building where you had that party in the empty loft space."

He threw her a skeptical look. "I never threw a party in Midtown."

"Yes you did. On Fifty-Third, remember? Halfway through the night, you went downstairs to get food and came back with the Russian guys you met on the street. And they ended up bringing a watermelon that was filled with vodka."

The memory was buried so deep it took a moment for Freddie to find it, but when he did, he smiled. "Holy shit, that's right. They made us go downstairs and buy more vodka for them. I think those guys still have my credit card."

Anne laughed. The sound bubbled out of her, so light and effervescent that he couldn't help but laugh, too.

"I can't believe you remember that," he said.

"Of course I do. You wrote me a note on the back of that vodka receipt. It was the first time . . . " Her voice suddenly faded along with her smile, while a deep blush rose in her cheeks.

It took him another minute to remember why, to recall what he had written to her that night so many years ago.

> *Annie— It's Friday, April 15th. You're upstairs on the roof, having an amazing time, and I'm downstairs buying three handles of vodka for five strangers who look like they could break me like a toothpick. If they do, please know I probably had it coming. Also: I am utterly and completely in love with you.*
>
> *—Freddie*

It was the first time he had said "I love you." It felt so right at that moment, like the most natural thing in the world. Now the memory left a deep hole behind, a reminder that something substantial had been there once.

"It's so odd," she said, her voice so soft he almost missed it.

He turned to her. "What?"

She turned to meet his gaze. Her expression was almost apologetic.

"I don't know how to be strangers with you," she replied.

He stilled. It was so honest yet so unflinchingly brutal that he felt like the air had been knocked from his lungs.

He'd spent years carefully locking away all thoughts of her. Forcing indifference into those places where love used to be. He'd even convinced himself that he wasn't angry about how things ended anymore. But here on this roof, he could feel those walls beginning to crack. Worse, he was reminded of how weak they had been in the first place. Paper-thin and just waiting to be ripped.

What was he doing? He already knew what it would look like on the other side of that. He had let himself be vulnerable with her before; he didn't know if he could survive it again.

"I should go," he said, his voice clipped as he turned toward the steel door they had just come through.

"Right." She nodded. "It's late."

They walked back to the door, then down the stairs in silence. Once they arrived down in the hallway, he turned toward the door to his apartment, and she pressed the button for the elevator.

"Thank you. For making me go up there," he said, breaking the heavy silence.

"Anytime," she replied.

A loud ding echoed around them as the elevator doors opened. She stepped inside.

"Anne," he said before she could press the down button.

She looked up, meeting his gaze.

He wanted to say he was sorry for how he'd acted that first moment he saw her at Cricket's apartment, for how he'd acted every moment since. But he didn't know how to apologize without dredging up so much else, things he had worked to bury for so long that he was terrified of disturbing them.

Finally, he just offered a somber smile. "Have a good night."

"You, too," she replied.

Then the elevator doors closed.

His chest ached when he walked into his apartment. He didn't go to the kitchen to get a drink, though. And he didn't go to his bedroom and change, get out of his suit and go to bed. No, he went to the spare bedroom and stared out the window at her view of the stars.

CHAPTER 13

Anne stood under the hot spray of her shower and sighed, forgetting for a moment that the tub she was standing in was rusty and the cramped walls felt like they were closing in on all sides.

Apartment 4B didn't have many highlights, but she had learned quickly that the shower was at the top of that short list. The water pressure was phenomenal, and with a radiator planted right beside the tub—which ensured the room was always a touch warmer than anywhere else in the apartment—it was all the motivation she required to get out of bed every day.

The comfort was doubly needed today. When her alarm went off at seven, she had immediately turned it off and curled back under her comforter. Anne was set to meet Sophie at ten, go over all the work she had done to organize the shop's finances, but that wasn't eventually what prodded her out of bed and into the shower. It was the memories of the night before. The play, the arrest, then everything that came after. She was concerned about Cricket, of course, but Ellis had been texting with updates all night, so Anne knew she was okay. No, the scene that played on repeat in her mind was the car ride home, the conversation, the way Freddie looked at her when they were standing on the roof, just like he used to...

Except he's not that Freddie anymore, she reminded herself for the fifth time since she'd stepped in the shower. In fact, he'd even told her that in the cab ride home.

It was like they almost resented who I am now and wanted me to fall back into that old version of myself from before I left.

She closed her eyes and stuck her face under the water again, trying to drown out the memory. She was so focused on it that she almost missed the sound of voices coming from the other room.

Her body tensed as she turned off the water, listening more closely.

"It's a travesty!" a shrill voice cried out from beyond the bathroom door.

Anne released a sigh of relief. Cricket was home.

She got out of the shower and dried off, wrapped her robe around herself, and stepped out of the bathroom.

"I mean, what about my civil rights!" Cricket exclaimed into her phone. She was over in the kitchen, looking through the cabinets over the stove, her phone wedged under her chin. She was still dressed in the fairy costume from the night before, but now she had an oversized blazer over it. Her makeup was streaked down her face and her hair was a mess, with only a lone pencil stuck through the center to keep it in a bun on top of her head. "I'm totally going to sue."

She turned around and looked like she was ready to make another proclamation to whoever was on the other line, but when she caught sight of Anne, she froze. "Oh crap! I didn't wake you up, did I?"

Anne would have thought her wet hair and terry-cloth robe would suggest no, but instead of pointing it out, she just mustered a smile and shook her head.

"Thank God," Cricket moaned. Into the phone she said, "I gotta go, call you later, bye!" Then she hung up and threw it on the sofa. "Anne, you have no idea how crazy last night was. They booked me. They took a mugshot. It was like I was a criminal!"

Anne was tempted to point out the obvious—that slapping a police officer did in fact put her in that category—but decided against it.

"Are you all right?" she asked instead. "Did they charge you?"

"Oh, they charged me! I'm out on bail and I have a hearing and I ripped my costume!" Cricket exclaimed, then frowned as if she were about to break into tears. "And now I can't find the coffee."

Anne made her way over to the kitchen, opening just about the only cabinet Cricket hadn't looked through, and grabbed the tin of ground coffee from the top shelf. Cricket sighed with relief, then waltzed over to the sofa and collapsed into it while Anne filled the percolator with water.

"They're accusing me of fare evasion and evading arrest and threatening an officer. Meanwhile, I hit my head and the police didn't even care!" Cricket cried, her arm thrown over her eyes. "They just threw me in the back of one of their cars and took me to the precinct. I was stuck in this holding cell for *hours* before Glen got me out."

Anne was about to pour the coffee grounds into the percolator but paused. "Glen from 2B?"

"I could have had brain damage!" Cricket continued, undaunted. "I could have died!"

"But you're okay, right?"

Cricket sighed, sitting up. "Yes, but they didn't *know* that."

Anne curbed a smile and finished pouring the coffee grounds, then put the percolator on the stovetop. "Ellis texted a few times, but he made it sound like you could be there for a few days."

"If it wasn't for Glen, I would've been," Cricket replied, her indignation gone and now replaced with a dreamy look. "Ellis called him and he came right up to the precinct. He said they had violated my civil rights! Can you believe it?"

Anne was about to ask what specific rights had been violated, when there was a knock on the door.

"Come in!" Cricket yelled.

The door opened and a moment later, Glen Rinnard appeared in the hall. "Hello? Is now a good time?"

"Glen!" Cricket exclaimed.

Glen smiled and walked forward, barely nodding at Anne as his attention stayed squarely on Cricket. "I just wanted to check in. See how you were doing."

Cricket stared up at him, eyes wide. "Better now."

Anne's gaze bounced between them. What was going on?

"I'm glad," he said, sitting down beside her. Anne had only ever seen Glen in the evenings at their board meetings, when he was just home from work and his suit looked like it had seen hell. Between that and his perennially tired expression, she just assumed he didn't do anything but work. But now, in jeans and a wool sweater that fit snugly around his middle, he actually looked relaxed. Maybe even happy.

Glen and Cricket stared at each other for a moment, and Anne was suddenly struck with the impression that she was very much a third wheel.

The percolator began to gurgle beside her, and Anne had never been more thankful for her antiquated means of making coffee.

"Glen, would you like a cup of coffee?" she asked, pouring some into a mug.

"No, thank you. I just stopped by to discuss the case," he replied, barely looking over to the kitchen before turning back to Cricket. "Maybe over brunch?"

Cricket's lips slipped into a smile. "I *love* brunch. I just need to change. And shower. And do something with my hair." The thought seemed to remind her that Anne was still standing just a few feet away. "Do you want to join us, Anne?"

Even without the flash of disappointment on Glen's face, Anne knew there wasn't supposed to be a third chair at their table.

"No, that's okay," she said, taking a sip of her coffee and starting toward her bedroom. "I'm actually catching up with a friend. She's opening a flower shop nearby and I ... "

By the time she reached the short hallway, it was clear that neither Glen nor Cricket was listening. She doubted they even remembered she was there. So she skipped goodbyes and slipped away into her bedroom to get dressed without another word.

∽

The storefront for the shop formerly known as Bruno's Blooms took up the corner retail unit on Twelfth Street and First Avenue, tucked between a dry cleaner and a bodega. Anne remembered when she was little it had been a candy shop, but now its tall windows were blocked with brown paper and its awning above was rolled up.

"You're here, you're here!" Sophie exclaimed as she bounded down the sidewalk to where Anne was already waiting on the front step. "Sorry I'm late. The trains were a nightmare. Ready to head in?"

Sophie unlocked the door and let Anne enter first. The hardwood floors were covered with a thin layer of dust, but she could see how they had been polished and where a long wood counter had been installed. Even with the windows covered, the morning light still streaked through, spilling over the brick walls and drop cloths.

"It's gorgeous, Soph," Anne said. And she meant it.

"Took us months to find the perfect spot," Sophie replied. "When I saw this one, I just knew."

"It's a great location," Anne agreed. "The light is incredible, too."

"Thanks," Sophie said. "Ready to dive in?"

Anne tried to calm her nerves as she set up her laptop on the workspace in the back. She had been so laser focused on creating a seamless workflow for the shop that she hadn't stopped to consider what Sophie might think of it until that moment. Not everyone found numbers and spreadsheets as fascinating as she did—what if Sophie hated it? Or what if Anne had completely misjudged what she was looking for? Sophie would be too polite to come right out and say that, but—

Stop spiraling.

Anne let out a shaky breath. Right. She could do this.

Sophie took a seat and listened as Anne began detailing her recommended budget and a possible bookkeeping system that would allow Sophie to avoid daily entry. She worked to keep her voice steady, but it was an effort, and by the time she finished explaining the online tracker designed to alert Sophie when a new order came in, she thought she might throw up.

"Okay, that settles it," Sophie said, eyes wide as she stared at the last slide of Anne's presentation. "You are a genius."

The tension Anne had been holding throughout her entire body released as she let out a relieved laugh. "Thank you. But 'genius' might be stretching it."

"Nope, you're a genius. This is exactly what I needed! I can actually wrap my head around the business side of things for the first time. Thank you."

"There's still more we can do, too," Anne said, then caught herself. "Or, I mean, more *you* can do. If you want."

Sophie smiled. "What were you thinking?"

"Well, there should probably be a long-term plan for growth. And in the short term, maybe a promotional campaign to announce the shop to the neighborhood. You could design some postcards, maybe even throw a party for the grand opening."

"I love that idea," Sophie said, her face lighting up. Then she looked around, as if seeing the potential there for the first time. "It's time to prove that Freddie isn't the only Wentworth that can throw a party."

Anne could feel her cheeks redden as she avoided Sophie's gaze and put her laptop away in her bag.

Another moment passed before Sophie sighed. "Please feel free to tell me to shut up if I'm out of line, but... what happened between you and him?"

There was an odd lurch in Anne's chest, and she had to work to keep her expression impassive. "He went to Argentina, so we decided to break up."

"Yeah, I know that bit," Sophie replied. "But what really happened?"

Anne sighed. "We were so young. We talked a lot about the future, but we never really *talked* about it. By the time we did, we were already moving in two different directions. Neither of them was wrong, but they couldn't coexist without one of us having to compromise."

Sophie's forehead knitted with confusion. "I don't get it."

There was a part of her heart that wanted to hold back the truth, keep it locked away from other people's judgment or critiques... but why? Keeping it secret hadn't protected her. If anything, it only left her more exposed, forced to relive and examine what happened over and over again all on her own.

"Sophie..." Anne hesitated, then finally let it go. "He said he was going to turn down the Buenos Aires program to stay in the city while I went to Columbia. He would have stayed because *I* would have stayed."

Recognition slowly bloomed across Sophie's face. "Are you serious? He wouldn't have started his company if he hadn't gone, or done half of . . . " Her voice faded as another wave of understanding hit her. "Holy shit, that's why you broke up with him. So he would go. How did I miss that?"

Anne tried to smile, but it faded almost instantly. "He would have lost out on so much. I couldn't have him make that choice. Especially when I had no idea what I wanted past my MBA. We loved each other, but . . . " She let her voice fade.

"I get it," Sophie said with a slow nod. "Sometimes love isn't enough to fix everything else."

Anne paused. "What?"

Sophie's head cocked to the side, like she was trying to find the right words to explain it. "Take me and Jimmy. We didn't fall apart because we stopped caring. It was everything else, the small things that got overlooked, the resentments we pushed down and ignored. We didn't talk about any of it, so it ended up festering until it swallowed us up." She paused, taking a moment to shrug. "Maybe it was because we had been together so long. We got together as kids, you know? And even though we grew up like we were supposed to, we still saw each other as those same kids."

"You still love him, though?"

"Maybe," Sophie said with a shrug. "But we never learned how to grow together. And if you can't grow together, you grow apart."

Another moment passed, then Sophie suddenly shook her head and stood up. "What the hell are we doing? Lamenting past relationships? We're literally here to plan for the future! And I think the first item on our to-do list should be that party."

Anne laughed. "How about we start with organizing your list of vendors and go from there?"

"Hey, I can multitask," Sophie said with a wink. "Okay, I'm going to lock up. Meet me out front?"

Anne nodded, throwing her bag over her shoulder and heading to the front room. She had just made it to the sidewalk when her phone pinged somewhere inside her bag. When she pulled it out, she saw a text waiting.

THEO

> Hey! Just checking in on those documents? Would also love to run my talent contracts by you. And get your thoughts on the post timeline? Maybe it's too aggressive, but you tell me.

Anne frowned. It seemed every time she finished reviewing one of Theo's spreadsheets, another one suddenly needed her attention.

ANNE

> Okay, feel free to send it along, but I'm not sure I'll be able to get to it until after Thanksgiving.

THEO

> That's perfect. Gives me an excuse to ask you out for coffee after I'm back from LA that week. I'm meeting with the network and if all goes well, I think I'll have a pretty good deal on the table.

She replied with a thumbs-up emoji just as Sophie emerged from the shop, pulling the large key ring from her bag and locking the front door.

"I'm already picturing the postcards I'm going to send out to promote this place," Sophie said, checking the handle one more time, then turning to Anne with a wide smile on her face. "There can be just an explosion of flowers and then big, dramatic font announcing the opening of..." Her expression deflated.

"What's wrong?" Anne asked.

Sophie looked up at the storefront again. "What the hell am I calling this place?"

"It doesn't have to be anything too complicated," Anne assured her. "Just something that hints at that feeling of getting flowers."

Sophie rolled her eyes. "Unfortunately, it's been a while, so I don't remember."

It had been a while for Anne, too, but she wasn't about to admit that to Sophie, especially since the last time she got flowers was eight years ago, from Freddie. The moment rushed back to her in an instant, and suddenly Anne could almost smell the lilacs, feel the soft petals under her fingers, see the triangle note attached.

Annie— It's a Wednesday and you just got a C for the first time in your entire life. Congratulations, I'm so proud of you. Who wants to be good at microeconomic analysis anyway?

—Freddie

She tried to put the feeling of that bouquet—that gift—into words. "There's the surprise when flowers arrive, the warmth when you realize why. The euphoria when you open the card..." Then she paused. "Euphoria and flora... That could be it."

Sophie's eyebrows stitched together. "What?"

"You could call the shop Eufloria."

A smile slowly spread across Sophie's lips. "That's really fucking good."

CHAPTER 14

Freddie spent the entire car ride uptown to his lunch meeting with Mark Segel trying to forget the night before. Yes, the play was awful, and Cricket's arrest had been harrowing, but that was easier to compartmentalize, especially after Ellis texted that morning with the news that his sister had been released. No, what he had a harder time ignoring was everything that came after. The car ride, the roof, how Anne had looked at him . . .

Freddie shook the thought away again. He needed to focus, especially since it felt like he had been actively avoiding thinking about this lunch all week. Maybe that was because he still wasn't clear on what the hell they were meeting about. In Mark's introductory email, he had said he just wanted to pick Freddie's brain about sustainable farming. Meanwhile, George had sent along a job description for an executive role Mark was looking to fill, just in case Freddie wanted to take a look.

It's just a meeting, he reminded himself as the car came to a stop outside the Butcher Block on Fifty-First Street and Fifth Avenue.

Still, his suit felt too constrictive, his leather oxfords too tight around his feet. Suddenly, Anne's voice filled his head again:

So altered I barely recognized him.

Freddie grimaced. It was going to be a long lunch.

The restaurant was worse than Freddie had expected. Walking through the revolving door, he was welcomed by tall, mirrored walls and every piece of décor draped in different shades of gray—gray marble, gray chairs, gray carpet. It looked expensive, and wildly impersonal.

The hostess smiled at him as he entered. She was tall and beautiful, and she escorted him through the dining room to a table by the far window, with a smile that suggested she was more than happy he had walked through the door.

Freddie recognized Mark from his minimal research. A lifelong energy man, Mark Segel had founded AirSoil thanks to a couple of patents by his engineers for soilless farming equipment, and he had been riding that through early seed funding. Freddie knew George was keen on their sustainable farming initiatives—it's why he had invested in Wentworth Hydroponics, too—and that was enough to drive Freddie forward to the table.

Mark stood as he approached, his salt-and-pepper hair perfectly combed away from his face, and his suit impeccably cut to accommodate his slight belly.

"Nice to see you, Wentworth," he said, extending his hand.

Freddie shook it. "Hope I didn't keep you waiting too long."

"I'm impressed you got here when you did. I was stuck in traffic for forty minutes," Mark said with a superficial laugh.

There were the usual pleasantries that Freddie had learned were a prerequisite for these types of meetings, inquiries that were friendly but ultimately superfluous. Then the waiter appeared with a couple of sparkling waters and took their food order. As soon as he was gone, Freddie opened his mouth to speak, but Mark cut him off.

"So, Wentworth, what do you think about AirSoil?"

Shit. He should have done his homework.

"Well, any company that's investing in sustainable farming systems is automatically interesting to me," Freddie replied tactfully.

Mark scoffed. "I can't imagine anyone not investing in it. It's one of the fastest growing sectors of green technologies right now."

And it's life-changing technology that has the potential to help solve climate change as well as the devastating impact of famine around the world, Freddie wanted to say. But he only smiled.

Lunch progressed slowly. Mark pontificated on his own achievements and AirSoil's impressive board of directors after they ordered. Freddie worked to stay interested once their lunches were served. The company sounded interesting, though after almost an hour, Freddie realized that Mark hadn't actually asked him another question over the course of their meal.

As their plates were being cleared, Mark leaned back in his chair and let out a sigh. "So, what do you think?"

Freddie blinked, quickly reviewing the last few minutes to see if he'd missed a key piece of information. "About what?"

"Coming on board." As if he could see Freddie's reticence, he leaned forward, waving it off before he could say a word. "I know George said you weren't looking for a full-time role right now, but the sustainable farming sector misses you. I think we could make a real impact together. I'm sure you miss it, too, right?"

Freddie was ready to say no. Thank him for lunch and call it a day. But Mark was right—he did miss it. And suddenly he had an image of his mom in her kitchen, so excited about the potential of her son having a real job that the thought of turning it down almost felt cruel.

"Let me think about it," he said, forcing a smile.

"Great. We'll set up a meeting to go over specifics," Mark said, handing the waiter his credit card before he had time to put the check on the table. "George should come, too, since he might have some leads we can exploit. There's a lot of opportunity here."

Freddie nodded, painfully aware of just how superficial the motion was. "Sounds good."

"And lucrative," Mark added, and laughed again.

As soon as the waiter returned with Mark's card, Freddie was on his feet, making his excuses and promising more discussions to come, before thanking him for lunch.

He didn't let the facade drop until they had said their goodbyes on the sidewalk and Freddie was in his Uber, heading downtown again.

He let out a long breath, one that he felt he had been holding in for an hour. A moment later, his phone began to ring in his jacket pocket. George's name was waiting on the screen when he pulled it out.

"That was a job interview," Freddie answered.

George laughed. "Yeah, Mark called me on his way back to the office. Said you were as good as hired."

Freddie sighed. "Great."

"You sound thrilled."

"Sorry." He glanced out the window, at the shop windows lining Fifth Avenue. It was only mid-November, but the Christmas decorations were already on display, an explosion of reds and greens and golds that bled into one another as his car headed downtown. "I guess I forgot how superficial these corporate meetings can be, especially when the bigwigs want to court you. I have to get used to it again."

"Only if you want to." George said it like it was nothing but an observation, but after working with Will for the past few years, Freddie could read the subtext.

"It's what's expected, though, right?" Freddie replied. "My mom is already picking me out a collection of silk ties."

George laughed. "Hey. I wear ties every day. They're not so bad."

"Right."

"Oh, I meant to ask you, how are things with Anne?"

Freddie's head fell back against the seat. For a moment, he considered telling George about the day before—the play, the debacle in the subway, the car ride home, the roof . . .

No, he wasn't doing this again. He had been working to keep Anne from his thoughts all morning, tamping down the feelings that had stirred last night. It had taken so long to lock them away; he couldn't risk them getting loose again.

"Why?" he asked.

"At the housewarming party, you two were staring daggers at each other. Just wondering if you kissed and made up."

A muscle in Freddie's jaw ticked. "We're not getting back together, George."

"I'm not talking about getting back together," he said. "Just getting to a place where you can stand being in the same room together. Who knows, maybe you could be friends."

"You sound like my mom," Freddie murmured.

"Well, she's a very smart woman."

Freddie let his gaze go to the window again as the suggestion turned over in his head. The last time he'd been asked to think of Anne Elliot that way was eight years ago, when she asked to be friends right after she broke his heart. He had blocked her number then, tried to block the idea entirely, but now the idea didn't seem so offensive. He had spent so much time and energy over the last few weeks trying to keep her at arm's length, he hadn't even considered anything else.

"Friends, huh," he mused. "That's interesting."

George chuckled. "No, Freddie, that's called growth."

CHAPTER 15

"So," James said from where he sat on his marble countertop, staring at his phone. "How's Freddie?"

Anne almost dropped the bag of flour she was pulling down from the shelf as her heart plummeted to the kitchen floor. James had called her a few hours before, asking if she had any cake pans, and now she was upstairs in his kitchen mixing the dry ingredients for a chocolate cake, while James pored over his monthly horoscope.

"What?" she asked, feigning ignorance as she did a survey of the array of measuring cups and ingredients laid out in front of her, the bright orange stand mixer and attachments at the ready.

"Freddie Wentworth," he repeated, looking up from the astrology app. "Has he come by the apartment looking for Cricket since she's moved on with Glen Rinnard?"

"No, I haven't seen him," she said, ignoring the annoying disappointment that accompanied the statement.

"Poor guy probably has whiplash," James said with a snort. "She was making the full court press the night of her play, then bam! She gets arrested and starts shacking up with her lawyer."

Anne threw him a disapproving glare over her shoulder. "She's not 'shacking up' with Glen."

"Oh really?" James cocked an eyebrow at her. "And when exactly was the last time she was home?"

Anne opened her mouth to answer, then considered. She wanted to defend Cricket's honor, but at the same time realized she hadn't actually seen her roommate all week.

James watched her expression change and let out a self-satisfied sigh. "Like I said, shacking up."

"Well, I'm happy for her," Anne said, thankful that the cake recipe propped up on her phone gave her something to concentrate on right now.

"So am I!" James countered. "But it's weird, right? The guy hasn't stopped talking about his ex-wife all year, and now Cricket's practically moved in."

Anne turned to him, offering him a slight smile. "Which one of them are you slut-shaming again?"

James did his best impersonation of someone truly offended. "In this house, we don't slut-shame, Anne. We slut-celebrate."

Anne laughed and turned back to the recipe. "Okay, I need you to focus, James. This is a surprise birthday cake for your husband, not mine."

"Right. Yes. Okay." James set his phone down on the counter and focused his attention on where Anne had meticulously lined up the ingredients on the counter. "What do we need to do next?"

"Once the oven is preheated, we need to mix the dry ingredients together, then the wet—"

James snickered.

Anne threw him a look, then continued. "And then we bake for thirty minutes."

"Perfect. Ellis is at work and I told him I was finishing up the Christmas decorations, so he'll probably avoid home for ages," James said with an eye roll. "He hates decorating."

From the looks of their apartment, Anne would not have guessed. It might have been the day before Thanksgiving, but James and Ellis's apartment was already decorated top to bottom for the holidays. Their wreath went up on the door on November first and, inside, their tree was set up in the living room just a few days later. The balsam was twelve feet tall and apparently from New Hampshire, with branches completely concealed below a layer of carefully curated ribbon and ornaments that coordinated with the room's décor.

James caught her expression. "What?"

"Nothing," she said, eyeing the plastic mistletoe hanging above the door. "I just usually wait until after Thanksgiving to tackle Christmas."

"I love Christmas. So sue me."

"Aren't you Jewish?" Anne asked.

Now James did, in fact, look offended. "This is a Chrismukkah household, Anne. There's a menorah on the mantel."

She smiled. "Well, it's great to see interfaith representation in the building. Even if it's a month early."

"It brings me joy," he said, lifting his chin defiantly. "And you should never delay what brings you joy."

Her head cocked to the side as she considered. "That's a good line."

"Thanks. It's my therapist's," he said with a wink. "But enough about her. We have a surprise birthday party in two days and all I have to show for it is a deconstructed cake."

"Which will be constructed soon," she reminded him.

"Right. Good." James let out a long breath. "So, Friday afternoon while he's at the gym, I'll go up to the roof deck and set up the table. The heaters are still working up there, right?"

She nodded. "They replaced the fuel a few weeks ago."

"I don't know what to order for food, so I thought I'd just get everything on the menu at Dim Sum Palace and pick it up an hour or so before the party. Can you lay it out upstairs?"

Another nod. "I'll use the freight elevator so I won't risk running into Ellis."

"And I texted Cricket to remind her to be up there at seven," James mused. "God, do you think she'll bring Glen?"

Anne cringed. "She might."

"Fine," James said with a sigh. "At least people will be there. I have residual trauma from the last time Ellis's birthday fell on the day after Thanksgiving and no one showed up to his party. We were eating canapés for a week."

"James. Focus."

"Right." He clapped his hands, causing his collection of rings to clink together. "Are you sure it's okay that we're baking the cake two days early?"

"Totally fine," she assured him. "Just keep it in the freezer until you want to ice it."

He nodded. "And how do I make that?"

"It's simple. Do you have any powdered sugar?"

He looked up, eyebrows knitted together. "You can powder sugar?"

She opened her mouth, ready to ask him if he had ever baked a cake before suggesting they do this one, when the faint ding of the elevator in the hallway sounded.

They both stilled, listening carefully to the barely perceptible sound of footsteps approaching, keys jangling. Then the distinct slide of the apartment's dead bolt.

"It's Ellis!" James yelped, shoveling up all the ingredients from the counter. "Hurry! Grab the evidence!"

"I'm hurrying!" Anne pushed the mixer back into place, then grabbed the lone box of baking soda James had left behind and shoved it in a nearby drawer.

"He wasn't supposed to be home until five!" James hissed as he threw everything in his arms into the cabinet above the sink. "What are we going to do? All we've done is line up the ingredients! I don't even have batter!"

"We can bake it down at Cricket's. Just come by later," Anne whispered.

"Yes! Right! Good plan."

Anne did a final survey of the kitchen just as Ellis called out. "Honey, you home?"

James looked around wildly, finally pulling a French cookbook from the shelf and pretending to read. But as soon as he cracked it open, he looked up, his face ashen.

"Oh God. What about the powdered sugar?" he whispered.

"I'll run out and pick some up," she replied. "It's fine—"

The kitchen door swung open and Ellis entered. He stopped in the doorway when he saw Anne and James huddled close over the cookbook, covered in flour and looking frazzled.

"Everything okay?" he asked. It looked like he was battling a smile.

"Hi, babe. You're home early," James said, his voice casual as he flipped to the next page, like this scene happened every day.

"The Jeselsohns canceled their showing, so I thought I would come home and help in case you were having another one of your tinsel emergencies," Ellis said warmly, then he turned to see Anne. "Hey, Anne. Are you staying for dinner?"

While James continued to feign interest in the text in front of him, Anne grabbed her bag from the counter and headed for the door as she stumbled over her words. "Nope, I have to go. Lots to do . . . around. You know how it is. Bye!"

"That's upside down, you know," Anne heard Ellis challenge James, before she shut the front door and hurried to the elevators.

～

Even though she knew exactly what she needed to get, Anne felt oddly unprepared when she walked into Helwig Deli a few minutes later. The bodega was her usual go-to for quick grocery items, along with a surprisingly wide variety of Korean snack foods, but usually she arrived with a detailed shopping list, or at least a Post-it. Walking the narrow aisles empty-handed felt unnatural, even though she found herself discovering things she had never noticed before. Had there always been a collection of toiletries on the wall?

Fifteen minutes later she had a bag of powdered sugar in hand at the register. She swiped her card, bracing herself until the small screen announced it was approved, when her phone started ringing in her bag. She pulled it out and saw her mother's picture illuminating the screen.

"Hi, Mom," she answered, holding the phone to her ear with one hand, as she grabbed her canvas shopping bag with the other and walked outside.

"Hello, darling!" Bianca replied, then paused. "Where are you? It sounds like a war zone."

Anne smiled, stealing a quick glance across the street at the workers struggling to control the tall pine tree now standing in the middle of Tompkins Square Park. Their truck was beeping, a steady anxious tone as the men yelled obscenities at one another, each with their own view of how to get the tree level. It was the same struggle every year, the East Village's own unique start of the Christmas season.

"They're putting up the tree in the park."

"Ah." Her mother knew the scene well. "Well, very apropos, because I wanted to touch base with you about Christmas."

Of course. How could Anne forget about Bianca's annual trip to Manhattan? Regardless of where she was traveling, her mother spent the month of December at the Carlyle Hotel on the Upper East Side. She usually had a packed social calendar upon arrival, slotted appointments with old friends and even older colleagues that were precisely scheduled, and then systematically checked off. It was a system Anne had observed every year since her parents divorced. From the age of ten, she had spent the holiday season sipping Shirley Temples at endless fundraisers and luncheons, trying desperately to blend into her mother's shadow. Thankfully, Anne was able to opt out of most of it now. Instead, she and Bianca usually planned a few excursions of their own, a dinner or two here or there. Just as long as it was in the schedule well in advance.

Her mother listed a number of dates, different events she had already planned. Then came one that required Anne's attention. "Oh, I have an event at Lincoln Center that Wednesday night, too. Black tie, very elegant. You should come."

Anne laughed softly, her eyes following the pine tree now listing dangerously far to the left. "No thank you."

"Fine," her mother sighed. "Then let's at least schedule our standing lunch at Le Bernardin for that Saturday. And Christmas we can do at the hotel like we usually do. Oh, and what about that Tuesday night? I have an invite for drinks at the Beekman."

Anne was about to offer her standard decline but paused, suddenly remembering the text she had gotten from Sophie the day before. She wanted to schedule the flower shop's launch party for that same night. For the first time in years, Anne had a conflict. "I can't. I actually have plans."

Silence. Her mother was as stunned as Anne. "A date? With who?"

"It's not a date. I just . . . I'm working with a friend to help her open her business."

"What kind of business?"

"A floral shop." Anne was aware of just how clipped her words sounded, how carefully she was parsing out the information to give.

"Well, *that* sounds interesting. Don't fifty percent of floral shops close after a year? Though if she can get a foot in the wedding market, she'll be *set*."

"Right." Anne nodded. Then another thought popped into her mind. "Would you want to come?"

"To pitch weddings?"

"No, to the party."

"I can try. Send me the details." A moment passed before she continued. "Who is this friend again?"

"Sophie," Anne replied, and clamped her mouth shut. There was no reason to keep Sophie's last name a secret—Bianca hadn't met her. She probably didn't even know Freddie had a sister. Still, Anne was hesitant to share more.

"Sophie," her mother repeated slowly. "Well, I hope this Sophie knows how lucky she is to have you. Now, what about Thanksgiving? Your father isn't expecting you to go all the way to Brooklyn, is he?"

Anne took a deep breath, letting the cold air fill her lungs. To be honest, she had no idea what she was doing for Thanksgiving. The last text her father had sent her was about getting the contact information for all the network execs in charge of *Divorce Divas*.

She had tried to dissuade him, but in the end he had gotten frustrated with her and stopped replying.

She understood why her mother assumed she would spend Thanksgiving with her father—that was the holiday he had locked in for years, thanks to their custody agreement. But as an adult, it suddenly occurred to her that the continuation of the invite had more to do with her proximity—and access to the caterers' numbers—than affection.

"I'm not sure yet," she replied, hoping her voice sounded breezy, as if she hadn't considered it yet. In essence, as if she were an entirely different person.

Her mother hummed to herself. She likely suspected that Walt was being difficult, but she chose not to prod. "Well, how's the tree looking now?"

Anne glanced across the street and cocked her head to the side, considering its current angle. "Conflicted."

Bianca hummed. "I still don't understand why they put it up so early. It's not even December yet."

More yelling, then the tree lurched sideways, standing straight at a right angle, beautiful and perfect.

"Maybe they're trying to spread some joy," Anne said, remembering James's words.

"That sounds like something my therapist would say," Bianca murmured. "All right, I have to go. See you soon!"

She hung up before Anne could say goodbye—not that she would have anyway. She was too entranced by the tree, how even unlit, it triggered a warm glow in the center of her chest.

Maybe James was right. Why delay joy?

CHAPTER 16

Twenty minutes later, as Anne shuffled around the corner of Tompkins Square Park with a five-foot-tall balsam fir on her back and a tree stand tucked awkwardly under her arm, there was only one thought going through her mind: *Joy is overrated*.

After hanging up with her mother, she had turned to walk back home, with James's words in her ears. She had never considered joy as an active word, just a random feeling that found you at fleeting moments. Maybe that was why she only encountered it sporadically. But if joy was a conscious choice, something she could reach out and grab, then why not start now?

That's when she reached the corner and saw the motley collection of trees lined up in a Christmas tree stall.

She walked by slowly, breathing in the crisp pine scent. Then her gaze fell on the *DAMAGED—50% OFF* sign. It hung over the last section of the makeshift sidewalk stall, and while the rest were full of healthy, dense Scotch pines and Douglas firs, this one only had one lone tree left. Anne wasn't sure you could even call it a tree, really, just a thick trunk with a few branches sticking out in odd directions. Still, it was tall and straight, as if begging to be noticed. Someone just needed to give it a chance.

It had seemed like a good idea at the time. The vendor had even thrown in the tree stand for free.

But now, two blocks from home and her grip slipping, it was clearly the stupidest idea she had ever had.

Where would she put it? The apartment was already crammed full of Cricket's stuff—it barely had room for the few things she had moved in, let alone a Christmas tree. And what about decorations? And cleanup? Even its minimal needles would be murder on her bare feet when they fell off in January.

This is why I always need to stick to the plan, she chastised herself. *The first time I try something impulsive and look where it gets me: sweating on a sidewalk, holding a tree.* She should have paused and thought this through. How embarrassing to be stuck like this without—

"Do you need help with that?"

The deep voice was so close and so familiar that her heart seized, and she straightened before she could think better of it. It was a quick motion that sent the stand and the tree falling to the ground, leaving a halo of needles around her on the sidewalk.

Freddie was standing in front of her, staring down at the tree with morbid curiosity.

"No, I'm fine," she managed to say. "I was just . . ."

Her words fizzled out as her eyes found Freddie again.

"You were . . ." he repeated.

Anne blinked. "Carrying a tree."

He looked down at the collection of needles at their feet. "Does it have a Do Not Resuscitate order?"

She laughed, but she was so short of breath that it came out sounding like a long wheeze. "That's . . . very funny."

He smiled, too. "You sure you don't need help?"

"No, it's okay," she said, waving him off. "I just . . . need to get it to the building. And into the elevator. And up to the apartment. It's fine."

She was almost impressed with how convincing she sounded, until Freddie threw her that look she had been so familiar with eight years ago, the one that told her she wasn't fooling anyone, then stepped past her to take hold of the tree and hoist it over his shoulder in one easy motion.

It was only slightly hot.

"You all right?" he asked when he caught her expression.

She gaped up at him, then finally managed to say, "Yes. No. I mean. It's a Christmas tree."

"Yeah. I picked up on that," he said, then motioned for her to walk with him toward their building.

She quickly picked up the tree stand and fell in line with his steps as they walked down the sidewalk to the Uppercross.

"Thank you," she said as they entered the lobby. "You didn't have to do that."

"I don't mind," he said. "I was heading home anyway."

She nodded as they made their way over to the elevator, even though part of her wanted to poke holes in his rationale. He didn't need to help. He could have walked by, and she wouldn't have even noticed as she struggled. Then again, she couldn't imagine Freddie ever walking by someone who needed help and not offering it. Even if that someone was an ex-girlfriend, or if he was wearing an obviously expensive coat that was now covered in sap, or—

"Oh my God," Anne blurted out when she saw the streak of sticky liquid across his shoulder. "Freddie, your coat . . ."

The elevator doors opened as he looked down at the dark gray wool. Then he shrugged. "That's all right. I never liked this coat anyway."

He pressed four and the doors closed. They rode up in silence until the doors opened again on the fourth floor.

"Thanks," Anne said, turning to him and moving to take the tree from his hands. "I can take it from here."

"No way," he said, stepping past her into the hallway. "Me and this tree have come too far. I need to see this through to the end."

"It's a Christmas tree, Freddie."

"It's my Everest."

She smiled, even as her heart stumbled. She reached into her bag, trying to find her keys and ignore a litany of questions that popped up in her brain.

But why are you doing this? What does this mean? What are we even doing here?

By the time she finally found the keys and unlocked the door, it was too much. She paused before turning the knob and looked back at him.

"Thank you for helping me," she said again.

"You're welcome." He grinned that familiar grin, the one that seemed to erase the expensive clothes and new haircut. The one that made him look like the old Freddie again. "Now, can you open the door? I can't feel my shoulder anymore."

"Right." She smiled and opened the door, staying close to the wall to make room for him to walk by.

The tree was deceptively tall, and on Freddie's shoulder it was almost a battering ram in Cricket's apartment, knocking over a coat rack, a collection of hats, and three plastic wineglasses before Anne found the right place for it in the corner. She set the stand down and helped him guide the trunk into it, finally getting it on the fifth try.

"Perfect," Freddie said.

She stood up and stepped back. It was bent at an odd angle, and she could now see that it had a grand total of six branches, but she had to agree. It was perfect.

She had never bought her own Christmas tree before. To be fair, she never really had to. Walt Elliot had a twelve-foot-tall fake tree he paid someone to haul out of storage each year. While Bianca had been in charge of decorating it when she was still with Walt, the responsibility fell to Anne after the divorce. Not that anyone ever asked her, of course.

But not this year, she thought and smiled. It may have been a broken little tree, but it was hers.

"Do you have to water it?" Freddie asked, moving to stand beside her.

She looked up at him incredulously. "Freddie, your entire company was based around hydroponic farming."

He looked almost offended. "Hey. Give me a break. The only Christmas tree I've ever had was that ten-foot silver monstrosity my mom puts up every year."

Anne's smile returned along with the memory. She had only spent one Christmas at the Wentworth home, but she remembered that tree in the window when they arrived, each needle made of silver tinsel, so its lights were almost blinding from the street.

"She doesn't still have it, does she?" Anne asked.

He nodded. "Oh yeah. I had to haul it up from the basement just a couple of weeks ago."

Anne laughed again. As the sound faded, a heavy silence fell, one that seemed to highlight the facts: The tree was here, it was up, and there was nothing left for Freddie to do.

But she didn't want him to go. It felt like she was finally getting the old Freddie back and she was afraid that something as simple as him leaving would erase all the progress they had made. She had no idea how to avoid it, though. So she just stared at the bare branches of her tree, hoping to prolong the moment before the inevitable.

"I think it needs something," he finally said.

Right. Of course. She had to decorate it. She didn't know how to explain to Freddie that she barely had the money to afford the tree, let alone ornaments. Then a thought popped into her mind.

"I have lights!" she exclaimed. "Wait here."

She started toward the hallway closet before he could protest.

Chloe's fairy lights were right where Anne had put them a few weeks ago, coiled up on the shelf.

She returned, holding them above her head like a prize catch, then plugged the cord into the socket by the tree. The floor lit up with a thousand points of light around their feet. She picked up one end and he grabbed the other, and together they found a rhythm passing the lights back and forth between them.

"This is going to look better than I thought," Anne said halfway through the process.

"Well, you cheated," Freddie said before handing the lights back to her to go around again.

"Excuse me?"

"You plugged the lights in before they were up. You're supposed to plug them in after you've covered the entire tree, then stand back, and say, 'Okay, ready!' Then someone plugs them in, so you get that real ta-da moment."

Anne rolled her eyes. "That's not something people do."

"It absolutely is." That grin pulled at his lips again.

She shook her head. "No one would waste that amount of time decorating a tree without checking to see if the lights worked first."

"It's part of the drama," he said. "The 'will they/won't they' effect."

She laughed. It felt like a release, like she had been holding it in for eight years, just waiting for this moment, so she didn't try to temper the sound. She let it bubble out of her until there were tears in the corners of her eyes. Freddie watched her, smiling, too.

A few minutes later, they were done. The room was darker now that the sun had set, and the warm glow of the tree made the room feel smaller, like a cocoon around them.

"We did it," she said, almost embarrassed by the sense of pride swelling in her chest.

"We did," he said with a nod.

A moment passed before she turned to him. "Can I ask you a question?"

He was still staring at the tree as he answered. "Sure."

"Why did you help me?"

His brow furrowed. "What do you mean?"

"I mean, why did you offer to bring this up here? Why did you stay to help with the lights?"

He stared at her for a minute, as if he was just considering the fact as well.

"I guess I don't know how to be strangers with you, either," he said. "So maybe we could try friends."

Friends. She had made the same offer to him eight years ago: It was all she'd asked of him after their breakup. His only answer then had been to block her number. Now, here they were again. She had felt so angry, so hurt back then, and she expected those same feelings to rise up now. But they didn't. Instead an old kernel of hope returned to her chest.

"I could be friends with you," she replied.

He stared down at her in the dim light, and smiled. In that moment, it almost felt like those eight years hadn't passed at all. That maybe...

WHAM.

"Finally!" James cried out, throwing the front door of Cricket's apartment wide open while balancing a big heavy box and pivoting into the kitchen, "I never thought Ellis would leave. Honestly, how many ways can you say 'get out' without just saying 'get the fuck out so I can make a birthday cake for you!'? I tried 'you should go to the gym, bring your new weighted vest,' and 'there's a secret sale at ABC Carpet, hurry!' I even made up a building HVAC emergency. The man is oblivious! I finally had to call Cricket to have her pretend she lost the keys to their office. Oh, did you get the powdered sugar?" He dropped the box on the kitchen counter and had already removed the flour and baking soda when he looked up. "Oh, Freddie! I didn't even see you there. Oh, and look! Cricket got a tree!"

"Actually, I got the tree," Anne said, pushing a few loose strands of hair away from her forehead. God, she didn't even want to imagine what her ponytail looked like right now. "Freddie was..."

"The muscle," Freddie added.

Anne swallowed down another laugh.

"Hmm, *so* helpful," James's eyes narrowed as his mouth quirked up playfully. "Who is Freddie Wentworth? Entrepreneur. Tree mover. I have so many more questions. For instance, do you know how to bake?"

Freddie chuckled. "Unfortunately, no."

James frowned. "That's too bad."

Anne turned back to Freddie. "It's Ellis's birthday on Friday, so we're baking him a cake."

"Throwing him a party, too," James replied as he unloaded the hand mixer and measuring cups on the kitchen counter. Then he paused, eyes wide like he had an idea. "Oh! You should come! Friday night, are you free? It's just upstairs on the roof deck."

Oh God. This was quickly going off the rails.

"I'm sure Freddie has plans," she said, waving off the invite.

"I'll think about it," Freddie answered as if she hadn't said anything at all.

"Fantastic!" James clapped his hands together. "Now, where's the powdered sugar?"

Anne turned to Freddie, ready to apologize, but he spoke first.

"I should get going. I didn't realize how late it was," Freddie said.

"Oh, okay," she replied, trying to appear nonchalant. "Well, thank you again. For helping me with the tree."

"No problem," he replied, then he turned toward the door.

"I won't tell Cricket you were here!" James called after him, but he was already gone.

Anne exhaled.

"That man has an air of mystery around him and it's so hot. Don't you think?" James asked as he opened the flour, sending powder all over the counter.

She shook her head, trying to curb her smile. "Let's start this cake already."

CHAPTER 17

Anne had just about come to terms with celebrating Thanksgiving alone in her pajamas with an order of Chinese food and a Christmas movie marathon on her laptop, when she received a text from her father.

DAD

> What are you doing for Thanksgiving? I have a res at Balthazar. 6:00pm.

The shock was only mildly embarrassing. It wasn't that she thought her father didn't care—though that was always a nagging question—only that Walt Elliot was the center of his own universe. While both Anne and her mother had come to terms with it in their own ways—Bianca had divorced him, and Anne tried to keep tight control of everything else in her life—it was only Anne who still harbored hope that he would eventually share a scrap of affection with her.

If that meant spending a holiday specifically designed to be celebrated at home at a swanky restaurant in Soho instead, so be it. It wasn't exactly a secret that her father adored Balthazar—at one point during Kellynch's heyday, he had the maître d's number and used the "bat phone" entrance, a privilege reserved only for the most exclusive clientele. The effortlessly chic brasserie, where New Yorkers and celebrities sat side by side on the long zinc wooden bar dining on rich French cuisine, was a place to be seen without being pretentious. It radiated a refined elegance—something Walt aspired to but could never quite grasp. Of course, if his continued attempts required Anne to enjoy a delicious gourmet meal every now and then—maybe even dessert—who was she to say no?

She had spent the last few weeks living off ramen noodles and the Korean snacks they sold at Helwig Deli, so while she got ready Thanksgiving morning, she daydreamed about warm French onion soup, crème brûlée, and one of those baguettes that was as long as her arm. It sounded glorious, even if it meant listening to her father's complaining—what was sure to be a never-ending litany about Brooklyn, his credit freeze, and his overall predicament, as if he had been merely an innocent bystander to it all. But she could power through.

Just think crème brûlée, she reminded herself.

She bundled up in her navy blue peacoat and knit hat, then headed downstairs at half past five to make sure she arrived on time. The air outside was brisk and an array of Christmas decorations dotted the different stoops as she walked across town. She moved briskly, like every New Yorker, but still let herself enjoy the walk through the Village, how the city shifted to avenues and cobblestoned streets lined with art galleries and boutiques. Soho welcomed her like every Manhattan neighborhood did, warmly and then with a blaring taxi horn. After she turned onto Spring Street, she made her way over to the prominent red awning of the restaurant.

She opened the black-rimmed glass doors to a wall of sound—conversations and laughter and clinking of silverware and glasses. She took off her hat and coat as she moved to the hostess stand.

While she waited for the couple in front of her to be seated, she felt a stab of guilt over not visiting her father in Brooklyn. For the past couple of months, she had been so concerned about cleaning up his messes that she had forgotten to worry about him. Yes, he was difficult and self-centered, but he was still her father, and she knew he defined himself by his social status. Now he was living in a different borough, MacKenzie was living in Ibiza, and his only source of income was in limbo. Suddenly, the prospect of dinner didn't seem so daunting.

The hostess reappeared and Anne stepped forward.

"Hi, I think my father has a reservation," she said. "Walter Elliot?"

The tall, willowy woman looked at the screen in front of her, then smiled. "Ah, yes. Follow me."

They made their way past the bar, then the cozy red leather booths, and into the heart of the restaurant. Then, suddenly, a high-pitched shriek sliced through the air.

Anne froze. She knew that shriek. It was the soundtrack to a hundred different nightmares over the past five years.

Denise Sinclair.

"Aaaaaaaaaaanne!" The star of *Divorce Divas* emerged from the far corner and started toward her, bumping into the chairs of numerous diners along the way. She was clad in a gold-encrusted designer wrap dress, the same color as her signature platinum-blond hair. The only thing different from the last time Anne had seen her was that her Pomeranian, Chanel, was decidedly absent from her tanned arms where he was usually perched.

"It's so good to see you!" she exclaimed as she locked Anne

in a tight embrace. As she pulled away, she smiled, her full set of veneers (purchased by production during season five) on display.

"I'll take it from here," she said to the hostess, shooing her away. Then she turned back to Anne. "I'm so glad you're joining us for Thanksgiving! We have so much to talk about!"

Anne blinked. *What is going on?*

"Denise." Anne finally exhaled, feigning as much enthusiasm as she could muster. "It's good to see you, too."

"Come on, come on, we're over here!" Denise sang. Her arm flailed out toward the long table in the far corner.

For a split second, Anne found herself looking around the restaurant for the production crew to appear, as if everyone was in the midst of shooting a *Divorce Divas* holiday special and she had just missed the memo.

When no one came, she turned back to Denise. It was impossible to tell this woman's age with all the work she had had done. Was she thirty or sixty? No one really knew. Her porcelain skin pulled tight over her high cheekbones, flawlessly layered makeup adorned her eyes and overly full lips, and her hair was inhumanly shiny. Her fitted designer dresses hugged her curves, and her gravity-defying cleavage was only pushed up further as she put one arm around Anne's shoulders and started walking with her to the table.

"Thank God you're here!" she lamented. "The manager said no cameras were allowed! Can you talk to her? We need content. Who knows what might happen tonight! We're missing television gold. I already said two quotable lines that if they were filming would go viral, I just know it."

Anne pretended to listen as she craned to see who else was waiting just ahead. "Is my dad here?"

"He's right there at the head of the table, sitting with me and my favorite sister, Angela—she cracks me up. I thought it would be fun to get the gang together again, like old times. Make sure there's no hard feelings. Your dad has always been there for me. At least I won't lose you!"

Anne frowned. "Excuse me?"

The woman's head fell back as she cackled. "You're so funny! My show, obviously!"

"The show is on hiatus, Denise," Anne said.

"Not *Divorce Divas*! *My* show! Or my *brand*, as Theo calls it. You know I don't keep up with all the different platforms and apps and whatever the hell they call it. That's why we have you. HA! Anyway, glad you're finally here. I'm just gonna use the loo, but go on! Everyone already had their appetizers. The oysters are to die for!" Denise squeezed Anne's arm before leaving her.

"Great." Anne sighed as the woman left her and bounded toward the ladies' room.

She felt that she had only just processed the appearance of Denise and now there was another show? Her stomach did an odd drop as her brain started to connect the dots. Was that Theo's project? The one she had spent so many hours working on?

"Anne!" The sound of her father's voice brought her attention back to the restaurant. She dodged a waiter and a dessert tray and finally arrived at the long table in the back corner. It was brimming with Denise's friends and family—she recognized them from unavoidable run-ins during production. It was a sea of sequins and animal print, and in the center of it all was Walt Elliot. He was indeed at the head in his best silk shirt, one elbow on the table as he laughed at whatever was being discussed, even as he caught her eye and impatiently waved her over.

Walt rolled his eyes when she finally arrived at the seat next to him. "Finally."

Anne sighed. "Happy Thanksgiving to you, too, Dad."

"Oh, take that look off your face. You know how much I hate it. It's a party. And the paparazzi might be here soon." Then he gave her his signature wince, the one that was supposed to work in lieu of an apology.

"There's paparazzi?" Anne asked, confused.

"Honestly, it's like you don't even care. Denise has a friend who will feed the pictures straight to TMZ. How the stars give thanks and celebrate the harvest, or something."

Anne looked around the busy restaurant again. "Dad, I don't think—"

"Can we get more oysters!" he called out across the room to no one in particular. "Make it two dozen."

A nearby waiter responded with a nod and hustled away.

"Dad," she said sternly, keeping her voice low so only he could hear. "What is going on?"

"What do you mean?" he said, as if he was still in awe. "Denise invited me as her personal guest to celebrate!"

Anne blinked. "Celebrate what? Did Marsha drop the assault charges?"

"Oh, who knows," Walt replied, rolling his eyes. "You're burying the lede! When I called the network to talk about the hiatus, they told me some fantastic news. *Divorce Divas* is headed to Turkey! Isn't that fantastic? The residuals are going to be astronomical." He took a deep sip of his drink. "And it all happened after MacKenzie signed the divorce papers, so she won't see a cent of this deal. I love it when things work out."

"Wait." Anne shook her head, trying to make the facts fit into place in a way that made sense. "What deal?"

"Aren't you listening? The licensing deal with Turkey! A top TV streamer over there wants *Divorce Divas*! Every damn season!

It puts me so far back in the black, it's obscene. Who says there's no money in television anymore? Ridiculous."

Anne's mouth fell open. "When were you going to tell me?"

"I just did! But you can't tell anyone else. It's all very hush-hush until the agreement is signed. Which reminds me, I have it on my phone so you can look it over and give me your notes."

What was happening?

Divorce Divas was still on hiatus, but meanwhile, its back seasons were headed to Turkey, while Denise was developing a television show with Theo that Anne may have unwittingly helped create. And it was coming to light at her family Thanksgiving with her dad, a plethora of oysters, and a table lined with zebra print and sequins.

"Dad, have you talked to Theo about any of this?" Anne hedged.

He scoffed. "Who?"

"The showrunner on *Divorce Divas*," she replied. "Because I think Denise has been talking to him about—"

"It's my company," Walt cut her off. "I know what I'm doing."

"Do you?" Anne whispered sharply. "You're celebrating a licensing deal while our staff and crew are at home, waiting for news of whether the show is going back into production or not. Even the star of the show is making other plans!"

Walt's eyes closed as if she were weighing on his last nerve. "Anne, don't make me regret inviting you. Honestly."

Anne's jaw tightened and she clenched her fists. She wanted to point out that he only asked her to come because Denise told him to. He never asked Anne anything, in fact. Instead he just assumed, took, overstepped, which is exactly how she ended up wasting the past five years of her life keeping his production company from falling apart, only to have him find a way to implode it anyway.

But before she could open her mouth, Denise appeared in front of them.

"Oh, look at us all!" She beamed as the entrees were placed on the table in a mad dash by the waiters. She took her seat across from Anne and raised her champagne flute, addressing the entire table, "To us, to family, to my brand!"

Anne glanced back and forth between her father and the reality show star. This wasn't a holiday—it was a business meeting. All her life, she had just wanted a holiday that wasn't consumed by ulterior motives, by fights and digs and money. She wanted her father to want to be in her presence, not require it for his own advancement. And she was so tired of fighting against that, of hoping anything would change, that suddenly the anger in her chest twisted and molded into something else entirely: indifference. They wouldn't change, and she refused to waste any more time expecting them to.

"Dad," she said, pulling his attention back to her. "I'm going to go home."

His smile faltered. "What?"

"I'm going home."

"Don't be silly. You just got here," he said dismissively. "There's five courses coming, and I need you to look over this agreement while you wait. There's something about backend residuals, and you know I don't know—"

"I'm leaving," she interrupted, then turned to Denise. "It was lovely to see you, Denise."

"Oh, Anne, I'll call you!" she replied, smiling like she was completely missing the tension in the air. She probably was.

"Right," Anne replied, pushing out her chair and standing. "And, Dad, I quit."

Her father's face went slack with shock.

Anne continued forward, skirting around a frenzied waiter, past the cozy leather booths filled with well-fed happy patrons, and headed out the front door to the fresh air to take the first deep breath she'd had in years.

CHAPTER 18

Freddie opened his refrigerator for the fifth time in ten minutes and, sure enough, it offered up the same view. Neat piles of Tupperware, each labeled with his mom's clear handwriting. Pumpkin risotto. Sliced turkey. Sausage stuffing. Scalloped potatoes.

The day before had been the familiar mayhem of every other Wentworth Thanksgiving. His parents' house in Queens was already bursting with activity when he had arrived that morning—his mom in the kitchen fretting about the ziti, while his dad fried the turkey out back. Sophie stuffing mushrooms and detailing her plans for the new floral shop with their Aunt Susan, who was reading a *People* magazine aloud. He had barely said his hellos before he was pulled to put the leaves in the dining table, only to lose the job when his Uncle Gus said he wasn't securing the latches underneath properly and pushed him out of the way to do it himself. The scene only became more chaotic when everyone began to arrive for the meal itself. Soon the Wentworths' narrow dining room was teeming with two dozen friends and relatives, all talking over one another, passing food in all directions, and raising their glasses at every invitation.

Per usual, the evening wrapped up much later than anyone intended, and Freddie spent the night in his childhood bedroom, trying to ignore the litany of concert posters that had been up since he left eight years ago. In fact, his parents hadn't changed anything except the sheets. His bookshelves by the door were still full of comics and textbooks. His desk still had his old computer and mouse. It was an odd time capsule that he usually found funny, but this time he noticed the bulletin board above his desk, filled to the brim with photos of Anne. His heart lurched.

As soon as the sun was up the next morning, he was out the door, making excuses to leave. He had a meeting scheduled with George and Mark Segel on Monday and he hadn't even looked at his proposed contract yet. To his mom's credit, she hadn't pried, only sent him out to his Uber with two huge bags of leftovers and strict instructions for reheating.

He opened the fridge for the sixth time, grabbed a beer from the door, then trudged over to the living room. The deep cushions of his sofa swallowed him up, and for a moment he considered grabbing his laptop and opening Mark's email.

It was only a moment.

Instead, he turned on the television, flipping through one streaming service and then another, trying to find something to drown out the nebulous anxiety. After a few minutes he landed on *SportsCenter* and leaned back, forcing himself to listen to the commentators and turn off his brain.

BANG.

The sound rang through the apartment so loudly it made Freddie jump.

He stilled, listening to see if he could tell where it came from.

BANG.

The same sound again, but this time it was followed by muffled laughter, a few unintelligible shouts. Then there was the low rumble of furniture being dragged across the floor.

He looked up. It was coming from above him, on the roof deck.

Freddie frowned and turned the television up. They were recapping a football game from earlier in the day, which he hadn't watched. To be honest, he didn't even care about the result, but hopefully the play-by-play would drown out the sounds of conversation and laughter now humming from above.

It didn't.

He groaned as he leaned forward, letting his head fall to his chest. He refused to be that guy who complained about other people having fun that was too loud, too unrestrained. Hell, he was usually the guy who was at the source of it. How many times over the last decade had he gotten calls from random front desks around the world, asking to please keep it down? Even before he left the city, he had reveled in being the life of the party. He wouldn't be the one to tell someone else to temper it.

Two minutes later, he turned up the volume on *SportsCenter* again.

Five minutes later, he was walking out his front door and up the stairs to the roof deck.

He pushed open the metal door, ready to put on his most charming, yet assertive voice, but paused. The table in the center was surrounded by people, each bundled up in sweaters and coats as they talked and laughed and drank from the numerous bottles plopped in between what looked like Chinese food containers. It was hard to see exactly who made up the party—not only because of the dimness, but because half the people had their backs to him—but then a familiar face leapt up from the head of the table.

"Freddie!" James called out, clapping. "You made it!"

Everyone at the table turned at once, including the person sitting next to James in the purple sweater and winter hat with a large orange pom on top. Freddie knew it was Anne before they even made eye contact, and he froze in place.

Shit. He had been so wrapped up in distracting himself, he'd totally forgotten about Ellis's party.

"You heard the chair, didn't you?" Anne asked. Then she turned to the table, her tone apologetic as she affected a loud whisper. Freddie remembered when she used to do that years ago, after she dared to have more than a few sips of a drink and entered the unfamiliar territory of being tipsy. "If there's more than two people up here, you can hear everything downstairs in that apartment. The ceiling is so thin and—"

"It's fine," Freddie said, waving off her worried concern. And, he was surprised to realize, it was fine. His annoyance had evaporated as soon as he'd seen her. "I just heard a bang and—"

"It was James," Bev announced. She was sitting across from Anne, slouched down and waving indiscriminately toward the end of the table. "He's an idiot."

"Thanks, Bev," James said, rolling his eyes. "See who defends you the next time one of your decorations falls out the window."

Anne smiled as she turned back to Freddie. "Sorry. One of the chair legs is broken and keeps tipping over."

At the other end of the table, Cricket cackled. "You mean the person *in* it kept tipping over."

"It was James," Bev repeated.

Ellis tried to cover his laugh with a cough, while James narrowed his eyes at the whole table.

"I hate all of you," he said, pointing around the roof. Then he got to Anne and his look of indignation melted away. "Except for you. You're perfect."

Anne laughed, then yelped as her chair almost fell over, too.

"Come on, Freddie. Join us," Ellis said, pouring more wine into everyone's glasses. The table concurred, laughing and lifting their own glasses, spilling their drinks over the remnants of the Chinese food spread out ahead of them.

Glen stood from where he sat beside a still-laughing Cricket, looking around the roof. "Here, let's find a chair for you."

"Oh, I don't want to put you out . . ." Freddie started, but it was no use. The roof was a flurry of activity—James leaping up and sending his chair slamming to the ground again, as Glen directed Ellis to a chair off in the corner and Cricket yelled down the table to Bev to make room. More shuffling, yelling, and the spare chair was at the table, slotted in next to Bev and across from Anne.

Freddie stole a glance at Anne then. The wine had made her cheeks flushed, and the lights above set off a glint in her eye. Or maybe that had been there before—he wasn't sure.

"Anne Elliot, are you drinking?"

She turned to him, wineglass hovering near her lips. "No."

He narrowed his eyes on her and bit back a smile, waiting.

"I've had *one* drink," she said, rolling her eyes. "But we're celebrating Ellis's birthday."

"Hey. You don't need an excuse," he said, holding up his hands in mock surrender.

Beside him, Bev's gaze bounced between them until she finally leaned forward.

"You went to college together, didn't you?" she asked.

They both paused before Freddie finally nodded.

Bev turned to Anne. "Did you two date?"

Anne had been in the middle of a sip of wine and began to cough. Ellis reached over and smacked her back until she released a nervous laugh.

Jesus. Freddie's mouth fell open even as he tried to work out what to say. Thankfully, James jumped in.

"What even constitutes dating in college?" he asked, waving his wineglass around and leaving splatters of pinot noir all over the table.

Cricket scoffed drunkenly. "What constitutes dating now?"

Glen looked momentarily confused, but didn't have time to ask any questions before Anne leaned forward, adding another splash of wine to her glass.

"Dating is whatever you want it to be. It's no one's business but your own," she said diplomatically.

Bev cocked an eyebrow at her. "Okay. Are you dating anyone?"

Everyone's attention was suddenly on Anne, their attention rapt.

"I'm not, no," she replied, then took another deep sip of her drink. "What about you?"

Bev sighed. "Not since Iggy."

The chaos of the party overwhelmed them again. James asked Anne for the forks, while Glen passed Ellis another glass of red wine and Cricket directed Beverly to give her the box of the leftover crab Rangoon. The older woman ignored her, though, choosing instead to turn her attention to Freddie.

"You're handsome," Beverly said, her voice raspy.

He chuckled. "Thank you."

"What do you do for a living?" she asked, throwing an arm over the back of her chair so she could face him fully.

"I used to run my own company, but I sold it last year. I haven't quite figured out what comes next."

She stared at him for a long moment, studying his expression. "You should model. You have the bone structure for it. Just like my friend Kenneth. He used to model for Andy Warhol."

"Really?" he asked.

The woman nodded. "They hired him to be a mime at the Electric Circus over on Saint Marks." Then she paused. "Come to think of it, I haven't heard from Kenneth since that place exploded."

Freddie's eyebrows bobbed up. "I'm sorry?"

"A bomb exploded," Bev replied matter-of-factly. Then she saw Freddie's worried expression. "Oh, don't worry. Kenneth's fine. It blew up years after that show closed."

"Well. That's ... good," he said, looking to Anne again. She just stared back, eyes wide.

Bev nodded, then switched her attention to James. "So, are we having cake or what?"

The question seemed to jog everyone's memory and conversation abruptly halted. Anne's attention snapped to James, and he quickly jumped up to his feet.

"We'll be right back!" he sang out, as the two of them scurried to a nearby table that had a bright pink cake dome in the center. They huddled together for a moment, then James lifted the dome and turned around with the homemade cake in hand. Anne quickly worked to light the candles dotted across the top while the table began to sing "Happy Birthday," each at their own distinct pitch. Within a few notes, the cake was ablaze.

James slowly placed the cake in front of Ellis and gave him a kiss just as the song concluded. Ellis's smile was broad as he looked from his husband to the rest of the table, to the slightly asymmetrical layers caked in buttercream in front of him. Then he leaned forward and blew out the candles. The table erupted in cheers.

"How old are you, Ellis?" Bev asked as he cut into the cake.

Cricket snorted out a laugh. "Oh my God, Bev. You can't *ask* that."

"Why not?"

"Because it's rude," Cricket replied, tossing her hair over her shoulder. "What would you do if someone asked you that?"

"Try me."

"Okay, how old are you?"

Beverly shrugged. "Seventy-two."

Freddie was impressed. He wasn't an expert on women's ages, by any means, but in the short time he'd known Beverly, he had come to see her as more of a contemporary. Not only in how she spoke—curse words and hilarious anecdotes—but how she carried herself. Even now, as she relaxed back in her chair, she was wearing Converse and oversized gray pants with a huge blazer on top of a T-shirt.

"Well, you look fantastic," Ellis said.

Beverly eyed him suspiciously. "Don't sound so shocked."

Ellis blanched. "Oh, I didn't mean . . . It's just . . ."

"You're very cool," James said, saving his husband.

"For a seventy-two-year-old," Beverly murmured.

Across the table, Anne let out a rueful sigh even as she smiled. "Bev, you're cooler at seventy-two than I was at twenty-two."

"I don't know about that." The older woman threw Anne a wry grin. "You know what they say, a woman can be hotter at twenty-nine than she was ten years before."

Anne laughed, even as her cheeks flushed even more.

The conversation moved on as pieces of cake were passed around the table. Ellis wanted to hear about all the changes Freddie was making to the apartment, while Anne listened to a conversation between Bev and Cricket about the current state of New York City's penal system.

"Our civil rights are at stake! And you should feel the toilet paper in the holding cells. It's awful," Cricket lamented.

Bev nodded solemnly.

For the first time in years, Freddie forgot to look at the time, letting the music and the conversation and the wine swallow up the night. By the time he finally pulled out his phone, it was one a.m. and the party was fading. Glen was trying to wake up Cricket, who was asleep on a nearby chaise lounge, and James was yelling at a pedestrian down on the sidewalk about public urination.

"That's my cue," Bev said, standing up and taking a bottle of wine with her. "Anyone else coming?"

Anne nodded from where she sat beside Ellis on the other side of the table. Her eyes were closed, and she looked only moments away from sleep herself.

Ellis sighed, looking down the table at the remnants of dinner and cake.

"Do you need help cleaning up?" Freddie offered.

"No, it's all right. I'll make him deal with it," he said, motioning behind him to where James was now flipping off someone below. Then Ellis nodded down to Anne. "Can you make sure she gets back to her place in one piece, though?"

"Sure," Freddie replied, working to sound nonchalant.

Ellis and James started to clean up while Freddie, Anne, and the rest of the party took the elevator down together. They did their best to ignore that Cricket and Glen were practically making out in the corner by the time the elevator arrived on the fourth floor.

"Good night, Cricket," Bev called as she, Freddie, and Anne stepped off. "Make sure he wears a condom."

"Good night!" Cricket replied. Then she smashed her face against Glen's again as the elevator doors closed.

Bev disappeared into her apartment across the hall, so by the time Freddie navigated Anne out of the elevator, they were alone in the hallway.

"Oh, I have keys," Anne seemed to remember, digging a hand into the pocket of her coat.

It took longer than it should have, but she pulled them out and unlocked the dead bolt, throwing the door open dramatically.

"I need to go to bed," she said, then she walked forward into the darkness.

Freddie hesitated on the threshold, but she didn't move to close the door behind her. It stayed open as she shed her peacoat, leaving it in a pile on the floor, then turned on the Christmas tree lights, flooding the room with a warm glow.

"You can come in," she called out.

So he did.

"Don't look in the kitchen. I haven't done the dishes. Cricket uses plastic cups, but I need *dishes,* you know?" Anne said. She was still wearing her knit hat as she walked out of the living room and down the hall. Then the apartment fell silent.

"Anne?" he called out. When she didn't answer, he followed where she had disappeared a moment before.

At the end of the hall, he came to an open door and stopped dead in his tracks.

Anne was lying face down on a bed, limbs flailed out like a starfish. The view was so adorable that it took him a moment to realize that the room itself was barely big enough to fit the bed. It also didn't appear to have any windows.

But then he started to notice the details.

He had dated Anne Elliot for almost three years, was in love with her for even longer than that, but this was the first time he had ever been in her room. He had imagined what it would look like so many times, but the reality felt different. There were layers and imperfections, each one hinting at a different part of her. The organized bins labeled for different office supplies above her small desk. The line of books about math and philosophy on the shelves.

His mind flooded with questions, all the details he had been too proud to pursue before, but with Anne still lying face down in bed, he realized now wasn't the best time, either.

"I like your room," he said, still standing by the door.

Anne mumbled something into her duvet.

"Sorry?" he asked.

She turned her head and sighed. "I said thank you."

Her eyes were closed, so she didn't see as he took a few steps inside. Next to her on the bed was a folder labeled *Eufloria*.

"What's Eufloria?" he asked.

Anne opened one eye to peek up at him. "Oh. It's nothing. Well, not nothing. It's something."

"That narrows it down."

She rolled her one available eye. "It's your sister's flower shop. But not really. That's just the name I came up with. She doesn't have to use it or anything."

He nodded.

"Anyway. It's coming along really well," she said. Then she pushed herself up to sit and pulled off her hat. The static electricity sent her blond hair flying out in every direction. A bigger man would have told her, but he rarely saw this version of her anymore, unpolished and imperfect. He had missed it.

"That's great," he replied.

"I'm meeting her tomorrow to go over all the last-minute stuff, so . . ." Her voice faded as she fell back against the bed again, this time facing up. Her eyes were closed, and for a moment he thought she might have fallen asleep, but then she said, "I just realized something."

"What's that?"

"You've never been in my bedroom before."

He considered. "That's not entirely true."

"No?"

"Your old bedroom is my office now."

Silence swallowed up the small room again. After another long moment, she opened her eyes again and sat up. "You know that window in the corner? The one that overlooks the park?"

He nodded.

"I used to have an old armchair next to that window," she said wistfully. "My parents had these long velvet curtains that I would drape over the arms. It made it feel like a little cocoon. I would curl up there with a book and read for hours."

He let the words sit in the air for a moment.

"Is it uncomfortable?" he asked, his voice low as he took a step toward her. "Having someone else live there now?"

She shook her head. "No. Just sad."

Shit. "I'm sorry, Anne. I didn't mean—"

"Wait." Her head tilted to the side, a drunken motion. "I just remembered something else."

He waited as she narrowed her eyes, like her brain was trying to catch the thought.

"You speak Spanish." She said it like it was a revelation.

His eyebrows bobbed up. "Yes?"

"When did you learn Spanish?"

"I lived in Argentina for seven years," he said, trying not to smile at the way her brow furrowed. "How did you know I spoke Spanish?"

She waved a hand randomly at the space between them. "After I graduated from Columbia, I created a fake Instagram account so I could follow you. In one of the reels, you speak Spanish."

An old scar along his heart began to ache again.

"I didn't know you were checking up on me," he said.

She rolled her eyes. "Just because you blocked my number doesn't mean I stopped caring about you."

His heart dropped. He hadn't thought she knew that. The only way she would have was if she had tried to call, if she had taken the time to notice that it rang and rang without going to voicemail, a telltale sign.

"Annie . . . " His voice faded.

It was the first time he had used her nickname in eight years.

He hadn't even meant to—it had just come out. Like it had been there on his tongue the entire time.

She stared at him, as if waiting for him to continue. When he didn't, she frowned, her eyes half closed. "I should get ready for bed."

She stood up, a slight sway in her stance before she started forward to a door. There were a million things he wanted to say in that moment, to stop her and pour out his thoughts and feelings, get the past eight years off his chest. But when she reached the doorway, all that came out was, "Annie . . . I didn't know."

She stopped and turned around. Whether she picked up on the old nickname was impossible to tell. She had always been hard to read, even after a few glasses of wine.

"If I had known it was your dad's apartment, I wouldn't have put in an offer. I wouldn't have done that to you," he continued solemnly.

"I know," she said, her voice soft. "That's my fault."

"How's that your fault?"

A slight shrug. "You would have known if I'd ever had the courage to invite you over."

Then she turned and disappeared into the bathroom.

Freddie listened to the water running from behind the closed door, working to regain his composure. The wine wasn't helping—his emotions felt raw and exposed, like the pinot noir had tilled a corner of his chest that had been neglected for too long. But it wasn't really neglected, was it? If he was being honest with himself, he revisited it more than he should—that small parcel that he had diligently kept alive over the past eight years. Every memory, every ounce of love for Anne, nurtured in the dark. Because as much as he didn't want to feel it, it also meant too much to him to ever let it die.

He looked around the small room again. It was like a scrapbook of the woman he had known, but with new layers he wanted to peel away and examine.

Anne shuffled back through the doorway before he could consider it. Her hair was piled in a messy bun on top of her head and her sweater and jeans had been replaced by an oversized T-shirt and nothing else. He darted his eyes away, careful to avoid staring at her long limbs as she threw back the duvet on her bed and crawled underneath.

He should go. She probably thought he had already left when she went into the bathroom. But before he could apologize, she moaned, her voice half muffled by her arm now flung over her face.

"Why did you let me drink so much?"

He chuckled softly. "Do you need anything before I go?"

"No," she said. At the same time, her other arm swung down and started feeling across the top of her nightstand. "Yes."

"What do you need?" he asked.

"My phone charger. The cord should be right here."

He did a quick survey of the nightstand. "I don't see it."

She groaned and her hand journeyed down to the drawers, fumbling with the handles while her arm stayed covering her eyes.

"Then it's in the drawer, in the thing," she said, her voice already starting to fade with sleep.

"Which drawer?"

"So many *questions*."

He sighed, and started at the bottom, pulling open the drawer to find a meticulously coiled phone charger, her earbud case, and a square container the size of a small shoebox. It was plastic, with a lid that covered the top, but next to it, half-hidden in the shadows, was an intricately folded piece of paper.

His pulse thundered in his ears, even as it felt like his heart had stopped.

It was one of his notes.

He was still for a moment, then slowly he reached over and lifted the lid on the small box.

It was full of them. Dozens of pieces of paper, each folded in their distinct way. He was so startled he pulled his hand back, letting the box fall closed again. Somewhere in his chest, a long-neglected pain sparked alive, that familiar regret over everything left unsaid between them, everything that had driven them apart.

It was eight years they would never get back.

"Is it in there?" Anne asked. Her arms were still lying across her face.

He grabbed the charger and quickly closed the drawer, then plugged it into the wall. "Yup. Right here."

She finally sat up but didn't appear to open her eyes as she took the cord from his waiting hand and attached it to her phone. Then she fell back into her pillows.

"Now I remember why I hate drinking," she whispered.

"You'll feel better in the morning," he said. He had to stop himself from brushing a few strands of hair from her forehead.

"What if I have alcohol poisoning?"

He almost smiled. "You don't have alcohol poisoning."

"But what if I do?"

"How much did you end up drinking?"

Her eyebrows scrunched together like she was having a hard time with the mental math. "Two and a half."

"Two and a half what?"

"Glasses of wine."

Her eyes were still closed, so he didn't try to curb his grin. "You'll be fine, Annie."

"Will you stay anyway?" she murmured. "Just until I fall asleep?"

He knew he should say no. He already felt too overwhelmed, too vulnerable. But he couldn't bring himself to admit it. All he could do was stare down at her, how her long lashes skimmed her cheeks, how her lips were already a little parted with sleep.

He reached out and finally brushed a lock of her golden hair from her forehead and sighed. "Yeah. I'll stay."

CHAPTER 19

There was no denying it: Anne was hungover. She had barely opened her eyes when the headache began pounding, each throb sending flashes of last night's dinner party to her prefrontal cortex like she was scrolling through a social media feed. She winced and turned her face into the pillow.

God, why had she drunk so much? She had promised herself she would only have one glass, but the pinot just kept coming. Then all she remembered was laughing with James, inhaling Ellis's cake, and acting like a complete and utter fool in front of everyone, including Freddie.

Her eyes shot open into the dimly lit room.

That's right, Freddie Wentworth was there. At Ellis's birthday party.

No no no no. Her mind flew back over what she could remember, trying to pinpoint if she had said anything embarrassing. It was a blur of wine and cake and laughter, but she was having a hard time recalling any crystalline moments.

She had to call James. He was the only person who would tell her if she had done something mortifying. Well, also Bev, but Anne knew that she didn't answer her cell.

The room was fairly dark thanks to the lack of windows, so Anne groped the top of her nightstand, searching for her phone.

Then something shifted on the bed beside her.

She froze, taking a moment to let her eyes adjust, then slowly looked over to the other side of the bed.

Freddie was sprawled out on top of her comforter, still fully clothed in his jeans and sweater, hands clasped over his chest. He was asleep, his mouth slightly ajar and each breath punctuated by a slight purr.

With lightning-fast reflexes, she lifted the covers to check what she was wearing.

Oh thank God. Her old *Trails End Camp* T-shirt and a pair of black underwear.

She shut her eyes and exhaled a breath of relief that she was clothed, retreating under her comforter again.

Freddie probably wanted to make sure she didn't puke before she passed out. That made the most logical sense. But why was he *still* here?

She snuck another glance at him. It was crazy to think she used to have unfiltered access to this view. Obviously not. Otherwise, why would she be so in awe of the slight curve of his full lips, or how his soft brown hair was mussed? It was all eerily familiar, but still completely new.

Suddenly her phone let out a loud PING from the nightstand.

Anne jumped just as Freddie's eyes shot open. It took a moment for his gaze to focus, but when it did, it found hers. Frozen in place, they took each other in for one long, drawn-out second.

Then came another PING.

"Let me . . . just . . . " She reached over to her phone to check the screen.

THEO

> Hey! Just double-checking that you'll have the production schedule all set when we meet for coffee tomorrow? The network needs it ASAP.

THEO

> Oh, and that possible crew list, if you're still up for making it? Thanks!

She rolled her eyes and turned her phone over, so it was face down. When she turned back to Freddie, he was sitting up, his back against the wall where a headboard should be.

"Good morning." He yawned, his expression still lax with sleep.

She offered him a small smile. "I'm sorry."

"For what?"

"Whatever I did that made you think you had to babysit me overnight."

He gave her a weary grin. "You didn't do anything. I escorted you home and you asked me to stay until you fell asleep. So I did."

That's right, she had asked him to stay. After she had talked to him about her old bedroom, her armchair, and . . . Spanish? The memory had still been sleeping somewhere inside her head, but now it was awake and loud and mortifying.

Her head fell into her hands. "Oh God."

He chuckled to himself. "It wasn't that bad."

"I told you about my fake Instagram account, Freddie."

"Yeah," he replied, itching his jaw. There was a dusting of stubble there now. "I was going to wait until after coffee to ask you about that."

She groaned. "Or we could just pretend I didn't say anything and never speak of it again?"

He threw her a wry grin. "You know me better than that."

She laughed softly, but then the full weight of his words settled in. She did know him better than that—or, at least, she used to. But now they kept finding themselves in this limbo of knowing everything about each other and not knowing each other at all.

The awkwardness felt thick now, and each passing second only added to it.

"I'm sorry, too," he finally murmured, leaning forward to run his hands through his messy hair.

"What are you sorry for?" she asked.

"I don't know how to do this, either."

Her mouth pinched, trying to decipher what he meant.

He caught her expression and sighed. "I don't know how to be strangers with you. But I also don't know how to be just friends."

Silence descended again. She wanted to tell him she knew exactly what he meant, that it felt so natural during moments like this, when for a second they forgot all the details that drove them apart.

"Freddie . . ." she whispered.

He stared at her in the dim light from the hallway, scanning her face, her mouth. She had the urge to just lean in, forget every concern she'd had over the past few weeks and . . .

Her phone pinged again from the nightstand.

Anne would have ignored it. She wanted to. But she knew Theo would only keep texting until he got a reply.

"Sorry, I have to just put this on silent," she said, reaching for the phone. But before she could flip the sound off, she saw the message now waiting on her screen.

SOPHIE

> Hey! One block away! See you soon!

Anne's stomach dropped. "Oh my God."

Freddie paused. "What?"

"It's Sophie! I'm supposed to meet her right now!" Anne threw the blanket off and stumbled out of bed. "She's going to be at the flower shop wondering where I am!"

She flew to her closet, barely looking at the jeans and sweater she tore from the shelves. She still had to review the spreadsheets and slides to make sure everything was correct before—

"Don't worry," Freddie said, moving to the edge of the bed to stand up. "My sister has never been on time for anything in her life."

Anne scoffed. "That doesn't mean I can be late. I'm never late. Being late is the worst! Especially since we have so much we need to go over. How will she be able to enjoy the launch party on Tuesday if she hasn't had a chance to review all the budgets and expense tracking?"

He threw her a doubtful look. "Have you met my sister?"

Anne held her clothes in one hand and reached for the Eufloria folder with the other. "Well, I won't be able to enjoy it. She trusted me to help her save her business and I take that really seriously. She's been through so much this year—I can't make her think that I don't prioritize her and her business and . . ."

He stretched as he was listening. It caused his sweater to rise up, and she caught a glimpse of his stomach, the soft trail of hair—

She darted her eyes away. Unfortunately, they darted to her own reflection in the small mirror hanging by the door.

"Oh my God. I didn't wash my face last night," she said, her hands running along the black smudges under each eye. "Why didn't you tell me to wash my face?"

He held his hands up in mock surrender. "You told me to stay until you fell asleep. I didn't think that included skin care."

How could so many things go wrong in just one morning? she thought as her gaze traveled to where her hair was knotted around her shoulders, the crease on her cheek from her pillow. There were too many things to be mortified by right now, too many details to remember and—

"Hey."

Anne whipped her head around to find Freddie now standing just a few inches from her. There was a lopsided grin on his face as he reached up and brushed a tangle of knotted hair behind her ear.

"It's going to be okay. Okay?"

His voice sent a familiar warmth around her body, loosening the tension and quieting her mind.

"Okay," she whispered.

"You go get ready," he said. "I'm going to head upstairs."

"Oh." She didn't know why she was surprised. Of course he would go home. He didn't live here. But that also meant that he'd be gone when she came back.

He watched her expression, then took a step toward her. "Come by when you're done?"

Oh. *Oh.*

Her disappointment was suddenly replaced by a myriad of emotions that she didn't know how to quantify. "Okay. I will."

"Good." He nodded toward the door. "Then you should probably hurry up. It's not very professional to be late and—"

She rolled her eyes and pushed him away before he could finish, barely tamping her laughter as she rushed to the bathroom.

CHAPTER 20

Anne almost walked by the shop. She didn't recognize it now that the parchment paper had been removed from the windows, which were now crowded with floor-to-ceiling flowers. The explosion of pinks and greens and blues, each petal overlapping the other, was so overwhelming that Anne almost missed the sign above the entrance. It looked to be one long piece of wood, polished to a high sheen, with *Eufloria* written across it in bold, black print.

It took a moment for Anne's brain to register it. Her gaze traced each letter, sure that she had misread them, that she was dreaming, or that there had been a mistake. But no, the name was there, so beautiful and perfect that Anne couldn't help the smile that spread across her face.

"Ta-da!" Sophie sang out, stepping out of the front door with a flourish. "Welcome to Eufloria!"

"Sophie," Anne said, shaking her head. "Are you sure? You could pick any name; it's your shop."

"And I did. Eufloria is genius."

A sense of pride tugged at Anne's chest. "Well, it's incredible."

"Wait until you see inside!"

The scent of fresh lilacs and roses consumed Anne the moment she walked across the threshold. The store was still in a state of disarray, but the dust that had blanketed the floor and walls during her last visit was replaced with fresh shavings from workmen framing the drywall partitions exactly as Sophie had described.

"It's a mess, but it will all be set by Tuesday night. I'm really good under a deadline. One of the pluses of having ADHD," Sophie said, then she looked at Anne again and frowned. "Are you okay?"

Anne finally pulled her attention from the array of flowers to turn to her friend. "Yeah. I'm great. Why?"

"You look flustered. Like you have a fever or were just ravaged or something."

Anne forced out a laugh, even as she felt her cheeks redden more. "No. No no. I'm just cold. It's cold. Outside. There's wind picking up and . . . the temperature fell. I think." She cleared her throat. "So, are you ready to go over everything?"

They set themselves up on one of the new work surfaces Sophie had installed in the front room. Anne presented her carefully organized slideshow on her entire vision for the shop's future. There were budgets she created against projected sales over five years, to illustrate the shop's potential trajectory, along with hard copies of all proposed vendor contracts and workflows. After an hour, Sophie looked as impressed as she was overwhelmed.

"Wow," Sophie said. "Now I know why Jimmy spent so much time in his office."

Anne smiled. She hadn't been as nervous as the first time she presented to Sophie. In fact, she was fairly proud of herself. She had worked out how to build something from the ground up, and even she had to admit she'd done an amazing job.

"Oh!" Sophie exclaimed suddenly. "I almost forgot." She

turned and leaned over the front desk, grabbing a piece of paper stuffed under the register. "I still owe you money for getting this place off the ground. I know we didn't discuss compensation, but hopefully this is fair."

Sophie held out the paper with a smile and it was only then that Anne realized it was a check. She slowly took it, feeling the smooth paper under her fingers, not even sure what to say.

Then she saw the amount.

"Sophie." Anne gaped at the number. "This is too much. I can't accept this."

"Why not?" Sophie looked genuinely confused. "You earned it."

"But ... I don't ..." Anne didn't even know what she was going to say, only that the moment required something. But the words weren't forming properly in her mind, so all that came out was: "Thank you."

"Don't thank me. This place is as much yours as it is mine. Which very conveniently brings me to my next question." Sophie cleared her throat and smoothed down her messy pink hair. Then she took Anne's hand and slowly went down on one knee. "Anne Elliot, will you be my business partner?"

A laugh erupted out of Anne before she was even aware that it was there. "What are you talking about?"

"You and me, running Eufloria together! Sure, I can create utter masterpieces with a few petals and stems," Sophie said, flipping her pink hair dramatically. "But you know how to actually *run* things."

Anne's smile faltered. "Does Freddie ... I mean, what does he think—"

"My brother doesn't know anything about this. It's none of his business, so don't let that factor into your decision." Sophie's smile broadened as she jumped back up to her feet. "We could set it up to be a fifty-fifty partnership, so there wouldn't be any weird power dynamics. I think it could be great! What do you say?"

Yes, Anne wanted to say. At that moment, she couldn't think of a professional move she had ever wanted more. But then a familiar anxiety rose up in Anne's chest, forming a litany of questions that needed to be answered: the whats and the hows and the whys. Yes, it might be what she *wanted* to do, but was it the most practical choice? Was it irresponsible to start an entirely new career in an unfamiliar industry, especially when Theo was still hinting that he wanted to partner with her on his new show? And then there was Freddie...

No spiraling, she thought.

"That's an incredibly generous offer, Sophie," she finally said.

Sophie's smile faltered. "Why do I feel a 'but' coming on?"

"No, no but," Anne said, shaking her head. "I just need to think about it. There are a lot of details to work out, and I want to make sure I've considered everything."

Sophie nodded. "Of course. But whatever you decide, you're still coming to the launch party on Tuesday, right?"

"I'll be there." Anne smiled. "And Sophie?"

Her friend looked up, waiting.

Anne leaned in and gave her a hug, big and all-encompassing. "Thank you," she whispered into Sophie's pink hair.

And her friend hugged her right back.

CHAPTER 21

Anne walked back to the Uppercross and went straight up to the eighth floor.

Freddie's door was slightly ajar, as though he had left it like that after she texted to say she was headed up. As she pushed it open, she could see that the apartment looked like it did for Freddie's housewarming party, though the details were clearer now—how the light played off the muted tones of the furniture, where the paintings hung on walls where her own family photos used to be.

The smell of fresh paint had faded, and a fire roared in the fireplace. The sofas had indentation marks on one side, as if Freddie had already chosen his favorite place to sit. Keys were strewn on the entry table. It felt broken-in, like life in this place had continued on after Anne left.

She didn't know if that made it better or worse.

The sound of glasses clattering together pulled her further into the apartment. She turned the corner into the living room and found Freddie pouring himself a glass of water. He paused when he saw her.

"Hi," she said.

He smiled. "Hi."

"Do you leave your door like that a lot?" she asked, biting back her own smile as she took another step into the room.

He shrugged. "Bev told me she'd seen the ghost of Joey Ramone in the building, so I was trying my luck."

Anne laughed and a bit of the tension in her shoulders melted away.

He came around the kitchen island, pausing in the middle of the living room. "How'd it go with Sophie?"

"Well. Really well." She thought back to the check in her bag and took another step toward him. "She paid me way too much for all the work I did."

"I would hope so."

"And she asked me to become business partners so we could run Eufloria together."

That gorgeous, lopsided smile she loved so much spread across his face. "That's amazing."

"I haven't said yes yet," she added quickly. "I have to weigh my options, make sure it's the right choice long-term."

"Of course," he said, nodding. "But do you want to do it?"

She thought for a moment. It was hard to move past the excitement in her chest, the anxiety swirling around with the possibility that made objective reasoning almost impossible. "I think so. I just need some time."

He tilted his head to the side, as if thinking hard. "A checklist, maybe. Or maybe a pros-and-cons spreadsheet."

Anne's mouth fell open and she tried to maintain some level of offense, but she couldn't help laughing, too. "Are you mocking my quantitative approach to decision-making?"

Freddie shook his head, even as he said, "Yes."

Her head fell back as she finally let herself laugh again, completely unencumbered. No one could ever make her laugh like Freddie.

After a moment, as her laughter began to fade, she finally looked over at him to reply. But the words dissolved on her tongue when she saw how he was watching her. His green eyes were dark, his lips parted slightly.

"I missed this," he said.

She paused, waiting for more, but he stayed silent.

"Missed what?" she asked.

"Us."

The silence seemed to vibrate in the air between them. She had never been more aware of her breathing, how it suddenly seemed to match time with her pulse as his gaze fell to her mouth, then back up to meet her eyes.

"Don't you miss it?" he murmured.

She nodded slowly. "Yeah."

For a second he didn't move. It didn't even look like he was breathing. "What do you miss?"

Her heart was a wild animal in her chest, slamming against her rib cage even as her whole body was still, frozen under his scrutiny.

"I miss talking with you," she said softly. "I miss laughing."

He took a step toward her.

"I miss coming home and smelling like you," she continued. "That mix of soap and sandalwood and that cinnamon toothpaste your mom used to buy."

The corner of his mouth twitched.

She smiled, too, but it faded just as soon as it appeared, swallowed up by the enormity of everything she wanted to say.

"I miss how you looked at me." Her voice was barely a whisper now. "I miss how you made me feel."

He took another step forward. He was only inches from her now.

"And how's that?"

She sighed, already ashamed of how pathetic she sounded. "Like I was someone special."

"Yeah. I know that feeling," he said, his eyes studying hers. Then he reached up and tucked a strand of hair behind her ear. "So, what should we do?"

God, it would be so easy to arch up and kiss him right now. Lose herself in him the way she used to. She could convince herself that if she held him close, it would erase all the resentment and pain that had been allowed to fester between them, fill the cracks that had existed at the heart of this for so long.

But then Sophie's words rattled in her brain.

Sometimes love isn't enough to fix everything else.

It was true, as much as she hated to admit it right now. If they really wanted to fix this, then they couldn't just rely on love. They had to put in the work.

"Let's go grab a coffee," she said. "And . . . talk."

He smiled. "Okay. I'll get my coat."

CHAPTER 22

Anne and Freddie had always been good at wandering. It was a habit they had picked up early in their relationship—meandering the city streets for hours while their conversation flowed through every topic under the sun—and now it came back to them like they had never stopped. Like it was second nature.

Anne couldn't ignore the subtle differences now, though. Like how Freddie didn't hold her hand. Or how she was so careful not to cut him off while he was speaking, or how he didn't crack the same jokes as he had done so many years before. Every step felt deliberate, like they were retracing their path to find something they had lost along the way.

This is fine, she told herself as they grabbed two coffees from Monkford Café. They were playing catch-up. That's what this was about, wasn't it? They had to work to get back to being friends—or whatever this was that was building between them. She just had to relax and trust the process.

She tamped down her anxiety as they made their way downtown, crossing Houston Street so they could roam through the Lower East Side. There was a snowstorm due to hit the city in just a couple of days, but for now the sky was clear and the chill mild enough for her peacoat to keep it at bay as they reminisced about punk rock karaoke nights at Arlene's Grocery and their favorite bars where they could always get in even without an ID.

By the time they reached Delancey Street and turned toward Soho, Freddie had started to describe his time in Argentina, how the very first installations of his hydroponics system were with indigenous villages in the north, and how they were so successful that he had garnered international attention.

"It was a lot," he said as they crossed Broadway, ignoring a group of tourists that passed. "Don't get me wrong, I loved it, but I also feel like I didn't come up for air for three years."

"Did you at least get a chance to come home and walk at graduation?" she asked.

He barely concealed his wince. "No. I actually forgot to complete a few credits."

She stopped in the middle of the sidewalk. "You *forgot*?"

"Hey. It's much easier to do than you think."

"Oh my God." She shook her head, as shocked as she was amused. "You're a college dropout."

He smiled. "I prefer 'matriculately challenged.'"

Then his hand finally found its way into hers, and the last of her anxiety disappeared.

At some point they must have turned uptown because a little while later they found themselves in Union Square, where the holiday shopping stalls were already set up and crowded with tourists. They navigated their way through, telling themselves they were getting a head start on Christmas shopping, but instead Freddie bought them hot chocolates, then peppered her with questions about Columbia, the hedge fund, and her years at Kellynch.

After they had exhausted the market's labyrinthine layout,

they started to head home, winding their way through the grid of streets, revisiting memories of stores long closed, and perennial mainstays that seemed completely unchanged.

Anne had no idea how long they had been walking, but by the time they arrived back at the Uppercross, the sun had dipped behind the buildings, and the smile on her face felt permanent.

How have you gone so long without this? she thought as he tugged her forward, fingers intertwined while they made their way through the lobby. It was so easy yet felt so vital. Like she'd had a limb reattached.

Then they stepped into the elevator and Freddie stepped forward to press 8 and then 4, and her smile slowly dissolved.

The rational part of her brain knew she had no right to be disappointed. Obviously, he wasn't going to assume she wanted to go upstairs to his apartment. The polite thing to do was drop her off on her floor and pick up tomorrow where they left off. She had her coffee with Theo in the morning, but then the rest of the day was clear. And Tuesday was the party at Eufloria! Maybe she and Freddie could go together. Like a date.

Maybe.

The elevator dinged then, and the doors opened on the fourth floor.

"I guess this is goodbye," she said as she stepped off, forcing a smile onto her face.

He remained in the elevator car as he nodded. "I guess so."

"You're coming to the Eufloria party on Tuesday, right?"

He nodded again. "I'll be there."

"Good." She swallowed, trying to think of something else to say. Anything to buy a few more seconds. "Well. I guess I'll see you there."

He smiled, though it looked superficial. "Bye, Annie."

"Bye."

The elevator doors closed again.

Their day was over.

This is fine, Anne thought. Better than fine, really. It was exactly what she wanted, wasn't it? She had spent the day with him, held his hand, and heard his stories—that should have been enough, right?

She turned and unlocked apartment 4B. It was dark when she entered and closed the door behind her, but she didn't turn on the lamp, just walked to her Christmas tree and plugged in the lights. It sent a soft glow across the room that she barely noticed. She was still buzzing from the afternoon. Every moment had felt vital and necessary, except now that it was done, she felt like a fundamental mistake had been made in the equation that got her from the elevator to here. Giving each other space was a smart and sensible thing to do, regardless of what she wanted...

That was it, the crux of the issue. Anne had spent her entire life being smart and sensible, putting what she wanted to the side while prioritizing everyone else.

She sure as hell wasn't going to do that now.

Anne dropped her bag on the floor, spun around, and flung open the door only to find Freddie staring back at her, mid-knock, his cheeks flushed with color after racing down the hall.

"Annie..." It was like how he used to say her name in those secret moments before, desperate and possessive. Like she was his.

The familiarity of it held her heart in a vise grip, refusing to let go until she arched up and kissed him.

He stilled, but only for a moment. Then a groan before he deepened the kiss, demanding, indulgent, and oh so familiar, as his hands slid under her sweatshirt to her bare skin. Calloused fingers dug into her hips as he pulled her against him, and the rush of how many times he had done that before came back to her like a wave. That's right—her body had always fit so perfectly against his.

"Get inside," she said against his lips. "Now."

She could feel him smile, but he didn't break their kiss as he started forward, pushing her back into the apartment, then kicking the door closed with his foot. His mouth traveled down to her jaw, brushing a soft path down to her neck, then kissed and licked a long, slow trail from her throat up to her pulse point, the one that was so sensitive beneath her ear, and sucked.

She gasped, adrenaline shooting through her. It was the same move he used to do once he found that spot, when they'd make out for hours around corners of the city, stealing every second they could with each other. The memory, the *feel*, dissolved every thought from her mind. All she could focus on was his mouth, his body, every point where they touched and every point where they should.

"Is Cricket home?" he asked between kisses. "Do we need—"

"No," she cut him off. "Just. Bedroom. Go."

A deep chuckle vibrated from him as he started forward again, this time past the tree and down the hall. She held tight to his arms as they wrapped around her, guiding her backward until finally her legs hit her mattress.

"Like this?" he murmured against her lips.

She nodded, staring into his eyes for a long moment.

"I want to take my time with you, Annie," he said, his voice so low it was almost a growl. "But I also know I can't hold back. Not right now. I . . ."

She sat up, cupping his hand in her jaw. That was the Freddie she knew, brimming with so much want and desire and love for her that he felt like he needed a disclaimer. Permission. So she gave it.

"I don't want you to hold back," she whispered.

He took a sharp intake of breath, and then his lips were on hers again, hard and demanding.

Suddenly her hands were clawing at his sweater, grabbing and stretching in a desperate attempt to get it off his body. He leaned back just far enough to help, pulling it over his head in one swift motion, followed by his T-shirt, to reveal his bare chest. He had always been tall, but he had broadened in the past eight years, wide shoulders and muscled arms that caged her in over the mattress, held her in place as he pulled off her sweatshirt. Her bra. Her jeans. Her underwear.

Then he stared down at her, his gaze so searing she could feel it as he made a slow survey of her skin.

"I remember these freckles," he said, tracing the cluster just below her left breast. "And that scar there." His thumb came up to graze the thin, pale line across her hip from when she fell on the sidewalk when she was younger. Then he shook his head, his green eyes finally coming up to meet hers. "I never thought I'd get this view again."

She reached up, running a hand down his chest. She wanted to say the same thing. How, even though his shoulders had broadened and his muscles had become more defined, it was still her Freddie there staring down at her. But when she opened her mouth, all that escaped was a sigh as his hand came up to trace her lips. Then he leaned forward, ghosting his mouth over hers. It was gentle, tentative, and she wasn't sure if this was who they were anymore, here in this foreign place between strangers and soulmates, but she also couldn't fight it anymore. So she reached up, threading her fingers into his hair, and simply stopped trying.

He groaned again, leaning over her as he deepened the kiss so much that she gasped. Was it a gasp? She couldn't even identify the sounds she was making, hungry and deep and so desperate she should have been embarrassed. She wasn't, though. She could never be embarrassed with him.

She wrapped her legs around his hips, feeling how hard he was between her thighs, his calloused fingers running up her back.

"I missed you so much," she whispered, pulling at his hair, trying to get closer, trying to get inside him, to get back to that place she loved most.

He leaned back enough to meet her eyes again, while his hand went lower, pushing off his boxers so there was nothing between them. God, it was the echo of a memory, so like that first moment they were together. But this time he entered her slowly, carefully, as if he were afraid she was made of glass.

"Are you all right?" he murmured, still against her.

She didn't answer, only brought her mouth to his, swallowing his moans in her own as his tongue danced with hers. He began to move his hips, the slow drag of him like torture. She let her head fall back, letting sensation take over. Her confusion and anger and worry were still there, but they were overshadowed by the building tension in her core. It tightened every tendon in her body as he continued his unyielding pace.

"Tell me you missed me again," he whispered into her hair. "Tell me you missed this."

"I missed you," she cried out, eyes squeezed shut as her head fell back. "I missed this. God, Freddie..."

His hand came up to push some hair from her face, a delicate motion. "I missed you so fucking much, Annie."

A muted whimper was her only response, but it was enough. His thrusts became hard, and his grip on her skin tightened. Then he leaned forward, nipping and kissing the length of her neck, whispering unintelligible things into her skin. But it didn't matter what he was saying; she could only focus on the building tension in her muscles.

She moaned. She was close. So very close...

The orgasm was like a bomb detonating in her body, a surge starting at her core and exploding out to every limb. She cried out and Freddie leaned back, watching it bloom across her face.

She closed her eyes and gave herself over to the feeling. How had she gone so long without this? Without him? She felt right and whole and suddenly there was nothing to hold back. Her muscles seized and her body exploded again, like sensation and light were shooting through her veins.

"Fuck... Annie..." Then he groaned, the sound muffled by her hair as he leaned down, then thrust into her again and again as he came. His breath was ragged on her skin, and she held him tightly until his body finally went limp. She raked her hand through his short hair, letting it tickle her palm. She could almost forget that eight years had passed since they had been here. It would be so easy to get lost in the immediacy of his body, his smell.

He turned his head, watching her profile for a long minute as his breath steadied.

"What's that look?"

She turned to look at him. "What look?"

"Like you're already thinking about something," he finally said.

She could tell him, list the concerns and worries and questions already beginning to bubble up in her brain. How this would work, what happened now... but she didn't want to. She wanted to stay lost for a little bit longer.

"You've got some new moves," she replied, suppressing a smile.

He laughed. She could barely hear it, but the vibration of it went through her body and made her shiver. Then he leaned back and swept his fingers delicately across her cheek. Even in the dim light she could see the new lines around his eyes. The deeper creases in his brow. But still, he was familiar. So familiar and real that for the first time in days she felt calm.

They lay in bed for hours. At some point he got up, the blanket wrapped around his waist as he went to the kitchen and grabbed food, which really only consisted of a bag of pita chips and hummus, then they curled up again, eating and talking and laughing until they finally fell asleep.

In the middle of the night they woke up and made love again. Anne wasn't even sure which of them initiated it, whose fingers began to venture over first, but suddenly it was all-consuming, their lips and tongues exploring every inch of each other's bodies, like they were making up for lost time. It was hungry and desperate, and perfect. It felt perfect.

Anne woke up the next morning to Freddie sitting up beside her in bed, staring at his phone.

"Good morning," she murmured, smiling.

He looked down and smiled, too, easy and relaxed. "Morning."

"What time is it?"

"Almost ten."

Anne's eyes widened. She couldn't remember the last time she'd slept past eight o'clock.

Freddie watched her expression and chuckled. "I know, I can't believe it, either." Then he leaned down and kissed her forehead. "What do you say we throw on some clothes and grab some breakfast?"

She was about to agree, because honestly, pancakes had never sounded so good, but she paused as her mind snagged on something she was supposed to do, an obligation she had marked down for today...

And then she remembered: She was meeting Theo at Monkford Café in an hour. They were supposed to go over the final documents for his show and a role for her in his company.

"I can't. I have a work meeting in a little bit." Her head fell back as she groaned again. She really wanted those pancakes. "How about tomorrow?"

"I can't," he said with a heavy sigh. "I have a work meeting, too."

"Look at us. We're so busy and important," she said with a smile.

He chuckled, leaning down and ghosting a kiss over her lips. "And chivalrous, which is why I'll let you have the bathroom first while I make us coffee."

Her brow furrowed. "Oh, I only have a percolator—"

"I went to school for environmental engineering, Annie. I can figure out a percolator."

For a second, she didn't move, trying to think of what to say. But then he gave her another look, and she could only turn, hiding a smile as she retreated to the bathroom.

She took her time washing her face, brushing her teeth, detangling her hair, all while listening to Freddie moving around in the kitchen.

Is this what it would have been like if she had gone with him to Argentina? A shared space they navigated together? The din of spoons and mugs and the occasional muffled curse? The sounds were so comforting and welcome that she couldn't believe she'd ever lived without them.

And you'll have to do it again as soon as he leaves, she reminded herself. They'd have to talk about their relationship, too, what last night meant, their expectations, where this was going and—

She caught her reflection in the mirror then, her blue eyes bright, her blond hair now pulled back.

Stop spiraling.

This moment was perfect, and if that's all she would get with Freddie now, that would be enough. She had to appreciate that.

With the resolution on repeat in her head, she opened the bathroom door to find Freddie dressed and in the kitchen. The percolator was disassembled in front of him and there were coffee grounds spilled across the Formica countertop.

"Okay, turns out I don't know how to work a percolator," he said, frowning.

Anne laughed, reaching for the filter. "Matriculately challenged is right."

She took over but he didn't move, standing close as she filled the tank, twisted the top back on and put it over the small burner on her oven. A moment later, she poured the coffee into two mugs, then added milk to both and a spoonful of sugar to his.

"You remembered," he said as she handed the coffee to him.

Oh God, she had. It wasn't even conscious, just muscle memory.

"Well, how could I forget?" she said with a shrug. "Every time your mom saw you do it, she reminded you that your grandfather had diabetes."

He chuckled to himself. "I like to live dangerously."

She smiled, too, but hid it under the rim of her mug as she took a sip. Freddie watched the motion, his gaze locked on her lips before blinking away.

"So what's your meeting tomorrow?" she asked, taking a sip of her coffee.

He shrugged one shoulder. "This green tech company wants me to come on board and run their sustainable farming division."

Anne paused. It didn't sound like something Freddie from eight years ago would ever have been interested in. But she wasn't in the position to question. Not yet.

"What about you?" he asked. "I didn't think Sophie was in the city today. What are you two working on?"

"Oh." She blinked. "No. Actually, I'm having coffee with the showrunner on *Divorce Divas*. He started his own production company and I've been helping. I think he wants to talk to me about coming on board, maybe working on his new show."

Freddie frowned. "Why?"

"What do you mean?"

"Why meet with him? I thought you hated TV?"

Anne's mouth fell open, but it was another moment before anything came out. "I did. I mean, I do. But it's where I have the most experience. And I need a job, so—"

"You have a job. Sophie asked you to be her partner."

"Right, but I don't know if that's the smart choice right now. For me."

His expression had lost all its humor. "Yesterday you said you wanted to do it."

"I do. But I can't base a huge life decision on how much I want it. There are other factors that need to be considered. For instance, my mom told me that fifty percent of floral shops close their first year and—"

Freddie let out a bitter laugh as he put his coffee mug back on the counter. "Your mom is still making decisions about your life?"

Anne's eyebrows pinched together as an old forgotten anger poked at her chest. "My mom never made decisions about my life, Freddie."

"Didn't she?"

The energy between them suddenly felt unstable, dangerous. A minefield they'd accidentally stumbled upon right here in the kitchen.

"No, she didn't. I might follow her advice sometimes, but—"

"What about Columbia?"

"I didn't know what I wanted to do after NYU," she said, eyes narrowing on him. "She suggested I get my MBA, and she was right. It was the best choice at the time."

His brow furrowed, and it was only at that moment that she realized how her words had come out.

"Funny," he said. "I didn't think your other choice was so bad."

She sighed. "But it wasn't really a choice, Freddie. Was it? You applied for the program and bought me that ticket without asking me about any of it."

"Are you serious?" He looked genuinely confused. "Annie, you'd already applied and been accepted to Columbia!"

"Because I thought you were staying in the city! You didn't know if I had other plans or—"

"And whose fault is that?" he cut her off.

The words landed between them with a heavy silence. God, it was almost a relief. An old Band-Aid finally ripped clean from the skin.

"I wanted you to come to Argentina with me," he continued, his voice low and angry. "I wanted to build a life with you, and you just cut me off like I meant nothing."

"So did you!" She was surprised by how loud her voice was, like the words had needed to get out for so long that they burst out of their own accord.

His eyebrows bobbed up. "What?"

"You blocked my number," she said, working to make her voice steady again. "You were my best friend, and I told you I wanted to hold on to that, and you blocked my number."

"Because you broke up with me!" Freddie's voice shook. "Do you know what that was like? Being told you wanted to be *friends*? You treated me like an obligation. Even your speech sounded rehearsed!"

"Because I was falling apart, too!"

"Then why do it?" he asked, stepping forward. "Why the hell did you end it before we even had a chance to try?"

Because you wouldn't have gone to Argentina if I hadn't, she thought. She couldn't say it, though. It felt like a cheap shot, leverage thrown in his face that he didn't even know existed. Her sacrifice used as some kind of trump card, when really there had been so many factors leading to the decision. She may have delivered the final blow, but all the things they had never discussed—their future, their plans, even what they wanted—had chipped away at their foundation long before that.

Sophie's words echoed back in her head then: *Sometimes love isn't enough to fix everything else.*

"We were so young, Freddie," she replied. "We were trying to read each other's minds, dreaming about the future while sparing each other's feelings, but all that meant was that we never talked about it. We never made those plans, and now we're here, eight years later, still stuck in this same loop."

"Fine, you want to hear something new?" he said, throwing his arms out at his sides. "You broke my fucking heart, Annie." His eyes narrowed at her. "And for what? Business school? A job at your dad's company?"

"No, to figure out what *I* wanted. To come up with a plan for my life."

He let out a sharp laugh. "Yeah, looks like that really worked out for you."

It was bitter. Worse than that, it was mean. The words of a hurt twenty-one-year-old. And maybe they were. Still, that didn't make them any less hard to swallow.

"Would it have been better if I followed you?" Anne asked.

"Maybe," he said, a mix of shame and anger rising on his face. "At least you would have taken a risk. Life doesn't care about your plans, Annie. Things go wrong and change; you can't predict it. When you try, you end up with a life that looks like everyone else's. Sometimes you need to get out into the world to figure yourself out."

"Right," she said bitingly. "That really worked out for you, too."

He blinked. "What?"

"What do you want, Freddie? You left because you didn't want to get stuck in a corporate job. You said you'd never sit in an office for eight hours a day. Wear a suit and smile through meetings. You were going to start a nonprofit and change the world on your own terms." Her voice was tinged with frustration, but she still stood resolute in the center of the kitchen, back straight and arms around herself. "And now, here you are in expensive suits and designer shoes. You left to forge your own path but still ended up where you never wanted to be."

Freddie's expression flattened, and she knew her words had hit like a bullet pointed right at the single chink in his armor.

"Well, at least we got it all out in the open, right?" he said, his voice like ice. "Anything else you want to say?"

I did everything I was supposed to! she wanted to scream. *I followed the rules and put everyone else first, and I thought that counted for something. I thought it would matter.*

But she could only stare at him, tears threatening at the corners of her eyes. He wasn't responsible for her choices. That was on her.

A long moment passed. Then he turned and walked out the front door, slamming it shut behind him, sending a tremble through the walls and Anne's plans crashing to the floor.

CHAPTER 23

Apartment 4B still smelled like Freddie an hour later. Sandalwood and citrus and soap polluted the bathroom. The bed. Even the kitchen.

Anne had curled back under the sheets after he left, letting the smell take her back to the night before. Her rational brain told her it wasn't productive. Pretending he was still here wouldn't bring him back; that required conversation. And even then, nothing was guaranteed. They thought they could pick up where they left off, but there was too much baggage, things that needed to be exposed to the sunlight and purged.

They needed to grow up.

She still stayed in bed a few extra minutes, though.

Unfortunately, reality eventually beckoned. She was meeting Theo for a coffee at Monkford Café soon and had to be ready for whatever he was about to offer.

So she went on autopilot—showering, getting dressed in a matching sweater set and jeans, then pulling her hair back into a ponytail. She felt adrift, so lost she could barely focus, but at least she could appear put together.

She left the apartment and locked the door behind her, then made her way down the hall to press the elevator button. That was her first mistake. Standing there gave her mind time to wander, and in seconds it found Freddie again, what she had said to him, how they had left things . . .

The elevator doors opened just as she was making her second mistake, pulling her phone from her bag. She knew she would talk to Freddie eventually. They both needed time to cool off, that was clear. But she also couldn't shake the hope that there would be a missed call, a text waiting.

There was nothing.

She swallowed down her disappointment as the elevator arrived at the lobby. A Christmas tree had been put up in the corner over the weekend and its branches sparkled, shifting points of light around the dim room. This was usually her favorite time of year—when she was little and her parents fought upstairs, she would come down and lie on the dark green leather benches here, watching the snow fall outside. Now as she walked across the room, her boots clicking against the marble floor, it felt hollow and sad. A diorama of the life she was trying desperately to hold on to.

She paused at the row of mailboxes. With everything going on, she had completely forgotten to check it all week. She quickly unlocked it and luckily found only a few pieces waiting—some take-out menus, a marketing brochure masquerading as a bill, and a couple of Christmas advertisements. But then one postcard caught her eye. Thick and square, it was covered with an explosion of flowers, all framing the logo for Eufloria, along with its business hours and phone number.

Anne froze. She didn't even know what emotion to assign to what she was feeling, only that she was still standing in the middle of the lobby when Bev shuffled off the elevator a few minutes later.

"Did you have a stroke?" she asked, eyeing her curiously.

Anne blinked. "What?"

"You look like you had a stroke," Bev said.

"No, I just . . . I got a postcard."

Bev glared at her, then at the mail in her hand. "Stroke makes more sense."

"Sorry," Anne said, holding up the postcard and shaking her head. "I just . . . I helped open this place. I even came up with the name and suggested sending out mailers like these."

Bev's eyebrows bobbed up as she glanced down at the glossy image. "They look good."

Anne nodded. "Thanks."

"Congratulations." She turned toward the front door again, then paused. "So what's your title?"

"Oh." Anne shook her head. "I don't have one. At least, I was offered one, but I haven't accepted it."

Bev stared at her like a stroke was still a possibility. "You don't want it?"

"No, I do, it's just that running a small business in the city can be so volatile, and it's hard to predict the market, so . . . " She let out a deep breath. "I don't know if it's the right choice."

Bev scoffed and started toward the door. "There's no such thing as a right choice. The only time you hear that is in government propaganda campaigns."

Anne blinked. "Really?"

"Like the war on drugs." Bev waved her hand in the air as she stepped outside. "That was some bullshit."

"Thanks, Bev," Anne called out, but the older woman was gone.

∼

Anne arrived at Monkford Café a few minutes later and found Theo seated at a table near the front. He waved her over the moment he spotted her.

"Anne Elliot," he said when she arrived at the table, and they exchanged a brief hug.

"Hello, Theo." She took off her peacoat and scarf, revealing her jeans and loose-fitting cashmere sweater set—either she was underdressed or Theo, in his tailored suit, had overshot the formality of the situation.

She sat down across from him, ready to trade pleasantries until she could find the right time to ask him about what she had learned during her father's Thanksgiving dinner, but Theo began talking before she could open her mouth.

"I have so much to catch you up on. Those documents you sent over were stellar, by the way. The network has some thoughts about where we might be able to cut corners, but we can go over those details later. The main headline is that they think there is real potential here, and . . ."

For the next fifteen minutes, Theo didn't come up for air. Anne did her best to listen, grateful when the waiter arrived to take their order, then returned with coffee. She nodded politely but found it hard to follow Theo's words. The clattering of the plates and the sounds of people enjoying their meals at the restaurant felt louder than she'd ever remembered.

Then she realized it wasn't that she couldn't focus on Theo's words. She didn't want to. All she wanted to think about was Freddie, their fight, the Eufloria postcard still in her bag. Her life felt so fundamentally different than it had just two months ago—but was that necessarily a bad thing? She'd been playing it safe for so long, but hadn't been happy. She'd barely been living.

Theo cleared his throat, and it broke Anne's reverie.

"There you are," he said with a smile. "Everything okay?"

She was sick of contorting herself to fit into everyone else's life. And she wasn't going to wait for the right time to call people out on it, either. "Theo, how long were you going to develop a series with the star of *Divorce Divas* without telling me?"

Theo's eyes widened, but he recovered quickly, letting out a short laugh. "You beat me to the punch. I was going to tell you today, along with the good news. We've got a series ordered. Eight episodes of *The Diva Code with Denise*."

He waited, like she should have had some reaction. All she could do was stare back.

"Congratulations, Theo," she said. "Good for you."

He smiled. "Good for us! Now that we have an approved budget, I can bring you on board."

She cocked her head to the side. "In what capacity?"

"Well, you'd have to start at a production manager level, just for the first season. You didn't get an official credit on *Divorce Divas*, so it's hard to justify a higher title, you know?"

She stared at him for a moment. "Theo. I created all the documentation that secured you this series to begin with."

"And I'm so grateful, Anne," he said, his expression morphing into something resembling pensive. "Really grateful. But you know how these networks are. They want to see every line item justified. But it would only be for one year, then the sky's the limit. What do you say?"

She should be angry. Or at least annoyed. But all she felt was relief. Of course he was trying to screw her over. Why had she expected anything else?

"No," she replied.

He paused. "Sorry?"

"I said no."

"Okay..." he said, looking confused. "But... why?"

"Because I've spent the past decade cleaning up everyone else's messes, handling everyone else's schedules. I have better things to do now."

He frowned. "Like what?"

"Selling flowers," she said, letting a smile take over her lips. "And hanging out with a college dropout." Then she stood up and took one last sip from her mug. "Thanks for the coffee, Theo."

"Are you seriously turning this down?" he asked. "It's locked and loaded."

"I wish you and Denise all the luck in the world. But I decline whatever it is you are offering." She put on her coat and scarf, then extended her hand to him.

He narrowed his eyes before slowly standing and shaking her palm. "You realize what you're giving up, right? If there's something you—"

"Goodbye, Theo."

At that, she pivoted and turned to leave the café. Her pulse raced as she made the trek across Tompkins Square Park, but it wasn't anxiety coursing through her veins—it was excitement.

For once, she didn't have a plan, and it felt fantastic.

CHAPTER 24

Freddie was late to his meeting with Mark and George the following day. It wasn't intentional, though he wasn't exactly looking forward to it, either. He still hadn't bothered to read the contract that AirSoil had sent over the week before, or even come up with any intelligent questions to ask about the position. It felt hollow, a title for title's sake, to show off on a business card or to his parents when they wanted to come by and see his corner office.

But that wasn't what kept him from looking at the clock. He had been distracted by the one person he had worked for years to compartmentalize, the same one he had been avoiding since yesterday morning: Anne Elliot.

Twenty-four hours ago, she had been his. For a fleeting moment, the distance, the anger, the resentment—it had all disappeared.

It was like coming home.

But there was another side of that coin, one he hadn't anticipated until it flipped right there before him. It was home, but one that hadn't changed, like his room back at his parents' house: nostalgic and full of love, but so stuck in who he used to be that it seemed intent on ignoring who he was now.

That's when the anger and resentment came back. Because it never really went away, did it? All of it was just tamped down, suppressed for the sake of keeping a fantasy alive.

Shit. He ran a hand through his hair. Was it a fantasy? Was the whole idea of him and Anne cursed from the beginning? Or had he broken it, sabotaged something he'd never find again?

What do you want, Freddie? Anne's words echoed in his head.

When he and Anne were together in college, he had known exactly what he wanted—to start a nonprofit to help develop sustainable farming techniques and take it around the world to those who needed it most. The when, why, and how were things he knew he'd figure out along the way. And because he'd left that open-ended, he had gotten sidelined for the sake of investment and growth. Wentworth Hydroponics was built on the ground where his nonprofit should have been. He hadn't even taken the time to mourn it.

So what did he want now? How the hell could he ask Anne to figure out her shit if he was in denial about his own?

His car pulled up outside AirSoil's headquarters on Fifty-Eighth Street, and he tried to ignore the crushing weight of that question as he headed inside and upstairs.

George and Mark were already waiting in a conference room when Freddie arrived on the twentieth floor. He barely remembered shaking their hands, saying hello. Then he sat down, trying to focus on whatever the hell Mark was saying. After a few minutes, Freddie still couldn't recall a single word. Not that it mattered. He had been in enough of these types of meetings to know that the first few minutes were filled with bullshit.

His gaze wandered to the large window against the far wall that gave a sprawling view of downtown. The snowstorm wasn't due to hit until tomorrow night, but he could already see the clouds swirling overhead, leaving a gray tinge to the skyline.

You left to forge your own path but still ended up where you never wanted to be.

Anne's words came roaring back, taunting him from the corner of his brain where he had tried desperately to store them away.

An abrasive laugh cut through the air, pulling him back to the conference table. He turned to find it was coming from Mark. Freddie had obviously missed the punch line.

Then Mark turned to him. "So what do you think, Wentworth?"

Freddie knew he should at least try to pretend that he hadn't missed the entire conversation, but he couldn't muster the effort. "About what, Mark?"

George cleared his throat. "Mark was just explaining how this new division wouldn't step into the markets already carved out for Wentworth Hydroponics."

"Wouldn't make much of a dent anyway," Freddie replied, maintaining a practiced smile that felt so sharp it could cut glass. "Part of the acquisition meant that the patents in that area entered the public domain. Those systems belong to whoever needs them now."

"And I appreciate your effort toward altruism, I do," Mark said, leaning back in his chair. "But at AirSoil, we need to think bigger."

"Bigger," Freddie repeated.

"Exactly," Mark said, tenting his fingers in front of him. "Wentworth Hydroponics is in developing communities around the world, and sure, that's great, but that's not where the money is. We want to make hydroponics a *luxury* item. Celebrity endorsements, expensive price tag, you get what I'm saying."

Anne's words were back, echoing through Freddie's skull. Suddenly, the anger and frustration he had been working for months to subdue began to swell, and he didn't care about containing it anymore.

"Did you ever read the mission statement for Wentworth Hydroponics, Mark?" Freddie's tone was calm but stern, the one he usually reserved for meetings with companies or municipalities more concerned with profit than the people they claimed to help. The one he wielded to ensure that, regardless of who bought his company, the patents for all his work would go into the public domain for anyone to use.

Mark's expression faltered. "Sorry?"

"It's okay, it was long. I'll summarize it for you." Freddie leaned his elbows on the table. "Leave the planet a better place than we found it."

Mark laughed again, as if this were a joke, even as George's expression became stoic. Unreadable.

"Listen, I know you're trying to keep that altruistic angle, and that's great. Really. But none of that matters now." Mark leaned an elbow on the table. "We're here to make money; you need to understand that. And if you don't, I need to know that now. Okay?"

"Okay, Mark," Freddie replied, donning a sharp smile. "Then I guess there's something you need to know."

George didn't say anything as he and Freddie left the building and walked out to their waiting Suburban. His expression was blank—he was good at that—so there was no way to gauge how pissed he was. But it was safe to assume he had to be. Freddie had left every feeling he had about the new CEA division on the table, calmly outlining his contempt for Mark and his entire idea, then segued into all the issues he had with the man's entire work ethic and approach. It had been cathartic, but when he was done and finally took in the expressions of the two men sitting with him, Freddie realized he probably should have at least discussed it with George beforehand.

The problem was Freddie hadn't planned on doing it. The idea never even crossed his mind. He had been too consumed with dissecting what Anne had told him, how she had torn down every excuse he'd made for himself in recent years until he was left with only the stark truth.

You left to forge your own path but still ended up where you never wanted to be.

After everything, he had assumed that she saw through his bravado, past all the posturing, the expensive suits and fancy furniture. That she could see the person he was under everything. And maybe she had, but the view left her unimpressed. Worse, she knew who he had been and could track the change. He might be able to ignore the compromises he had made along the way, but she never would.

Unfortunately, he had chosen a shit time to realize it.

Freddie sighed, running a hand through his hair as he watched Midtown fly by through the window. Then he turned to the man seated beside him. "George . . ."

He knew he had to cobble together an apology, say something to quell his friend's inevitable anger, because Christ, it was warranted.

But George shot him a glare before he could continue. "Don't."

"Come on. I had no right—"

"Don't apologize. It's fine."

"No, it's not. I should have talked to you first."

"You did."

Freddie paused, eyes narrowing in confusion.

George smiled. "Freddie. Do you remember our first business

meeting? You walked into my office in a T-shirt and cargo pants and called me 'bro.'"

Freddie smiled. He hadn't thought about that day in a while. When he had arrived at the offices of Knightley Capital, George had looked at him like he was there to deliver his lunch.

"I had barely said hello before you made it clear that you didn't care about profits, you just wanted to make sure the technology was open-source and available to everyone. You were there to make a difference," George said. "I admired that in you. That's why I invested in Wentworth Hydroponics. It's why I introduced you to Will when you decided to sell. No matter how much this business tried to bend your moral compass, you didn't let it. Don't start now."

"I don't know. I think that ship already sailed when I bought my first suit."

George scoffed. "Freddie, you just called their CEO a neocon. You're fine."

Freddie laughed, punctuating it with a sigh as he leaned back in the leather seat. "What the hell am I doing?"

"Depends. What do you want to do?" George asked.

The question was so big, so cumbersome, that for a long moment all Freddie could do was stare out his window, letting every possibility run through his brain. He wanted Anne back. He wanted to build a life she would be proud to share with him.

And then his brain returned to the very thing he had said to Mark just a few minutes before.

"Leave the planet a better place than we found it," he said. Then he turned and gave George a wry grin. "Is that lame?"

His friend shrugged one shoulder. "Only if you don't actually do it."

"Great. Got any ideas?"

"I don't know, Freddie," George said with a sigh. "You were going to start a nonprofit back in college, right? Do that."

Huh. The idea landed in Freddie's brain like a bomb, detonating and clearing out all the cobwebs.

"That's not a bad idea."

George shrugged. "There's no money in it, but on the bright side, you won't have to court another job offer in Midtown again."

"Thank God," Freddie murmured, letting his head fall back against the headrest.

Freddie didn't head back to the Uppercross. His emotions were still too raw and the idea for a nonprofit was fizzing in his brain, shooting from one possibility to the next too fast for him to nail down. So he did what he always had to when he needed to untether his brain—let it roam and work until it came up with a plan: He went to Queens.

By lunchtime he was helping his mother in the garden like he had for so many years. Everything had been moved into her small greenhouse near the garage, and together they repotted seedlings, debating whether to plant spinach again next summer. Then he went to the basement, where his dad still had Bertha going, churning out oregano and parsley year-round.

It was good to have his hands in dirt again, back where it all started. His body went into autopilot while his brain examined every angle for his nonprofit, coming up with idea after idea until he finally had to head upstairs to grab one of his dad's small reporter's notebooks to jot them down.

An hour later, he was sitting in his parents' living room, the Jets game on TV and a beer in his hand while he filled page after page, mapping out the first steps for his charity. He only paused when his dad shuffled around the corner in his pajamas and carrying a beer of his own.

"What's the score?" he asked.

"Nineteen–three, Rams," Freddie answered grimly.

"Goddamn it." Fred Sr. landed heavily in the recliner beside the sofa. "So, what are you still doing out here? Did your mother find that Santa in the basement?"

"No. I just needed a change of scenery," Freddie replied, tapping his pen against his leg. "Where's Sophie?"

"At the shop," his father replied, waving a hand toward the front door and, somewhere beyond it, Manhattan. "The launch party is tomorrow so she's working on some last-minute details."

Freddie nodded, even as the reminder of the launch party triggered a shot of anxiety. "Are you and Mom going?"

His father threw him an incredulous glare. "We don't go into the city after dark. You know that. We'll go in during normal business hours. You kids have fun."

The Jets turned the ball over with ten seconds left in the quarter and Fred Sr. grumbled to himself as the game went to commercial.

"Your sister has been singing Anne's praises for the past few weeks," his father said after a moment. "Sounds like she did a real bang-up job with all the accounting."

"Yeah."

"And Sophie asked her to be her partner?"

"Yeah."

"That's good."

"Yeah."

"Why'd you two break up again?"

Freddie's head fell back. "Dad, can we not—"

"Hey, just asking," his father said, holding up his hands in mock surrender.

The game returned, and they sat in silence as the Jets were intercepted, as the Rams missed a field goal. Freddie tried to watch, to get lost in the game and forget everything else, but instead, everything else felt like it was going to swallow him whole. He had to say it, hash it out, or he would end up exactly where he was eight years ago, broken and confused and having no idea what to do with it.

"I'm still in love with her, Dad," he finally said.

He didn't look surprised. If anything, a new tinge of sadness swelled in his eyes. "Does she know that?"

Freddie shook his head. "I had the chance to tell her, but I fucked it up."

"How did you fuck it up?"

He almost wanted to laugh. "Instead of trying to move forward, I brought up everything that had been eating away at me for the past eight years and threw it in her face."

His dad let out a low whistle.

Freddie sighed. "Yeah."

"You should apologize," his father said.

"I don't know if an apology is going to cut it," Freddie murmured, scratching at his jaw.

"Depends what you say."

Freddie's brow furrowed. "Other than I'm sorry?"

"Anybody can say I'm sorry. You have to put those words into action. Talk things out. Learn from it. Otherwise, what the hell are you doing?"

"It's more complicated than that."

"How?"

Freddie let out a long sigh. "There are still a lot of things that I don't know if we'll ever resolve."

"Then you gotta pick your things."

Freddie's brow furrowed. "I don't get it."

His father threw him an exasperated glare. "Those things that bug you, maybe even drive you crazy, but you can live with because you're living with her. It's like that tree." He pointed over to the towering silver monstrosity in the corner. "That is the ugliest goddamn Christmas tree that God ever put on this earth. But every November for the past twenty years, I help your mom put it up."

"So why don't you say something?"

"Because she loves it. And I love her," he said. "That's a thing. Get it?"

Freddie stared at the metallic branches, the twinkle lights that were almost blinding. "Yeah. I get it."

Silence descended then. They watched the third down, then the fourth, before his father spoke again.

"Have you turned down that job yet?" his father asked during the next commercial break.

Freddie's gaze snapped to his dad. "How'd you know about that?"

"I didn't." He shrugged. "But you were never gonna be happy behind a desk, Freddie. We've known that since you locked your kindergarten class out of the classroom and tried to convince the other kids to stage a revolt."

Freddie laughed. "Yeah. Mom's going to be disappointed, though."

"Oh, please. She still has that painting you did of that kindergarten class up in the kitchen. She's always proud of you. She just also has a lot of opinions." He got distracted by the game for a moment and cursed under his breath before turning to Freddie again. "What are you gonna do now?"

"Well . . . I was thinking of finally starting up that nonprofit to fund the implementation of cost-effective sustainable farming techniques in underserved communities," Freddie continued, trying not to wince.

His father narrowed his eyes on him. "So... still unemployed." A moment, then Fred Sr. grinned. "At least some things never change."

Then he clinked his bottle with Freddie's and turned back to the game.

CHAPTER 25

YOU ARE CORDIALLY INVITED
TO THE LAUNCH EVENT FOR

Eufloria

@EUFLORIA.FLORALS

TUESDAY, DECEMBER 2, AT 8 P.M.

FESTIVE COCKTAIL ATTIRE
RSVP REQUIRED

Anne stared down at the invite on her phone, then back at her full-length mirror, narrowing her eyes. She had loved this dress in the fitting room of the store, and even now she marveled at the way the deep-green satin fabric draped over her body and around her neck to create a halter, highlighting her shoulders. The color even matched her mother's emerald drop earrings that she liked to wear on special occasions.

Is it festive cocktail attire, though?

Considering how much she spent on the dress, it better be, Anne thought. Besides, it was too late to change now. The party was starting in a matter of moments.

She gave herself one more once-over, then grabbed her coat, all while completely ignoring her shaking hands.

What was wrong with her? She'd attended her fair share of parties in the past. Between premiere events for *Divorce Divas* to her father's lavish soirees to celebrate a new season (or even just a Tuesday), she had gotten good at pretending to enjoy herself in a crowd.

Maybe that was why her heart was racing right now. Tonight's party wasn't to celebrate someone else's project or achievement, it was about Eufloria, of which—as of two days ago—she was the co-owner.

Anne had called Sophie to accept her offer as soon as she got home from her meeting with Theo. Once her friend was done screaming, she told Anne that she had been over at the shop since dawn, getting everything ready, so Anne threw on her coat and joined her.

The next forty-eight hours had been a blur. As promised, Sophie already had the partnership agreement ready, and Anne had pored over it, trying to imbibe all the details and marking up her questions while they ordered pizza and put the finishing touches on the shop. By the time Tuesday arrived, Eufloria was ready and Anne was a co-owner.

Her hands hadn't stopped shaking since.

So she did what she did best: stayed in motion. She sent a quick text to her friends in the building, inviting them to the launch party—James and Ellis. Cricket and Bev. She didn't really expect them to show up, but she needed to ask, if only to let them know that while she had been working so hard to support them, she had been doing something in the background that was worth celebrating, too. Then she went shopping for a dress, making sure to stay deep in the sale section, and even found a pair of heels in her budget, too.

By the time she got home and started to get ready, she had expected to feel panicked. Even scared. But instead, she was giddy. God, when was the last time she'd felt giddy? It was ridiculous, but at the same time, she felt alive. There was still an incredible amount of work to do, of course: She and Sophie still had a number of agreements to negotiate with vendors, talk to their landlord about upgrading the plumbing in the back workspace, not to mention going over the receipts for the very party she was about to attend, and then—

She shook the thought loose. All those plans could wait for tonight. Right now, she wanted to hold on to giddy for as long as she could.

Because yes, there was a good chance she would fall on her face, fail in the most public way possible, but that was still better than doing anything else.

She just hoped Freddie showed up so she could tell him.

～

The snow had already begun falling when Anne arrived at Eufloria, leaving a soft dusting over the sidewalks and streets. The storefront glowed against the darkness, and she paused across the street to take in the full effect of the entrance. It looked perfect. Tucked between the asphalt and the subway grates, the small floral shop burst with color and life. Uplights illuminated the ivy and evergreen branches that surrounded the entrance, and tall potted plants flanked an attendant who stood by the door to welcome guests.

Through the tall front window, she could see there was already a crowd inside. She took a deep breath, watching it curl in the air before her like a cloud, then she stepped forward toward the front door.

The soft, humid air of the shop enveloped her as she entered, and as the attendant took her coat and hung it up on the rack with a few others, Anne's breath caught in her throat. It was better than she could have imagined. Lush foliage, broad green leaves, and pink and yellow blooms crawled along the raw brick from the lines of pipes running up the walls. The cement floors had been polished, and a long, gnarled piece of varnished olive wood ran across the perimeter, then cut into the center of the room. The register sat at one end, and on the other was a small bar set up for the party. Sophie was there, directing the catering staff in a burgundy pantsuit with her hair pulled up in a twist, a serious look on her face. When she saw Anne approaching, she broke out into a smile and ran over to give her a hug.

"It's so beautiful, Soph," Anne said.

"It better be, given how much work we did," she said with a laugh. "Now I just need to keep drinking these super-strong negronis to chill out or I think I might have a panic attack."

She picked up one of the dark red drinks lined up on the counter and took a swig.

Anne grabbed one, too, and did the same. She regretted it immediately.

"You okay?" Sophie asked, watching Anne's pained expression.

"Yeah." Anne coughed. "Just nervous."

"Okay, now listen. Everything is perfect. You're perfect. This is the most perfect flower shop launch party in the entire world."

Anne paused. "Have you ever been to a launch party for a flower shop?"

"No, but . . . " Sophie's voice faded as her eyes locked on the front door again. "Holy shit, it's Eloise from the Style section of the *Times*. And she brought Rachel from DesignLife." Sophie squealed as she put her negroni down on a passing tray. "I knew this party was a good idea. This will be all over TikTok tomorrow. Come on. Let's go mingle."

The crowd grew, and Sophie circled the room, introducing Anne to potential clients, friends, and press. Hors d'oeuvres were passed on trays as smartly dressed waiters made sure everyone had a drink. The music faded behind a wall of conversation, dozens of people admiring the space, complimenting Anne and Sophie's work. Still, Anne's eyes kept darting to the door, looking for a familiar face.

Then someone tapped her on the shoulder.

Her heart tripped as she turned around. James and Ellis stood behind her, each with a glass in their hand.

"You came," Anne said as she released a breath she hadn't even realized she was keeping in.

"Of course we came," Ellis said, embracing her.

"This place is incredible, and I'm so mad at you for not telling us about it sooner," James said, looking mildly put out, even as he leaned over to give her a hug as well.

Anne laughed. "If it makes you feel better, this place has only been half-mine for two days."

James seemed to think about it. "It does. A little."

"Being a business owner suits you," Ellis said. He was smiling so broadly, Anne actually believed it. "You look gorgeous."

"It's either that, or some tall drink of water has swept you off your feet," James said in agreement, waving a hand in front of her face. "You're all flushed and bubbly."

Anne rolled her eyes, working hard not to check the doors again. "It's probably because I had a sip of whatever that drink is that they're passing around and nothing to eat today."

James sighed. "That's my favorite diet."

"ANNE!" a voice rang out from the crowd.

They all turned just as Cricket emerged from the crowd. Her long curly hair was piled onto the top of her head, and she was wearing a gauzy lace dress that almost looked like a negligee with a faux fur coat over her shoulders. She was waving her arms so frantically that Anne almost missed Bev behind her, wearing cargo pants and a wool sweater, and looking around at the painfully stylish crowd with disgust.

"We made it!" Cricket announced when she finally arrived at the trio. "Bev said we would be late, but I told her it's okay because we had to make a fashionable entrance."

"This place got firebombed in the seventies," Bev added, still looking around the space.

"Cricket, what the hell are you wearing?" Ellis asked, looking down at his sister's almost-transparent dress.

"What?" Cricket looked down, too, concerned. Then her attention went to the coat and her lip curled. "It's not *real* fur, Ellis."

Anne smiled, her chest filled with so much joy she didn't know what to do with it. She had spent so much time showing up for everyone else, she never considered how much it would mean when they showed up for her, too. "This is amazing. I can't believe you all came."

Bev looked over at her like she had lost her mind. "Why the hell wouldn't we come?"

"Oh! Tax fraud," Cricket replied. "That's why Glen isn't here. One of his clients did some embezzling or something?"

Anne opened her mouth to ask one of the numerous follow-up

questions she had, but was cut off by Bev, who was now waving down a passing waiter with a tray of the hors d'oeuvres.

"Are those crab cakes?" she yelled.

"Hey!" Sophie's pink hair popped into the group, her smile wide. "Sorry, I have to steal my partner for a sec!"

Sophie pulled Anne from her friends to introduce her to the other guests. They talked about their business plan and hopes for the future, posed for photos with the flowers and other patrons. It was dizzying, and Anne was about to excuse herself to get a few moments alone in the back, when she turned around and froze.

"Hello, sweetie," Bianca Russell said, a smile on her red-lined lips. She hadn't taken off her long cashmere coat, and there were still snowflakes on the shoulders as if she had just come in. It was a telltale sign that she wasn't staying long, but Anne didn't even care. Regardless of how much time her mother would spend there, she came.

Anne blinked, and it took another moment before she replied. "Hi."

"What's wrong?" Bianca said, releasing her. "Is it the eyebrows? I just had them reshaped."

"No. They look perfect," Anne replied. "I just can't believe you made it."

Her mother frowned. "You invited me."

"I know. You're right." Anne nodded. She didn't want to mention that she'd invited her mom to a lot of things through the years—from high school science fairs to a simple coffee date—but it was always questionable as to whether she would be able to fit it into her schedule. Instead, she motioned around the room. "So, what do you think?"

Bianca took it in with a careful eye. "It's very nice."

Not exactly the ringing endorsement Anne had been hoping for, but she'd take it.

"It is," Anne agreed. "And as of two days ago, it's fifty percent mine."

Bianca turned back to face her, those newly shaped eyebrows bobbing up ever so slightly. "Really?"

Here we go, Anne thought.

"Yes, really. I quit Kellynch, last week. I'm now co-owner of Eufloria."

"Is that so." Bianca looked around the room again, her gaze more astute this time. "Well, if you—"

"I'm not looking for your opinion, Mom," Anne continued. "But I wanted you to know."

A moment passed before her mother nodded. "All right. Fine. I just didn't realize this was something you were looking to do."

"Neither did I," Anne said. "But I've spent the past month helping Sophie open this place, and it's been more fulfilling than anything else I've ever done. I've loved it. And I know you want me to go back to finance, to get some high-paying job that will look good on a résumé, but that was never me, Mom. It never will be."

A few people walked by, laughing and crowding the small space they had carved out in the center of the room, but neither Anne nor Bianca moved.

"I never wanted you to work in finance," her mother said, looking slightly offended.

Anne's eyebrows knitted together. "But the MBA—"

"You're brilliant, Anne," Bianca continued. "But you didn't know what to do with it. And I didn't know how to help. I wasn't here where I should have been; I didn't know how to be a mom like you needed." She sighed. "And let's face it, I'm terrible at math."

Anne couldn't help but smile.

"I gave you the advice I was capable of giving: Go to school and be selfish." She paused. "Was it bad advice?"

"No," Anne admitted, looking around the shop again. "I probably should have started following it earlier."

Bianca smiled.

"There's something else," Anne said, pausing to let out a shaky breath. "My business partner is Freddie Wentworth's sister."

She tried to temper the flush in her cheeks, the nervous way she tapped her foot and darted her eyes around the room, waiting for her mother's response.

Bianca watched her, gauging every movement, then her lips turned up in a smile. "You're still in love with him, aren't you?"

Anne sighed. "Mom—"

"Is he here?"

"Mom—"

"I just want to say hi."

"He's not here, Mom." A sharp ache hit her chest with the words.

"Well, that's too bad," Bianca said, looking around the room again with a new glint in her eye. "Because this is definitely worth showing off."

A bit of the tension that had been building in Anne's shoulders released. "Thanks."

Another moment passed, and then her mother's astute eye found her again. "I'm proud of you, Anne."

"Yeah?"

"Of course I am." Then Bianca lowered her voice just enough so no one around them could hear. "Fifty-fifty?"

Anne smiled. "Yes."

Bianca's eyes narrowed. "With equity?"

"Of course."

Her mother nodded sagely. "Of course."

Anne could feel tears welling in her eyes and she tried to blink them away. "Thank you for coming. It means a lot."

Bianca must have seen them, too, because she stepped forward and gave her daughter a hug, a brief motion before she righted her Chanel coat. "Don't cry. You'll ruin your makeup."

Anne nodded, finally letting herself laugh.

"All right, I have to leave. I'm going to that cocktail party down at the Beekman and promised I'd be there by nine. I'll see you Saturday at Le Bernardin, right?" She leaned in and gave Anne a kiss on the cheek. "Those earrings look wonderful with that dress, by the way. You should wear more green."

Then she turned and started for the door.

As a woman on the verge of thirty, Anne may not have needed her mother's approval, but it felt good to finally have it. She only had a moment to truly appreciate it, though, before she was pulled back into the celebration, a continuous cycle of conversations and congratulations, so overwhelming that she almost forgot to look to the door for Freddie again.

Almost.

CHAPTER 26

The snow was falling heavily by the time Freddie emerged from the subway at First Avenue. The storm wasn't supposed to get bad until after midnight, but there was already a thin layer of white across the city, muting the sounds and smells as Freddie passed shop after shop, each decorated with garlands and Christmas lights. He couldn't slow down to appreciate it, though—he had to stay in motion or the anxiety might eat him alive.

The Eufloria launch party was set to start at eight o'clock, and if the New York City Transit system functioned normally during bad weather, he would have arrived early. Unfortunately, the subway was delayed even more than usual, so even though he had left Queens with time to spare, he was now forty minutes late. He lengthened his gait, just making the light to cross the avenue, and cursed under his breath.

He had spent last night at his parents' house, staying up until sunrise, working out what was likely the first detail-oriented plan he had made in his entire life. Even more surprising was that he wanted to. With all that corporate structure out of the way, he felt like he was finally getting back to the person he used to be, and the dream he used to have.

Of course, he would be the first to admit that he was new to this and that some of the details were still, for want of a better term, lacking. But the bones were there and for a first draft of a life plan, he thought it was pretty good.

1. Establish a sustainable farming nonprofit
2. Apologize to Anne for storming out of her apartment like an asshole and put the work into rebuilding our relationship

For the first time in years, Freddie felt like himself. It wasn't just the jeans he was wearing now, or the threadbare wool sweater that had been his favorite since high school. He was finally moving in the direction he had always thought he would, high on the idea that he knew where he was going and choosing it for himself.

He could hear the party even before he turned the corner and found the shopfront glowing on the corner of Twelfth Street. There was a small crowd milling around the sidewalk outside, and the muffled sound of music and conversation wafted out every time the door opened to let another person in. He stopped before walking inside, letting his gaze wander up.

Eufloria

The wooden sign above was fashioned out of a long, curled piece of wood and backlit against the building's brick exterior.

Pride swelled in his chest for a moment. While he had been wallowing in his own shit, he hadn't stopped to notice how his sister and Anne were moving mountains. In just over a month they had taken the empty storefront and made something truly special—a bright, vital thing that was brimming with life, right in the middle of the East Village.

He stopped on the sidewalk, staring through the large front windows. The inside was brimming with people, so it was hard to see anything other than a cluster of bodies and the wall of flora rising up on the far side of the room, an explosion of greens and pinks and yellows against the rough brick. Yes, the wall was almost made entirely of plant life, so much so that Freddie's gaze stayed locked on it, studying how they might be attached or . . .

"It's impressive."

The voice came from beside him. He had been so entranced by the view that he hadn't noticed the woman who had approached and was now standing just a foot or so away. He turned to her, and in the darkness it took a second for him to recognize her face, for the details to snap into place.

It was Bianca Russell.

"Anne tells me it's your sister's store," she said, nodding to the window.

"It is," he said, his tone flat.

"And that she's decided to come on board as partner."

He couldn't help his wry smile as his eyes went back to the window. "Did she now?"

Bianca nodded. "I think the two of them have something really special here."

"So do I," he said.

Silence swallowed them up then. The sounds of the city were alive on the corner of Avenue A, but the heavy flakes dulled them. In that moment, it almost felt like the world had stopped, waiting for what would come next.

He turned slightly to look down at her. She was small like Anne, with the same blue eyes, but hers still had that hard edge he remembered from all those years ago.

"You never liked me very much, did you?" he asked.

"I never knew you, Frederick," she replied.

"Right." He nodded. "But that never stopped you from sharing your thoughts about our relationship, did it?"

A moment passed as she seemed to think about it, then she turned to meet his eyes. "Do you know how I met Anne's father, Walter?"

Freddie didn't reply. He was worried about what he might say, so he just turned back to the window.

"I was a junior at Barnard," Bianca said, letting her gaze slide back to the shop window. "One night my friends and I went out downtown and I met this guy. He was a film student. Tall, so good-looking... he even played in a band. For a girl who grew up in Connecticut and was majoring in prelaw, he was like lightning in a bottle." She paused for a moment, like she was pondering the memory. "I believed him when he said he would make documentaries that changed the world, so when I graduated and it was time to apply to law school, I chose to help him start his own production company instead. I didn't even like production, but I did it because it was his dream, and I loved him.

"We got married. Had Anne. The company slowly changed. There was more money in television, so that's what he focused on. We grew apart. And when the stress finally became too much, I left."

Freddie's jaw tightened. "Anne told me."

"I'm sure she did. But she doesn't know that I never dreamed of being a wife. Definitely not a mother. Before meeting Walt, all I wanted was to be a lawyer. But I gave that up for him, and I can never get it back."

Freddie stilled.

"I'm sorry that I never made an effort to know you, Frederick," Bianca said, turning to meet his gaze again. "Anne was desperately in love with you, so I should have. But when she told me about you, your plans and your dreams... it all sounded eerily similar. I knew how that story would end. And I didn't want my daughter prioritizing your future over her own."

"So you told her to break up with me?"

Bianca laughed, but it faded when she saw his grim expression. "Oh, I see. You never figured it out."

"Figured what out?"

Bianca stared up at him as if she was seeing him from a different perspective. "She didn't follow my advice to be selfish, Frederick. She broke up with you so you could be. She did it to make sure you went to Argentina, so *you* wouldn't have to compromise anything. And, from what I've heard, you should be thanking her for it."

His brow knitted together as some old puzzle piece began to slide into place in his mind. "But what about Columbia?"

"I encouraged her to apply," Bianca replied. "And I told her that if you really loved her, you would stay. But she made sure you never had to make that choice."

He wanted to argue with her, dismantle what she was saying piece by piece. But just as quickly, he realized that he couldn't. Because he would have stayed. He would have given up his position in the Buenos Aires program, missed out on every opportunity over the past eight years, if Anne hadn't ended things. Anne had saved him from himself.

That truth landed like a lead weight in his gut.

Another moment passed, then Bianca turned to face him fully. "It wasn't that I didn't like you, Frederick. I just wanted what's best for my daughter. And she only wanted what was best for you. So now the question is: What do you want?"

He let out a long breath. "Her."

Bianca nodded. "Good. Then don't fuck it up."

Then she turned and started down the sidewalk. He watched her go, letting the epiphany rattle through him again.

Everything he had accomplished since college—his work in Argentina, his company, his professional success—was all thanks to Anne. She'd given up their shared future so he could have one of his own. It seemed so obvious now, and the fact that he hadn't realized it back then triggered an urgency that bordered on panic. He turned back to the shop.

He had to go inside and find Anne.

But just as the thought entered his mind, there she was, standing in the center of the crowd inside. He could see her through the tall window.

She was talking to a small group and hadn't seen him standing just outside, so Freddie let himself take in every detail. Her blond hair pulled up in a ponytail that highlighted the long slope of her neck. The green dress that played off the color of the vines and flowers around her, making her skin glow and her blue eyes vibrant. She had always claimed not to enjoy parties, but right now she looked so relaxed, like this was her natural state whether she knew it or not. Completely unaware that maybe the only thing that had been missing that entire time was a party celebrating her.

Someone must have called to her from the other side of the shop, because she craned her neck to look, then turned back to the people she had been standing with, smiling as she offered what he could only assume were apologies as she disappeared back into the crowd.

He didn't move, though.

How could he go in there right now? Yes, he needed to talk to her, apologize and work out all the shit he should have eight years ago, but tonight wasn't about him. This was *her* night, one she had worked her ass off to make happen. No matter what he said, if he went in there, it would quickly be about him, them, a recentering of the party's focus that seemed so unfair he couldn't even consider it. But he also couldn't leave without letting her know how he felt, that he was here and, from now on, he wasn't going anywhere.

That's when he felt his dad's small notebook in the pocket of his coat. He had slipped it in there when he'd left his parents' house, so he could continue jotting down his thoughts about the nonprofit on the train home. But now it needed to serve a different purpose.

He pulled it out and began writing. The snow was coming down more heavily now, but he didn't care. He bowed his body over the page and scribbled line after line, then tore out the sheet. He wasn't sure he would remember how to do it—he hadn't even considered it in eight years—but before he could recall the steps, his fingers did the work, carefully folding the small sheet into a perfect paper triangle.

He held it tight in the palm of his hand, then pulled out his phone to text his sister.

FREDDIE
Hey. Can you come outside? I need you to do me a favor.

CHAPTER 27

Anne never thought she liked parties, but as she leaned against the long wood counter and watched the last of the party guests make their way to the exit, laughing and blowing kisses before disappearing into the snowscape outside, she realized that maybe she just hadn't had enough to celebrate before.

People knew her name. They commended her work. It was as exciting as it was jarring, so much so that she had barely been aware of the time. One minute it felt like she had just arrived, and then suddenly Sophie was making her speeches, thanking everyone for coming, and wishing them a good night.

And it *was* a good night. Maybe one of the best she'd ever had. Except for one thing.

Freddie hadn't shown up.

The party had been so overwhelming, at some point she had forgotten to look for him until the very end. She had just taken for granted that he would be there, that at some point he would tap her shoulder, maybe even take her hand, and that would be it. She would apologize, he would, too, and they could start working toward building back everything they had lost over the past eight years. But he never did.

It hurt, in a tender way she hadn't felt in a long time.

"Well, I would consider that a success," Sophie said with a satisfied sigh as she strode over to stand beside Anne.

"I think that's the understatement of the year, Soph," Anne said, smiling.

Sophie nodded, surveying the empty glasses strewn on the counter, the empty hors d'oeuvres platters. "Yeah. I think you're right."

Anne pushed off the counter with a groan. Not only had she been too distracted to feel her heart break all over again; she hadn't felt how sore her feet were in her heels until a few minutes ago.

"Should we bring all these dishes into the back or ... " Anne paused when she saw Sophie's expression. Her friend was watching her with concern, as if mentally debating something. "What is it?"

"I just want to preface this by saying that he made me promise not to say anything until the party was over."

Anne narrowed her eyes. "Okay."

"Okay." Sophie let out a long breath. "Freddie was here earlier."

Anne's pulse stuttered in her veins. "What?"

"He didn't come inside because he didn't want to distract you or something? But he wanted me to give you this."

She reached into her pocket. When she unfurled her hand, Anne could see a small paper triangle sitting in her palm.

Suddenly, it was like the world had been put on pause.

Anne reached for it, holding it between her fingers tentatively.

"I'm going to go in the back and talk to the caterers about cleanup, okay?" Sophie said, sending Anne a knowing smirk. She didn't wait for an answer before she disappeared through the door.

It was a long minute before Anne unfolded the note. Even

then, the sight of Freddie's handwriting, smudged here and there along the page, was almost too much. And then she began to read:

It's Tuesday, December 2nd. You're standing in the window of Eufloria, surrounded by people waiting to congratulate you and talk to you, and I'm standing outside watching in absolute awe. You're a revelation, Annie. Don't think of ever telling someone you don't like parties again, because they will never believe you.

It's snowing hard now, and I can't feel my feet. I know I should go in and join that crowd congratulating you, but I also know that I can't. Because tonight is for you, about you, and if I'm there I would just insert myself in the worst way possible, because there's only one thing I will want to say.

I love you, Annie. I have never loved anyone more than I love you. You pierce my soul every time you so much as look at me. I am half agony, half hope when you walk into a room.

And I know I don't deserve you. I've been resentful and angry. And I could apologize a thousand times and it might never be enough. But please know I never stopped loving you. I don't think I ever could.

I'm asking Sophie to wait until the party's over to give you this. And after you read it, if you feel even a fraction of the way about me as I do about you, come home. I'll be waiting for you.

—Freddie

Anne looked up at the empty shop, eyes wide and heart thumping against her ribs.

"Sophie!" she yelled. "I have to go. I'll call you tomorrow!"

"Not too early!" Sophie called back. "I'm treating myself to a room at the Bowery Hotel tonight and I plan to sleep in!"

Anne smiled and started for the door.

She didn't realize she forgot her coat until she was already out the door. After just one block, her hair was covered in snow, her dress was soaking, and her heels—

BEEP!

A taxi slammed on its brakes and narrowly avoided her as she stepped into the street. The driver opened the window and flipped her the middle finger.

"Sorry!" she called out loudly over her shoulder, running onto the sidewalk, dodging piles of wet accumulation, and jumping past people congregating outside a bar, huddled together as they vaped.

"Go get 'em, girl!" one of them yelled.

She could see Tompkins Square Park in the distance, and it looked empty tonight except for the towering lit Christmas tree, the colored lights sparkling as the snow fell, but she didn't have time to admire it. When she reached Avenue A, she turned and darted inside the lobby of the Uppercross.

It was blessedly warm when she burst inside and rushed over to the waiting elevator. She pressed eight and waited, rubbing her arms for warmth as she watched the numbers slowly light up above the doors as she ascended.

The doors slid open again once she reached the eighth floor, and Anne burst out, but stopped just as quickly. The door to 8A was slightly ajar, with the soft light of the fireplace bleeding through the crack.

She approached slowly, her teeth no longer chattering, and pushed open the door.

Inside, the apartment was warm, with only the fire lighting the space. And sitting on the long sofa in front of it was Freddie. He was facing the fire with a drink in his hand, so he didn't notice as she stepped forward into the center of the room.

"Freddie," she said.

He turned at the sound of his name, his expression stoic. Then his gaze darted down her body and concern knitted his brow. "Annie—"

"I'm sorry," she blurted out. "I was so busy at the party that I didn't see you. I didn't know you were just outside, or that you came, or—"

"Annie." His deep voice cut her off as he stood up. "Where's your coat?"

She looked down. Her skin was covered in goose bumps and the delicate green fabric of her dress was sodden and sticking to her body.

"At the shop. I think."

His eyebrows bobbed up. "You walked all the way from the shop in heels and no coat during a snowstorm."

"Well, I got your note, and I had to talk to you, so I didn't really have much time to plan things out."

A grin began to tug at his lips, crinkling the corners of his eyes. "Anne Elliot without a plan?"

"I know," she said with a soft laugh. "It's been a big week."

His smile faltered, as if he was considering the full weight of the past few days. Then he started toward her, reaching over and pulling a thick wool blanket from the arm of the sofa on his way.

Anne stood like a stone as he made his way across the room, keeping his gaze locked on her. It felt like her heart was beating outside her body, like he would be able to see if he looked close enough. But his eyes never left her own.

He stopped inches from her, close enough that she could feel the heat of his body on her freezing skin. Then he lifted the blanket and gently wrapped it around her, tucking it up close to her neck and cinching it tight across her chest. It was so warm she almost groaned, closing her eyes and letting the smell of his cologne surround her as she began to thaw.

"You broke up with me so I would go to Argentina."

Her eyes snapped open again to find him still watching her, studying her reaction.

"How do you know that?" she whispered.

"Your mother told me."

Anne's mouth fell open. "What?"

"I ran into her tonight outside the shop."

Oh God. She tried to think of what to say, words that might mitigate his hurt, or anger, or whatever he was feeling, because—

"I'm sorry, Annie," he said, interrupting her thoughts.

She blinked. "What are you sorry for?"

"That I didn't figure it out sooner. That you were put in that position to begin with." He sighed. "That I didn't listen for so long before that or talk about the things we needed to. But I'm here now and I'm not going anywhere. I want to discuss all of it, plan everything, do the hard stuff, but do it together. If you'll let me."

She stared up at him for a moment. The strong line of his jaw. The varied shades of green in his eyes. The messy brown hair. And then, she saw him. Her Freddie, the one she thought she had lost eight years ago. He was staring down at her, battle-worn and bruised, but it was him.

She smiled. "We don't have to plan *everything*."

He took a step closer, bringing his body almost flush with hers. "No?"

"No. In fact, I learned recently that it's okay to be spontaneous once in a while."

His grin returned. "Is that so?"

She nodded. "Yes, I can give you some pointers."

"I'd like that." He reached up and brushed a strand of wet hair away from her face, tucking it behind her ear. "I love you, Annie."

Joy swelled in her chest, so bright and warm that she couldn't feel her cold skin anymore. She could only see him. "I love you, too, Freddie."

He let out a long breath. "God, I missed hearing you say that."

She couldn't stop herself anymore. She stood up on her tiptoes, angling her mouth to his, and kissed him, warm and slow. He stilled, then his arms were around her, kissing her back like he had been starved of her. Then he lifted her up and she wrapped her legs around his waist as he started toward his bedroom.

The door flew open and suddenly they couldn't get close enough—wet clothes and ruined shoes were torn off and abandoned on the floor as they fell into bed, their hands exploring their naked bodies, desperate and needy.

"I love you so much," he murmured in her ear.

She tilted her head back and arched up into him as he moved down her body, licking and kissing her collarbone, her breasts, her sternum.

"My perfect girl," he whispered. His kisses started to trail lower, words spoken into her soft skin so quietly she could barely hear him. Then his hands gripped her thighs, nudging them apart.

She looked up, her gaze steady and locked on his. He was beautiful, cheeks flushed, hair a mess, and pupils blown as wide as his dark green eyes. She forgot how this felt, to have Freddie Wentworth's complete focus. He would do anything for her right now, and that power was heady.

She closed her eyes, lying back and relaxing into the feel of his touch, his breath warm on her damp, sensitive skin. His strong hands bracketed her thighs as he peppered kisses down her body until his tongue teased her core. She disappeared into the feeling of him between her legs, as soft moans fell from her lips. With each sound, his fingers gripped her thighs harder, and when she arched her hips to his mouth, he let out a low growl.

"Do you know how many nights I fell asleep dreaming of this?" he murmured against her skin.

She shuddered; her lips parted and her breathing picked up as he sucked right where she was aching. Everything tightened and pulled taut, then snapped in one fluid moment. Her hips jerked up as she came, but he held on to her and didn't stop as the warm pleasure coursed through the nerve endings of her body. She came down slowly, relaxing with a long exhale and releasing her grip in his hair.

"Oh my God," she breathed heavily, her hands flying to cover her heated face.

She could feel him smile as he slowly kissed back up her body to lie next to her, pulling her against him.

"We're not done yet," he whispered into her ear, nipping at her cheeks, her jaw, while his hand traveled over the swell of her breast, to her hip, before repeating the journey back up again.

She tried to utter an intelligent thought, but it came out in unintelligible words, pleading and begging in syllables and sighs until his hands finally gripped her hips, pulling her under him. Her legs clasped around his hips easily as he positioned himself at her entrance and then he moved, slowly pushing into her. God, she'd missed this. She'd missed him.

He was unhurried at first, then steadily faster until each thrust rattled the bed against the wall. She raked her hands through his hair, closing her eyes and giving herself over to it. She couldn't think, she could only hold on to him, arching up to meet each of his thrusts.

He moved purposefully, with one hand pressing into her hip to help the movement of her body while he kissed up her neck, murmuring against her skin.

"I'm never leaving you again, Annie. Never."

She arched her hips up, and he rocked down against her, faster and harder, the friction too much. Her breath stuttered, her pulse thundered in her ears, as her thigh muscles tightened around him.

"I'm gonna—I just need . . ." she tried breathlessly, her thighs shaking. Her breathing fast and shallow.

She didn't need to finish the sentence. He already knew. His hand moved between them, rubbing small circles at her center as he rolled his hips harder, the dull ache in her core growing warmer and warmer.

She could feel the heat blooming across her skin, building again at her center, moments away from going off.

"Fuck," he cursed under his breath.

He angled deeper, and she moaned desperately as her mind and body swam. She fisted the sheets, wrapping her legs tightly around his hard body as her orgasm lingered on the precipice. She was so close, he just needed to say the thing.

"Come for me," he finally whispered, his voice low and deep.

Her entire body shook when she came. She gripped her hands into his hair, arching up against him, and rode out her second orgasm of the night in complete ecstasy as he worked her through it. He buried his face in her neck, breathing in her hair, his movements becoming erratic with each of his ragged, shallow breaths. He thrust once, twice, before climaxing with a low groan, and a muffled curse into her ear.

He held on to her tightly, both of them slowly drifting back to the present. After a moment, he fell beside her, their legs still tangled together as their breaths fell into sync.

She was just dozing off when he spoke again.

"You were incredible tonight at the party," he murmured, reaching over and running his hand over her hair.

She turned to him, eyebrows knitted together. "I thought you didn't come in?"

"I didn't. But I watched you through the window for a while. You were in your element."

She laughed softly. "I'm more surprised than anyone."

"I'm not surprised," he said, turning enough to look into her eyes. "You never realized how people looked at you at my parties. How you commanded attention. You were always incredible. I just think tonight was the first time you realized it, too."

She let her gaze linger on his, a smile on her lips as the realization slowly took hold. "Maybe you're right."

"I'm always right."

She laughed and leaned in enough to give him a kiss.

"Okay, I have a new plan for us," Anne said. "We are never leaving this bed. We have to stay here forever."

His chest vibrated with his chuckle. "Oh really?"

"Yes."

"I don't know. This sounds like it needs a bit more detail," he murmured in her hair. She could hear the smile in his voice.

"Maybe," she whispered against his skin. "But it's a good start."

EPILOGUE

One Year Later

Freddie asked Anne to marry him on a Thursday.

It wasn't something he planned to do. In fact, as he stood in the back room of Planet Rose, surrounded by a crowd of friends and barely recognized acquaintances, each waiting to take the small stage to sing karaoke, it didn't even enter his mind. All he could think about was how Will was beside him, still trying to maintain a conversation over the din of the room. By the time Cricket and James climbed onto the stage and began singing "I Got You Babe" at the top of their lungs, he was practically yelling in Freddie's ear.

"What?" Freddie replied, leaning closer to his friend as the song reached its chorus.

"I said we might take off after the girls' next song," his friend repeated loudly.

Freddie frowned. "It's only eleven."

"And?" Will asked.

George appeared from the crowd then, just as Cricket and James wailed "BABE!" in unison. Freddie was almost surprised to see him return so quickly. When he had excused himself a few minutes ago to refresh his drink, he barely made it two feet before he was pulled into a conversation with Birdie Carrington, who needed his help to convince a slightly tipsy Bianca Russell to move back to New York, and enlist Birdie as her Realtor. Freddie knew that was only the beginning. The party was filled with longtime friends, all of whom George would stop and say hello to, ask about their families and jobs, make them feel seen and listened to before worrying about himself. The fact that he had managed to return to them already, drink in hand, was something akin to a miracle.

Freddie didn't point that out, though. Instead, as soon as George stopped at his side, he motioned to Will. "He says he's leaving."

George turned to Will, giving him the same frown that Freddie had just a few moments before. "It's only eleven."

Will looked mildly annoyed. "Why are you both obsessed with the time?"

"Because it's a New Year's Eve party, Will," Freddie said, clapping his hand on his friend's shoulder, like he was breaking some difficult news. "Those typically run until midnight."

Will's expression remained flat. "And have you tried getting a car after midnight in New York on New Year's?"

George chuckled. "Touché."

The room broke into applause as James and Cricket finished their song with a flourish. They bowed and stumbled off the stage, Cricket into Glen's arms and James into Ellis's lap, just as the DJ's voice came through the speakers overhead.

"All right, next up we have Anne, Emma, and Lizzy," he announced.

Another cheer rose as three heads popped up from the long zebra-print upholstered bench across the room and the women made their way to the stage. Emma led the charge, her long dark hair swaying along the back of her pink fitted satin jacket. Behind her, Lizzy marched in time to the music, her oversized New

Order T-shirt hanging off one shoulder and her red hair pulled over one shoulder.

And then Anne appeared, her blond hair pulled back in a ponytail and lips wide with a smile as she adjusted the very chic—and very expensive—oversized blazer Emma let her borrow for the night. Even under the spotlights, Freddie could see how her blue eyes scanned the room until they found him. Then her smile broadened.

It had been a year since Eufloria's grand opening. Twelve months since they had both finally grown up and admitted everything they had been feeling over the eight years that preceded it. And yet, when she looked at him like that, he still felt his heart struggle to operate, tripping and catching like a motor caught in the wrong gear. No matter how much time had passed, he still felt like that eighteen-year-old freshman who had spotted her sitting alone at the Half Pint, reading a book about the history of mathematics, and known his life was about to change forever.

"'FREE BIRD'!" Sophie screamed from a few feet away, her arm thrown around Bev's shoulder. The two had gotten surprisingly close over the past year, especially after Bev revealed that she used to do all the floral bouquets for Andy Warhol's Factory. She started working part-time during the Valentine's Day rush last year, and now that Sophie and Anne were busy opening a second Eufloria location uptown, Bev was practically managing the original location on her own.

Anne laughed as she looked across the room. "Right. Before we get to our song, I just wanted to say thank you for coming out tonight and celebrating New Year's with us."

Another cheer rose up from the crowd, and Freddie's heart swelled so much his chest hurt.

A year ago, he had thought he was done throwing parties. It wasn't that he disliked them, only that the motivation behind them was moot. But just a couple of weeks after the Eufloria party last year, Freddie had taken Anne to a Christmas party hosted by George and his girlfriend, Emma. Apparently, Emma's family threw one every December, and when they pulled up to the imposing townhouse on East Eighty-Third Street, it looked warm and festive, yet also utterly intimidating. But then the front door had swung open and Emma was there alongside Will's girlfriend, Lizzy. They had swarmed around Anne and ushered her inside before he even had a chance to introduce them. The three women had been inseparable ever since.

That's how, during a late-night karaoke session at this very bar back in May, the idea for this party was born. Tradition dictated that Emma Woodhouse throw a Christmas party uptown but New Year's Eve was fair game, so after a few songs at Planet Rose—and half a vodka and soda for Anne—the plan was hatched. A New Year's Eve party with all their closest friends, right there at that downtown bar. George had agreed, and Will, too, but only because he was sure all the alcohol meant the three women would forget the idea by morning. Freddie wasn't so certain. Sure enough, just a few weeks later, Anne had invited Lizzy and Emma to a text thread about organizing the event, complete with links to the appropriate spreadsheets.

"For those of you that have known me for a while, I've never been one for big parties," Anne said. "But right now, I can't think of anywhere I'd rather be."

Lizzy let out an unbridled "Wahoo!" and the crowd laughed.

"The New Year is a time for new beginnings. And I'm a big fan of those," Anne continued, a smile still teasing her lips as her eyes found Freddie's again. "So Happy New Year's, everybody. Thanks for spending it with us."

Another cheer, but this one was from the whole group, punctuated by smiles and hugs and raised glasses all directed at the incredible woman standing before them.

Freddie raised his glass to Anne, too, not even trying to curb the look of adoration on his face. Back in college, he had been known as the ringmaster behind some of the most legendary soirees in NYU history. But he hadn't thrown those parties just because he enjoyed them. It was also an attempt at coaxing Anne out of her shell, so the world could see what he saw. In the end, he didn't need to worry about that. She didn't know how to follow someone into a party. That didn't mean she didn't know how to lead them.

The music kicked in then, a tinny, instrumental version of "These Boots Are Made For Walkin'," and Emma stepped forward. She looked more tipsy than her cohorts as she leaned into the microphone, gripping it tightly with both hands and squinting against the spotlights.

"Where is my boyfriend?" she said, her voice loud and muffled.

George smiled as he yelled out, "Over here."

Emma's gaze darted over. Then she pointed at him. "Knightley. This one's for you."

Knightley chuckled as the three women started singing, each at a completely different pitch.

"Did I miss something?" Will asked.

George shook his head, still smiling. "I asked her to marry me again and she said no."

Freddie laughed. George had asked Emma to marry him a dozen times since they finally admitted they loved each other three years ago. And even though she had officially moved in with him over the summer, she was still adamant about never walking down the aisle. Freddie never really understood why, though, and last summer, while the six of them were out in the Hamptons staying at Will's house in Montauk, he made the mistake of asking Emma.

He ended up spending the next hour listening to her pontificate on how people's antiquated notions of marriage were detrimental to the advancement of women in the twenty-first century.

"Why do you keep asking her?" he asked.

George sighed. "Is it weird if I say foreplay?"

"Yes," Will murmured, taking a sip of his beer.

George smiled again. "All right. Maybe it's just a way of letting her know that I don't care either way. I know she doesn't want to, and I'm all right with that. But if she changes her mind, the offer is there, too." He took a sip of his drink and nodded to the stage, where the three women had abandoned the lyrics in a fit of laughter. "This isn't Regency England. They don't need us to survive. They'll flourish either way. So then, it's really up to them if they want it."

Freddie turned to Will. "What about you and Lizzy?"

Will looked at him as if this was a stupid question.

George chuckled. "So what are you waiting for?"

"We're not in a rush," Will said, his gaze drifting back to the stage. His expression softened a bit when his eyes met Lizzy's. "Besides, her older sister is getting married soon, so she doesn't want to take any attention away from that."

George nodded again, then turned to Freddie. "And what about you?"

"What about me?"

"What are *you* waiting for?"

Freddie considered. He and Anne had talked about getting married. Of course they had. Back in college, it had seemed like a sure thing, an inevitable future that they didn't need to plan for, so they took it for granted. Now, so many years later, they understood the gravity, the nuance. But most importantly, they both appreciated the time. Not only how much was ahead, but how much had passed. They had wasted years already and the idea of spending any more time apart sent a unique panic through his bloodstream.

Suddenly, he couldn't remember what he was waiting for. Unlike Emma, Anne wanted to get married. She always had. And unlike Lizzy, she didn't have any major milestones she was waiting to accomplish. Anne had moved in with him last spring and reclaimed her old bedroom as her office. They even started a tradition by picking the worst Christmas tree on the lot again this year. Its almost-bare branches were still decorated in their living room.

As for Freddie, he had wanted to marry her since the first moment he saw her freshman year. Everything was right there, just waiting to be realized. And suddenly his mind zeroed in on the note sitting in his wallet. The one that had been there for more than a decade.

The song reached its crescendo and the room was cheering so loudly it was impossible for the men to continue their conversation. Not that they would want to, anyway. Anne, Lizzy, and Emma had stolen their attention, swaying together as they practically yelled the song's final lyrics.

"Are you ready, boots? Start walkin'!"

Applause erupted around them as the women bowed, then stumbled from the stage directly to where the three men were standing by the bar. Anne leaned into Freddie's side while Emma fell into George's embrace, planting a kiss on his lips. Lizzy stopped in front of Will even as his arms encircled her waist.

"Well, that settles it. I'm quitting journalism so we can take this act on the road," Lizzy said, tossing her red hair over one shoulder.

Will hummed to himself, a small grin tugging at the corner of his mouth. "Right. So that job that's waiting for you at the *Times*..."

Lizzy shrugged as she let out a deep sigh. "I'm sorry, but the public demands it."

Will stopped trying to school his expression then and tugged her forward to kiss her.

Freddie turned to look down at Anne. She had her chin resting on his chest, gazing out across the room with a look of contentment that made Freddie's chest constrict again. From joy, yes, but also an odd anxiety that sometimes needled his heart at moments like this. A reminder that this could have all ended so differently. The series of events that brought them back together could have just as easily kept them apart. The what-ifs were almost overwhelming. And suddenly, the idea of waiting any longer felt ridiculous.

He leaned down, his lips close to her ear. "Take a walk with me?"

She turned to look up at him, her eyebrows pinched together. "Why?"

"I have to ask you something," he murmured.

She smiled but didn't object, just turned back to the two other couples. "We're heading outside for a sec."

This was enough to pull Emma's lips away from George and give a disapproving look to Freddie. "It's cold out."

He glared back. "We have coats."

"Whoever told you that incivility was the essence of love never made their date stand outside in below-zero temperatures, Frederick," Lizzy said, working hard to make her voice sound deep and stern.

Emma let out a drunken snort. "You called him Frederick."

Then they both laughed.

Freddie sighed. "We'll be right back."

He took Anne's hand and led them through the crowd to the front door, then out onto the sidewalk. He kept a firm grip on her hand as they continued down Avenue A, around the corner to a quieter section of Thirteenth Street. The sound of the city faded a bit as he leaned them up against the brick facade of the building.

"Hey," he said, leaning down, his face just inches from hers.

"Hey," she whispered back.

"Do you know how much I love you?" he murmured.

Her smile broadened. "Is that what you wanted to ask me?"

"No. I'll get to that. But first, I have a confession," he said.

"What's that?" she asked, staring up at him, her lips still quirked in a smile, and he had to stop himself from leaning down to kiss her.

"You know those notes I've been writing to you for a while?" he asked.

Her eyes narrowed slightly. "I'm familiar."

"Well, there's one that I never got around to giving you."

She paused. "What do you mean?"

His heart tripped as he pulled her closer. "Remember the night we first met? You were sitting alone at the Half Pint, reading a book at the bar. I was there with friends, but I couldn't take my eyes off you. I spent over an hour getting up the courage to go over and ask you what you were reading."

"And when I told you it was *A History of Pi*, you spent ten minutes talking about whether cheesecake is a cake or a pie."

He chuckled. "I thought you were just really into baking."

She let out a soft laugh, too. "You were very charming when I corrected you."

"And then we talked for hours," he said, brushing his nose against hers.

"Until last call," she whispered. He could feel her warm breath against his cold cheeks.

"Then I walked you out to make sure you got a cab," he replied. "But before I left, I went back inside and wrote this."

He straightened enough to pull his wallet from his pocket, then reached inside to retrieve the flimsy paper triangle still slotted inside. He knew she would recognize the shape, but the small details seemed to give her pause. The corners that were worn down, the thin paper, almost like it wasn't paper at all. More like a napkin.

"What's that?" she asked, her eyes wide now.

"The only note of mine you don't have yet. The first one."

She reached up and slowly took it from his fingers. "You held on to this for over a decade?"

He nodded. "It was in my wallet. Everywhere I went, it was there with me."

Her attention was still on the small piece of paper, and it took her a moment to blink away and bring her gaze up to his. Tears were already forming in the corners of her eyes.

"I want you to read it," he said, his voice low. "And when you're done, I have something very important to ask you."

She smiled. And suddenly, he could feel tears in his own eyes, too. Yes, it could have all ended so differently. But it hadn't. She was his once more, and he would never let her go again. And with that thought, he watched as she slowly unfolded the napkin and began reading.

Annie—It's Friday, December 19th, and a little while ago, you were sitting at the bar reading a book and I interrupted you. I had no idea what to say, but you didn't ask me to leave. And then we had one of the best conversations of my life. You left a few minutes ago, and now I'm back in the bar, wondering when I'll be brave enough to tell you what I knew the minute you smiled at me: I'm going to ask you to marry me someday, Anne Elliot. And I've never looked forward to something more in my entire life.

—Freddie

ACKNOWLEDGMENTS

When we first began writing this book, we had no idea what kind of year we were about to face. While we ended up creating amazing memories with friends and family—and squeezed in some truly epic trips to Comic Con and to Texas—it ended up being the most personally challenging year of our lives. Yet no matter what life threw at us, we had Anne and Freddie. Escaping into their world of serendipitous Manhattan run-ins, hot-chocolate holiday shopping, floral shop launch parties, all-too-familiar television production mishaps, and their small crew of quirky characters in the East Village became our lifeline—a place for joyful light during an unexpectedly dark time. This second chance love story, set in our cherished New York City at Christmas, had the happily ever after ending we truly needed.

But we didn't do this alone. As we navigated this past year, we feel so much gratitude for the support of so many along the way. Above all, it's our friendship that made this book possible, which is why we dedicated it to each other. This is a tribute to all best friends—the ones who stand by you and make life's hardships more bearable. When everything feels insurmountable, facing it becomes a little easier with friends by your side, helping to steer the ship forward. We are both so incredibly lucky to have each other—because without that, this book would never have happened.

There are so many people who showed up for us during this time—some who knew just how much their support meant, and others who may not have even realized the impact of their presence—and we love you for it.

To Joëlle Delbourgo, who is not only our agent but our friend. Your constant belief in us has meant the world, and we are endlessly grateful for all you do.

To our editor, Molly Gregory, thank you for helping shape this book in so many ways. We're not even sure you know how much your steady guidance meant to us! And to the entire team at Gallery Books—Jennifer Bergstrom, Sally Marvin, Carrie Feron, Lucy Nalen, Fallon McKnight, Matt Attanasio, Heather Waters, Christine Masters, and Stacey Sakal—thank you for supporting us through every step of this process. This book came to life in your hands.

To Rich Green, Ellen Goldsmith-Vein, and the team at the Gotham Group, who fight in our corner every day—you're incredible and we don't know what we would do without you. (Seriously, you're miracle workers—you have to share your secrets.)

To Whitney Tancred, for standing by us with tenacious support and brilliant ideas. Thank you for going above and beyond. To Molly Lyons, for your belief in us always. To Molly and Becca of *Pod and Prejudice*, for your shared love of Austen. To Arden Myrin, for all the podcast book giveaways. And a big thank-you to our close friends Jenna Helwig, Nicole Page, Jessica Winchell Morsa, and Zoran Zgonc, who continue to make us laugh and impress us daily with their accomplishments.

From Audrey

In the middle of writing this book, I received a life-altering diagnosis completely out of the blue. In an instant, everything changed.

I could hardly process the words when my doctors delivered the news. How could I possibly have *stage four* lung cancer? It didn't make *any* sense—I had no real symptoms, had never smoked, and had been healthy—with perfect blood work and even roller skating for my birthday just weeks prior. But I quickly learned that this disease doesn't discriminate.

If you have lungs, you can get lung cancer.

Lung cancer kills 1.5 times more women than breast cancer. Isn't that wild? Right now, there's no screening for early detection. Unless you're high-risk, CT scans are not handed out willy-nilly.

I'm incredibly fortunate to have a type of lung cancer called ALK positive, caused by a change in a gene we all have. *Anyone can get this.* Regardless of smoking history, health, lifestyle, or age. For now, I'm able to take targeted therapy—pills that didn't even exist just a few years ago. There's much more to my story, but the short version is this: At the moment, thanks to my extraordinary medical team and these treatments, I actually feel better than I have in years.

So many people stepped in during this surreal and truly frightening time and continue to do so. Things became even more difficult when, within days of my diagnosis, we lost my dad—our anchor—to Parkinson's and related complications. Old friends, new friends, and my incredible family dropped everything to show up for me as we all tried to navigate this new reality together.

I don't know if I'll ever be able to thank everyone fully. But I'll start here . . .

ACKNOWLEDGMENTS

To the very best dad in the world, a true gentleman in every sense, thank you, Donald A. Bellezza, for ensuring my life was filled with so much love and so many possibilities. Any success I've achieved is a direct result of the foundation you provided. Know that I miss you and love you, always. I'm eternally grateful for the truly wonderful childhood I was so fortunate to have, and all the Bellezza memories that came with it. I know you're working your magic.

A heartfelt thank-you to my amazing family, who never once said no, always put me first, and gave me endless love and boundless patience. Thank you for being by my side when I needed you most. We have each other to lean on, and for that, I am forever grateful and incredibly lucky. To my wonderful loving husband, Michael Pierantozzi: What a year, and thank God it's you next to me. You are truly amazing. Thank you for loving your lemon/dream girl so much—love you back. To Bear and Dex: You are my inspiration, and it's all for you. I'm very proud of my boys. To my brilliant and loving mother: Thank you for all that you do, Elizabeth Stoll Bellezza. You are my first phone call, my biggest cheerleader, and the person who is always thinking about me. To my incredible brother, Philip Bellezza: A big thank-you for uprooting your life to make me a priority and being a rock of support for us all. Love you so much. You make me hopeful for what's possible. To the kindest sister, Veronica Bellezza: Thank you for reading my mind, making me laugh, believing, and caring so deeply. Love you. To Diana Diriwaechter, a true cousister and inspiration to me. Thank you for being there when I needed you most. I'm grateful for your sound advice—love you. To Whitney Tancred, thank you for being my best friend forever, since I was two, and upending your life to try to fix mine. I'm now a plant mom. To Yana Trushina, I'm so deeply grateful for you. Thank you for being there for me and the boys. To Mike Gardes and little M, I am so thankful for you both. Ella Burr, Adam Burr, Rainer Diriwaechter, thank you for all the love and support. Ellen and Thomas Diriwaechter, it never feels like you're far away because you are always checking in. Wynn and Barbara Burr, your invaluable guidance and support has been such a gift, I'm not sure how to thank you both enough. To Mike and Mary Pierantozzi, you have been a constant and loving support to me always. I'm so thankful and lucky to be part of the fun. And to the entire Pierantozzi family, thank you. Christine Ramsey, Michele Pierantozzi-Cassel, who matches my energy, and Denise Mapes, your support means the world to me—love you.

To my friends who helped me, loved me, and supported me during this time and always: Know how deeply I appreciate you and love you back, just as fiercely. To my favorite, most perfect ex-boyfriend and BFF, Mason Pettit, and Lindsay Fram, his brilliant wife, for their extraordinary support, moral compass, and delicious food—it's everything. To Meg Wolf and Jesse Gordon and Oz, thank you for being a source of strength and for trying to restore my vitality. To Karen Axmaker—I treasure our friendship. Thank you for the podcast phone calls, and Paris. Amanda Young and Jake Schmidt & Abby Jenkins and Jeff Boal—what would we do without all of you? NYC, Fox Hill Farm, VT, the love, the farm-to-table food—you lift the entire family up; we love you all and I thank you for always being there. Rachel Knobelman, the best and funniest roomie, thank you. Amy and Chris Dorrian, for all your help and constant support always, thank you. Sam Bradford and Allison Song—I'm so lucky to have met friends like you way back when—thank you. Tanya Jones, your light and positivity is everything, and Katie Kramer, for the years of friendship.

To my Mountainside pit crew: Heather Grondin and Marcia Stypa DiNorscio, for the incredible self-care now and forever friendship since grammar school; love you for never giving up. Katie Schumacher, the BFF keeper of the memories, for always trying to make me laugh, and the perfect closet. Molly Lyons, I'm so grateful for your guidance in all things. And to Debbie and Chetan Vijayvergiya, for caring so much since the beginning. To Thomas Tancred, Brian Courville, Mike Debbie, Gemma Lyons, Jean Pascuiti, and Barbara Weinberg, thank you. And to ALL my parents' wonderful friends and the Mountainside book club ladies, who have supported Elizabeth and me through this time, just as they have since I was little.

To my Fairfield U. Shangri-La girls, being with all of you so much has been too much fun and an absolute joy. Your energy, expertise, and support have made all the difference. Thank you, Rachael Rowley McQuillan, Christine Loftus Collins, Bethany Wind Verret, Erin Sheehan, Lynn Jacobowski, and Maura Kenney-Kieran. To Mike Troncale and Kate Waters, thank you for being there for Don and the family, always. To Eva Churchill, for listening. To Stephanie and Todd Leslie, Melissa and Fred Eltringham, and Mike Dolan, I appreciate you all and everything you do; a big thank-you. To Carolyn and Dan Jeselsohn and our girl R, you made everything so much easier—thank you. To Sarah and Matt Guiney, not sure what we'd do without you. To the Maplewood Back and Front Roaders! Thank you for the support. Appreciate it all so much. To Siu Ping Negrin, for your healing hands, guidance, and the gift of qigong; to Freddie Jeck, Lyda Ely, and everyone in the Heal From Within community—my deepest, heartfelt thanks. A thank-you to *Office Ladies* and the '95 BBC *P&P* for a vital escape. And to Jessica, Nicole, Jenna, and Zoran—so grateful for you all, always. Thank you to anyone I may have missed who helped and supported; it meant everything.

And finally, a huge thank-you, and XOXO ∞, to my exceptional writing partner and best friend, Emily Harding. You are my Ann Perkins, and to quote Leslie Knope, "You are the most beautiful, talented, brilliant, powerful woman I've ever known, and I'm lucky to know you. *Emily Harding*, you're the best thing that's ever happened to me." There's so much more praise I want to give, and I will say it often, beyond these pages. Thank you for keeping us on course and always making it easy because that is what I needed. For driving through snowstorms, road-tripping to the Hamptons, literally holding me up at Comic Con, connecting the dots with your medical deep dives, and listening to me for hours. I'm beyond grateful for you and your beautiful family. Thank you, Tom Harding, for always being there when we needed you—your support, and that accent, were always a welcome break. And a big hug and thank-you to Poppy and Henry. Em, you're an incredible person and I will never be able to thank you enough for everything you've done and continue to do for me. Thank you for loving me like Mary loves field slugs. Love you just as much.

From Emily

There are so many people I could thank here, but those people know how much they mean to me. They also know that there's one person who deserves it the most. Audrey, you've gone through hell this year, and done it with grace, compassion, and, honestly, such badassery that I'm in awe. I am so proud to be your friend and so honored to be at your side through it all. Even amid the worst of it, we found joy and laughter (and a real-life Jack's Surf Shop in East Hampton!), and I promise there's so much more to come. Thank you for being there for me even when you were totally overwhelmed, and for allowing me to be there for you. You're stuck with me forever, so get used to it. Xoxoxoxoxoxoxoxoxo

The silver lining in this devastating ordeal is the creation of Love4Lungs, a nonprofit born from this journey. If you'd like more information, or to follow Audrey's journey, use the link here:

www.love4lungs.org

@ourlove4lungs

ABOUT THE AUTHORS

Audrey Bellezza is a two-time Emmy Award–nominated TV producer and writer with over two decades of experience in television production. A proud graduate of Fairfield University, she studied art history and English before building a career producing and directing nonfiction series for networks and streaming platforms. She lives in New Jersey with her husband and two children, where she continues to write and chase down magic.

Emily Harding is one half of the writing duo behind the For the Love of Austen series, in addition to the author of *How Freaking Romantic*. She is a graduate of Emerson College with degrees in both creative writing and film. After working for over fifteen years in television development and production, she found her way back to writing. Emily lives in Dallas with her husband, two children, and an incredibly spoiled Texas heeler.